To VKggg

Where Sings the Skylark

With Jen.

Peter Wright

Pet Clay

Number Two in the Brocken Spectre Series

BY THE SAME AUTHOR:

Ribbon of Wildness – *Discovering the Watershed of Scotland,* pub 2010.

Walking with Wildness – *Experiencing the Watershed of Scotland,* pub 2012.

Nature's Peace – *A Celebration of Scotland's Watershed* – pub 2013.

Wright's Roots – *A Comprehensive Family History (private),* 2012.

Waking the Sleeping Giant – *A Novel,* pub 2017.

DEDICATION

To the adventurous spirit.

First Published 2022, by:

Ribbon *of* Wildness

To start your own journey of discovery . .

ISBN: 978-1-4709—1730-2

Cover photograph by Peter Wright

Typeset: main text 12-point Baskerville Old Font

BIOGRAPHY

Having left school at the age of fourteen, Peter Wright got his first job as a labourer in a chicken hatchery. This was followed by a year of Liberal Studies at Newbattle Abbey College, which he describes as *life changing*. A career in youth work followed, and he became manager of the Duke of Edinburgh's Award Unit in the City of Edinburgh Council; a post he held for over twenty years, during which he was awarded MBE.

With his mantra of *volunteering makes the world go round*, Peter has been an exemplar of this throughout his adult life. From this, a diverse range of organisations and programmes, mainly charitable, have been variously founded or developed by him. This has included projects for young people – especially the disadvantaged, in heritage and environmental action. More recently he has been an activist in supporting the provision of education for girls amongst the Maasai People in Kenya.

Writing was an accidental outcome of his epic 1,200km walk along the entire Watershed of Scotland when he was in his fifties, and he has been glad to share his experiences with ever-widening audiences. `Clearly, you are having a love affair . . . with the landscapes of Scotland`, was the perceptive comment by one of the editors of his first book, and he is known to be more than happy with this accolade.

Where Sings the Skylark

1.

Engulfed in a cacophony of noise and blinding dust, Andy stood rigid with fear, as the roof of the old stables building collapsed around him. Worm-eaten timbers, slates, nails, a century or more of accumulated mess, and even bits of furniture from the loft, suddenly disintegrated on top of him. Unable to see or even breathe properly, he had taken a few hits from some of this debris; he feared his curiosity would now be the end of him.

Slowly, it seemed like an eternity, an eerie calm began to come over the scene of destruction and the dust settled enough for Andy to realise he`d survived. As he looked up, blinking, he saw daylight through what remained of the loft floor. Most of the joists supporting it had survived the onslaught. Although he was in some pain, there seemed to be no broken bones. Sweating profusely with the terror of the whole experience, he became conscious of streams of muck running down his face, and trickles of blood mixed with it settled on his hands and arms. The thick hat on his head had probably been his salvation.

A pheasant squawking somewhere on Spurryhillock estate brought back a growing sense of reality and jolted him into action.

A quick assessment of the joists, as he blinked many times to get the grit out of his eyes, suggested that most were still somehow in place. But holes in the loft floor that they supported, showed clear blue sky above; one end of the roof had indeed collapsed. What might have caused it, was at this stage impossible to tell. Whilst he knew that the roof would have needed replacing anyway, its sudden, unannounced collapse, apparently of its own accord, had not been in the plans.

He`d survived though, and his curiosity about the building returned.

What looked like a hatch door in the floor above, had been forced open with the blast and dangled menacingly on just one rusty hinge almost over his head. He could see that some of the roof remained in situ, through the gaping holes, and yes, inviting further investigation. He knew that when the time came to tell Lizzie about this escapade, she`d be dismayed that he`d got himself into this extreme danger in the first place. But a quick investigation of what was left of the loft, was surely a must; before he got banned from endangering himself anymore. A wooden ladder beside the stable wall offered the best means of quickly satisfying his curiosity. It was placed to point through the ragged hole above him.

Gingerly making his way up the ladder, he looked around, in a mixture of alarm and interest. Bits of the shattered structure lay everywhere: rafters, broken sarking, slates, and even part of a chimney pot that must have dislodged from somewhere. Chaos.

But one thing amongst it all, that had survived, and caught Andy`s eye immediately, was what appeared to be a framed painting, its image obscured by a thick layer of dust. There was too much grime to make out any detail, but there it lay defiantly propped against the tottering gable.

Determined to at least get something out of this near disaster, Andy grabbed a sheet of corrugated iron, pushed it up through the gaping hole, laid it across the chaos, crawled along it, and nervously salvaged the painting.

The only witness to this bizarre spectacle was his faithful, loyal dog Bramble, who sat in the doorway looking on in fearful alarm, ready to bolt back to the house.

`Just wait till Lizzie sees this`, he thought, with his heart thumping in a mixture of excitement and lingering panic.

In a kind of three-way celebration, responsibility for Spurryhillock had been a gift from Archie to Lizzie and Andy. Firstly, he had retired from his career in law and had been keen to reduce his responsibilities at the same time. His smart three-piece suit had been laid aside for only occasional use. Although he wanted to continue several chosen voluntary roles, none of these was onerous.

"The next generation can now take up the challenge of doing something useful, and perhaps even profitable with the estate", he had said, as he handed Lizzie a box of files, maps, and weighty documents.

"Eh, thank you, Dad, this is quite a gift and an even bigger responsibility you are giving Andy and me. We`ll certainly try to do our best with it. Though what that best might be, we haven't a clue yet." Lizzie said rather cautiously, whilst thinking, we`ve just been saddled with years of neglect, I fear. Archie may have had a great legal career, but he wasn't the most practical of guys.

Secondly, in addition to paying for the entire renovation of Lizzie and Andy`s new flat in Warrender Park Road in Edinburgh as a wedding present from himself and Marissa, he felt it would give them a fresh start in their new life together.

And finally, he added rather mischievously, that after the great turmoil of solving the mystery of the Seven Signs, as he cryptically called it, and the fall-out from that escapade, there would be great value in a practical joint project to get their teeth into as a vibrant partnership.

"Perhaps it will keep you out of mischief Andy, as you've had quite enough to last you a very long time, dear boy."

So Spurryhillock estate; house, ruins, woodland, and fields, entered a new, uncertain chapter in its long history.

Life had become one enormous roller coaster of experiences for Andy and Lizzie.

2.

That dramatic Police stake-out in Perth, in which Jamie and his accomplice Jock had been arrested, was just the start of a lengthy process culminating in them both being given hefty prison sentences. So, although much of the evidence necessary to charge them with numerous offences was already in the bag, as they were driven off in handcuffs from the centre of the city, it took many more months to assemble the rest of the case of wrongdoings, which the Crown Office demanded to secure a watertight case.

Both Lizzie and Andy were heavily involved in this and found they were being interviewed again and again in various Police stations, by an assortment of Officers. Often, it seemed, like it was going back over old ground that they thought had already been covered very thoroughly, a frustrating process. For Lizzie, the focus was on her relationship with Andy, and indeed also, her brother Jamie, one of the accused. Archie, her father, was very good at being present for as much of this interviewing as possible. This was to give his daughter plenty of moral support, but also to ensure, that there was what he regarded, as `fair play`. There was, however, nothing amusing in any of it.

For Andy the questions poured in as he pondered; what he had been doing in those strange locations; did he have permission to be there; had he in some way set out to stir up the conflict; did he know Jock Tweedie before this; how he got on with Jamie; why he had attacked and assaulted him in Glentress Forest; and who was this mysterious Spirit character he kept referring to. Surely this was just fantasy? And so, it rolled on week after week, an inexorable grind of gruelling questioning.

`If this is what they are giving Lizzie and me`, he surmised, `I just hope that they are giving those two bastards, who caused all the problems in the first place, a much harder time. `

They were.

Many a time, Jamie`s otherwise smooth veneer crumpled, and the argument that he had fervently believed justified all his actions, fell apart in a heap of empty confused words.

Jock was a bit tougher to crack, his military training had prepared him for interrogation, or so he thought. But, bit by bit, he realised he`d been living a fantasy of his own making, rooted in sand or historical myth. He too succumbed to the rigour of the questioning he was experiencing. Without the need for any violence upon him, he disintegrated into not much more than a jabbering wreck.

Although not entirely ethical, Archie managed to get an inkling of the case being constructed against the two, through a friend in the Crown Office.

Over lunch one Sunday, in which the case was being discussed, Archie observed: "they`ve gone into every nook and cranny of what happened and why, squeezed every ounce of evidence out of it, and put it into a case that defence and prosecution questioning notwithstanding, will see these guys put away for some time."

"Such tragic waste of two otherwise harmless lives." Marissa ventured. "Even if they do and should, get what's coming to them."

A roller coaster like no other.

After all the turmoil of Andy`s Seven Signs escapade, Lizzie initially found it quite difficult to refocus on her work.

Major changes in the structure and content of the University courses she was expected to be delivering, and then the impact of Covid, together made it all much less appealing to her. The one good thing to emerge in all this though was the response she had had to her exhibition in The Three Sisters. Almost all of it was very positive. It gave her creative work a new edge and enabled her to develop a distinctive business. Responding to the opportunities opening in front of her, with online marketing, the combination of her landscape photography and painting style, she created a range of mounted and framed products that seemed to appeal to an ever-widening market. Commanding a reasonable price, she had been able to build up a worthwhile reserve, give herself a modest salary, and expand her workspaces in both the flat in Edinburgh and at Spurryhillock. The large walls and high ceilings in the flat provided excellent display space, so the offerings she was putting up on her website Landscapes by Lizzie, seemed to attract a lot of hits. From that, she then started to utilise social media to good effect. Lizzie was becoming a brand.

She liked to play with the theme Symbols of Wildness.

"I know you were very disappointed that the previously proposed plan for a documentary never took off, my love. That would have been such a good one for you. But they seemed to dither around for so long, not make decisions, and then came Covid. So that was the end of that one."

"Yeh, it did indeed have the promise of something great in it, but you know, out of one failure or disapointment, success can grow and flourish. We are doing not too bad now really."

11

From high to low and back again, their resolve was tested.

Daily attendance in court during the gruelling trial of Jock and Jamie, or `the two J`s as Archie had dubbed them, to try and add a bit of levity to the otherwise tragic business, took its toll on Lizzie and Andy. Having to re-live each episode, brought back all the fear he`d experienced and the distress it caused her, as each chapter had unfolded before Judge and Jury.

"This is all far too real," she said. "Oh, I know it all happened, of that there can be no doubt. But this cold question, answer, and evidence-building, just really brings it back into focus. The judge sitting up there taking copious notes, and the whole thing recorded, written down somewhere, gives it all an even greater reality. It's ghastly"

One morning, as they were waiting for the proceedings to restart, Lizzie took Andy by surprise, as she turned to look him in the eye, and spoke quietly but deliberately: "I love you, and I need you Andrew Borthwick, so let's get married?"

Suddenly all the horror of the case seemed to be put on hold. Doing all that they could to conceal their excitement, Andy just nodded and ever so quietly said "Yeah, let's do it."

The rest of the case seemed much lighter to bear, as day by day, the plans had been laid.

3.

Carefully wrapping the painting in an old bit of sack, Andy had carried it back to the house; his trophy, or so he hoped. Bramble dutifully trotted along immediately behind him, stopping occasionally to shake herself and try to dislodge the stables dust from her black coat.

"Hey Lizzie, my love, just look what I've salvaged from the remains of the stable. Who or what do you think this might be?" as he carefully unwrapped it.

She was not to be distracted in any way, from the sight that greeted her though.

"My God Andy, what's happened to you? You look like you've been in fight. What`s going on? Are you OK?" as she rushed forward to survey the mess, he was in.

Streaks of dirt-encrusted sweat ran down his face and soaked into his shirt front. Blood and dirt were all over his arms and the back of his hands.

"Is this some kind of sick replay of the fights you got into a couple of years back? I thought, hoped, we`d put all that behind us, man."

"Eh, I was about to investigate the stables, which we want to convert for more useful purposes, when half the roof collapsed on top of me. It's a bit rotten I think, Lizzie. We`ll have to replace it altogether."

"That's as maybe, but you seem to be in a very sorry state. Firstly, are you injured in any way?"

"No, I don't think so, I`m lucky just some bruises and cuts, oh, and a load of dirt. I`ll clean up OK, I`m sure."

"Off with those clothes then, and get yourself into the shower, for a start. Here. Let me take that picture off you." As she grabbed hold of it and put it against the wall of her workshop that they were in.

"Let's get out of here, you are making a bit of a mess on the floor. Sorry, you are much more important than the floor, but let's try and contain the mess a bit."

So, Andy went out into the back lobby, and through to the boot room, which had a shower in one corner. Slowly removing all his clothes, he left them in an undignified heap and went into the shower. The cuts on his hands and arms were painful in the hot water, and he became more conscious of the bruising on his shoulders and back. Turning down the heat a bit, he slowly washed off all the grime, noting that most of the bleeding had stopped. At least he felt better for being clean once more, but suddenly the memory of the collapsing roof returned, and he shuddered at the thought of how lucky he was to escape without much more serious injury.

Lizzie returned with some clean clothes for him, and he emerged from the shower to get dried.

`This shower here, which Archie had installed is a godsend.` Andy mused. `Saves leaving a trail of muck right through the house.`

Lizzie had made some tea for them, so they moved through to the big kitchen to enjoy it together.

"How do you feel now? What injuries have you got? And what on earth happened?"

Filling her in on an edited version of the saga, Andy assured her that he was pretty much OK.

"Might need a couple of plasters for the cut on my left wrist. But that's about all."

Lizzie gave him the First Aid kit, to sort himself out.

"I reckon if I hired a cherry picker, I could get the remaining slates off that roof, and dismantle it, in a more organised fashion"

"We`ll see about that, cos that's for another day. While you were showering, I quickly removed the picture from its frame, and it looks a bit clearer now. I wonder who on earth this young man that's in it is, and why he`s holding a box?" As she lay it down flat on the kitchen table.

A rather stained face from the past, presenting many more questions than answers.

When Ronald arrived a few days later, Lizzie and Andy looked forward to his convivial chat and general catch-up. The sound of a car on the gravel at the front of the house, brought them out onto the doorstep, along with Bramble, to greet him.

Lizzie quickly announced: "Welcome to Spurryhillock, Ronald," as he got out of the car, stretched, looked around, and smiled warmly at both.

"Well, this is a lovely rural-looking spot you have here. I`m sure you just love coming up for a break, whenever you can. Thank you for inviting me, and I`m looking forward to seeing around the place. How many acres did you say you have?"

"Oh, it's about fifteen hundred, and quite a mixed bag too. But hey, that's for tomorrow, pal."

"Your timing is perfect, Ronald. Dinner will be in about an hour, so time to come in, have a wee cup of tea, and get settled into your room. That's it up there at the central window. You are our first guest here, so this heralds more of all the new beginnings Andy, and I are enjoying."

"Here, give me your bags, and I`ll take them in for you. Lizzie`s cup of tea awaits."

With the sound of a light breeze in the trees and late afternoon birdsong, the trio went in to enjoy each other`s company.

"Here we go, sitting room this way." As Lizzie ushered Ronald into the sun-filled room.

"Do have a seat and make yourself comfortable after that long drive. I do like the look of your car, by the way. What is it?"

"Eh, it's a BMW. Very suitable, as I do have to drive quite a lot for my work. Oh, and to get to the mountains too, of course."

"Oh yeah, the mountains. I had a bit of an overdose of those a year or two back. I guess I need to overcome that soon."

"You sure do pal, and Lizzie too. The three of us should go up to something steep and high, before the year`s out. This is a lovely room guys, is the whole house as smart as this? As homely as this?"

"Yep, Dad had it all done up just a couple of years ago. The rest of the estate may be a bit neglected, but not this abode. He did a grand job on it. No Andy and I need to try and make something of the whole place, the estate, I mean. It's nowhere near even earning its keep. What do you take in your tea?

"Oh, just milk thanks. Ooh, it's nice to stop driving, relax, and be with you guys. Don't think I've seen much of you since you're wedding at Newbattle or was it the end of the trial? No matter, we have a few days to put the catching up to rights, and probably put the world to rights too. Well perhaps, but we`ll give it a damn good try."

"We sure will pal, and lay a few ghosts too, I don't wonder."

"Do you know what this eejit did the other day, Malcolm?" said Lizzie. "He brought half the roof of the stable building down on himself. Said he was just investigating it, cos we want to convert all those buildings into self-catering units. But he must have sneezed, or something, cos the next thing he knew he was being showered with slates, bits of rafters, and a hundred years of accumulated stour. Could have killed himself. But he came back with a trophy. Hang on and I`ll go and get it."

"My god you do like adventures, Andy. Your CV of adventures seems to be growing. Is that sticking plaster your wee reminder of this one?"

"It is, but as Lizzie has hinted, it could have been a whole lot worse. I blame the pigeons that were living in the stable loft. They hadn't paid their rent, the buggers."

Lizzie returned clutching the painting, which by now she`d cleaned up a bit. So, handing it to Malcolm, she quizzed: "Whom could this be, we are wondering? There was no name on what remained of the frame, and I can't make out the signature, or should I say brush stroke squiggle, on it. The loft was full of disintegrating furniture and stuff, so I`m assuming it was some of the unwanted contents of the mansion when it was abandoned to the elements many years ago. This picture seems to have been one of the few things that were in any way recognisable. Am I right, Andy?"

"Ae, after half of the roof fell in on me, the only thing I did was to retrieve this. But briefly, the rest looked completely past it."

"He`s a fine-looking young man," Malcolm interjected. "Early to mid-twenties perhaps, what would you say the style is, Lizzie?"

"I'd say it's Edwardian, though hard to be certain about that."

"And what's this box he's holding? That's surely quite unusual for a portrait. It must have some significance, as these things were not done just by chance. Oh, I see some lettering on it. Yes, BLB 8497. Do you know what, I think the BLB stands for British Linen Bank, you know, as in Stevenson's Kidnapped? If I'm correct, then that is a safe deposit box of some kind. Oh Ho, you've stumbled on a big mystery here."

4

"That was truly delicious folks," Ronald said, as he sat back after the meal. "Thank you, you do make a great culinary team."

The conversation over dinner had been about many things. The trial, Ronald`s recent mountaineering exploits, the wedding, and yes, Jamie`s death. There had certainly been no awkward silences.

"Glad you enjoyed it, so let's have coffee and dram through in the sitting room," said Lizzie, as she rose from the table. "We`ll clear this mess up later."

"There`s a jug of good coffee, and a choice of Highland Park, Port, or some liqueurs, Ronald. What would you like?" Andy ushered him to a seat beside the log fire. "This is a special occasion, so let's have something to match it."

"Could I start with coffee please, milk and none, and have a Highland Park to follow?"

"Sure thing," as Lizzie poured the coffee, and handed Ronald his cup.

"We were all very upset when Jamie took his own life in prison, and so soon after our lovely wedding,"

Lizzie then said, clearly with a heavy heart. "Oh, he got what he deserved, with that seven-year sentence, after all the damage he`d caused. He`d already cut himself off from the family well before the violent saga even ended. Hermione and the girls were of course upset that he seemed to have lost his mind or gone crazy, but they started to build a new life without him. And the way things are now, with Malcolm and Hermione, is wonderful to see. She`s happier than she ever was, with yon dangerous eejit."

"The fantasy that he was living, as a self-appointed adjunct to the landed gentry, was a sad betrayal of reality. The more he got into it, the worse he got. And finding that numbskull Jock was the beginning of the end. So, when he was incarcerated in prison, absolutely everything in his mind fell apart, and of course, he just couldn't cope with it at all. Dad did visit him a couple of times, he`s such an admirably kind man, but all he said after each visit was that Jamie was wrecked, and sadly it was all his own doing. Sorry for raising this just now, but I suppose I just wanted to get it out of the way, boys."

"Hey, that's perfectly OK Lizzie. It does help us to move on right enough." Replied Ronald, as he sipped his coffee. "You must have remembered how much I like good coffee; this is lovely. And besides a blazing log fire, now that's hard to beat."

"Did you manage to use your journalistic skills to find out any more about how that Jock character is doing inside? Filled with guilt and remorse, I hope." Andy asked.

"Only that he had caught Covid early on and although it didn't kill him; it might have been better if it had. He`s still got long Covid, I believe. Pretty incapacitated, going mad if he wasn't mad already, and as timid as a mouse."

"Thanks for the update, Ronald, let's leave that sad saga be, for now. Have you visited Lizzie`s website recently? She`s got some lovely creations posted on it, and they are selling quite well. There`s a load of orders for her, I mean us, to deal with when we get back to Edinburgh in a week or so. Our new flat there is lovely, but I have to say that carting packages up and down the three flights of stairs are a bit of a challenge. Up go the materials, and down come the completed and wrapped orders, en route to the post office. If it continues to grow, like this, we`ll need a warehouse."

"Is that you complaining Andy, my man? This is my revenge for your jacking in your career three years ago, without any warning." Lizzie said with a loud guffaw. "And anyway, it keeps you fit."

"Only joking love, I know that you didn't get to this stage on a whim. `Lot of hard work and amazing creativity went into it."

"Of course, I follow your great reviews Lizzie, and yes, I do love your website. Very imaginatively put together it is. There`s one picture on it that I love, think I`ll need to buy it, as there`s a space on my living room wall where it would look perfect. It's the one where you somehow captured the spirit of that standing stone in its surrounding landscape. Lots of dramatic movement in the wide sky, echoed by the texture of the hills and moors. Gosh, now I`m getting carried away with descriptive jargon, but I`m sure you take it all as the compliment that you so rightly deserve?"

"Thanks, Ronald, I do appreciate your comments, I do. It was an interesting process of photography, painting, and yet more use of the studio camera that produced the final creation. Yeah, I`m rather pleased with it. Whoever erected that stone all those years ago, did so for a very good reason. Its place in the Orcadian landscape is mysteriously special. Makes you think. Well, I hope it does."

"That was a night and dawn like no other," Ronald exclaimed, as he appeared for breakfast.

"Did you not sleep well?" Andy asked, somewhat puzzled. "Thought all this fresh air would knock you out for the night."

"Oh, I`m certainly not complaining pal. The outdoor show was a joy to see. I`d got up in the night, and before I went back to bed, I looked out of the window to see what all the commotion was. Perhaps that's what woke me in the first place. Anyway, as I looked out, two badgers were tearing around in circles on the lawn, by moonlight. Round and round they went. I watched for ages. You may have to repair the lawn, cos there are now big circular tracks, where the badgers have torn it up. Man, that was a sight to behold."

"Not long after I went back to bed, I heard another strange noise out there, so I got up again to investigate. What a delight because Mrs Fox was watching her cubs playing. Rolling over each other they were, pretend biting, and yelping. That show must have lasted almost half an hour, and it was every bit as captivating as the badgers."

"Back in bed, I dozed, I guess, but after some time, the dawn chorus woke me. It echoed around the big trees, bounced off the house, I suppose. A wonderful sound of nature`s fullness right outside my window and into my bedroom through the open window. Haven't heard as full a chorus as that in a long time. You laid it all on in full dear Lizzie."

"Can`t take any of the credit, as you know Ronald. It's just the way things are here, and as you can imagine, it's a great joy to experience it all. We love it, and hope that in time we can share it with many others when we get the self-catering part of the business up and running."

"You`ll have people beating a path to your door, I`m sure," Ronald exclaimed enthusiastically.

"Hopefully yes. Long way to go to get there, as you`ll see when we venture out this morning. Neglect and Nature in Harmony is the current strapline," Lizzie added.

"What would you like for breakfast Ronald? There`s cereal or porridge here," as Andy moved over to a cupboard. "Or there`s a fridge full of the usual stuff for cooking,"

"Just a light breakfast please Andy, porridge, toast, and coffee. That`ll set me up for the day very nicely thanks."

The trio then sat around the great old kitchen table and continued the catching up they craved, and that helped the breakfast go down rather well. Once again, the air was filled with the babble of friendly voices, and the aroma of coffee.

"Hope you've brought your boots, pal. Because I`ve planned a fine treck round the estate for you. Probably take all morning to get around all the points of interest, and we can then have a picnic at the top of the hill. How does that sound?"

"You're the host Andy. Well, no, I`m sure it's very much a joint lairdship you have here. What's the title or name for that, I wonder? My goodness, I`m not normally stuck for words, but this has me rather beat. In this day and age, we do need a suitable description. `Need to think about it. P`raps after I've seen around the estate, I'll get some inspiration. That breakfast has sure set me up for exploration."

"Brilliant, will we be ready to leave in about half an hour, meet out the front," Andy suggested.

"Yep, ready to stride the marches then."

Warm sunshine and more birdsongs set the scene for this exploration, and as Ronald strode boldly out, he blinked briefly, stretched, and stamped his feet, as is in readiness for whatever lay ahead. "Ready as you two are, I`m so looking forward to this, and with two excellent proprietorial guides to lead me. What more could a man ask?"

"We`ll have a great walk, I can promise you that. Your walking poles will be fine; the place may be neglected, and run a bit wild, but I assure you, no machete necessary." Andy said reassuringly.

"This place has been in my family for two or three hundred years, perhaps more. It may have been a bit larger at one time, but I`m not certain of that yet. Anyway, we`ve got almost fifteen hundred acres, and I`d say that's enough to be going on with. Over two hundred and fifty of that is woodland of one sort or another. There`s a let farm, as you`ll see, but the tenant no longer lives on it permanently. The changes in agricultural subsidies that are coming may mean a radical opportunity to manage the land in a more biodiverse kind of way. It's early days for that though.

As you`d see on your way up the drive, there are the ruins of a substantial mansion, mainly early Victorian, but that was abandoned to nature, a good many years ago. Probably just after the last war. So, the dower house is what we now live in. And it's big enough for most things.

Oh, and we think the original money for this place came from banking in Edinburgh, so the family probably had a house, or residence in that city too. But wherever that was, it's long gone. Mum and dad live in the Grange area as you know."

"Hey, that's enough of an introduction for now. Let's wander through the woodland, past the old loch, ruins of the big house, and so on," as Lizzie led the way.

"We keep this route as open as possible, so an industrial strimmer is a godsend. Andy`s a dab hand with that. Aren't you, my love?"

"Eh yes, a good full day of hard exercise or graft a couple of times a year. I tell myself it will get a bit easier, as I gradually defeat the wildly overgrown vegetation. We very disrespectfully call it `Archie`s neglect."

The trio took the single file, as they left the drive, and fell silent briefly. Crossing a slightly more open area, they stopped in front of the ruins of Spurryhillock house, or castle, as Lizzie told the group it was referred to on a few old maps.

"So, you can see, it's in a sorry state Ronald. Andy assures me that the main walls are surprisingly sound, but I`m not so sure. What would we describe it as? Early baronial? Probably, but I think there are the remains of something a lot earlier in amongst it. Is certainly unsafe, so you won't mind if we don't try to get into it?"

"Aye, we are fine here. Must have been quite a place. I`m sure it's been written up somewhere, so with that, I could easily imagine the interior, as it was. Is it haunted?"

"Story of a green lady, but I've yet to be introduced to her, Andy said with a chuckle. The huge early Victorian part of it seems a bit oversized for this estate, so I do rather wonder where the money for that came from. A wee puzzle which may never be solved, I fear."

Sounds of the breeze soughing in the trees above and all around had a mesmerising effect on the group; a gentle swaying in the boughs seemed to mirror their movement as they walked, captivated by the woodland magic. The dappled light where glints of sunlight broke through then faded till the next, illuminated their nodding heads, lightly swaying shoulders, and the rhythm of their walking. Their gaze fell into a pattern of looking ahead at the track to judge where their next tread would touch the ground with safety, whilst admiring the great trees all around.

That silence between them was only broken when Andy commented that many of the trees would have been planted when the big house was built. "The family that envisioned and built it probably never saw the real fruits of their great plan. Some trees that would have been even grander standing alone, like the cedar of Lebanon and oak, or copper beech, are now

25

crowded in amongst the rest as the years of neglect confused the original planting. No matter though, because I`m sure you'd agree it's a delight to experience where nature now seems to have free reign."

"I do indeed, and this winding splashing burn that we seem to be following close bye, completes what the birdlife sounds it is well pleased with." Ronald ventured.

"Oh my, you guys are getting quite lyrical in your observations. I love it."

At this point, they crossed an old stone arched bridge, which signalled the way ahead to a somewhat sorry-looking folly, designed perhaps to look like a small classical pavilion. A spreading tree growing up through its heart had somehow laid claim to the formality it had once pretended.

"Yes, my forebears liked to put on a little of a show of learning, or was it just romantic fancy? True, it now looks a bit overwhelmed, but even as it is, it has a certain flair about it, I`d say."

Admiring it, very much in passing, the explorers then followed the path up a small rise to the remnants of the walled garden. Beside the gateway, there were the remains of what must have been a gardener's house, potting sheds, and boiler house. Nature once more was laying claim to these, and what had been the garden within had succumbed too. A few very neglected apple trees and semi-collapsed glasshouse frames against one wall of the gently sloping land was but a hint at what had once been.

"What could we do with this, I wonder?" Mused Andy. "It has lots of tantalising promise, but with a price tag, I fear. The whole estate is littered with little gems like this, which surely have a future in the business plan that Lizzie and I are trying to put together."

"We may have to part with something, a small field or two perhaps to raise the capital that we`ll need. And there are a couple of these that are at the lower extremity, somewhat detached, with views down the rest of the valley, which would be ideal for modest housebuilding, if planning permission can be got. So, we are indeed starting to think ahead, about what might be. I've sketched a few rough plans already, which are over at the house, and if you are interested, you can have a look and see what you think. Add your ideas too, please Ronald," said Lizzie.

"I will of course be delighted to see them because I'm already getting caught up in the potential of this beautiful place. It needs to balance change, with regeneration, whilst also being desperate not to destroy the very wildness that is so appealing, my friends. Lead on please."

Further up the valley, a small loch had been created to provide something useful; fishing perhaps, water to feed a mill or just the magic of water in the woodland. The trail skirted around the edge of this, past the barely discernible remains of a boathouse on the far bank.

"Now wouldn't that make a wonderful, very romantic little self-catering unit, if it was rebuilt?" Andy ventured. "A honeymoon spot like no other, I`d say."

"Access by boat only, of course, guys. For an undisturbed honeymoon. I like it," quipped Ronald. As he almost tumbled over a fallen tree, lying across the trail.

"Oh, do watch your step," Lizzie advised. "As you can see, Andy`s still got a way to go with the trailblazing. We go up across a couple of fields, or should I say, rough grazing, when we leave the woodland. Then we`ll be at the top of the hillock part of Spurryhillock. We`ve still to identify a spurry though. It's a wildflower in the pink family. I think the farmer has taken his bull out of this area," she added, as they clambered over a rickety style, out into the open.

"I do hope so, Lizzie, as my last encounter with a bull somewhere up north, was a bit alarming. You`ll see that I survived it though. Just left the bull snorting angrily at me from the other side of a fence I`d cleared quicker than you could say, close shave."

Several big, rounded stones on the hilltop, provided good seats for admiring the view and having some lunch. Andy had his stove out, as the first essential.

"Tea OK, on this occasion folks," Andy enquired. And as the others nodded loudly, Lizzie handed round the sandwiches.

"So, a business plan is in the making, is it? Unlike you to be as organised as that, Andy," Ronald teased.

"It's Lizzie in the driving seat for that, but she`s right. We must start making some money out of this place, and of course, we still have major commitments in Edinburgh too."

"I have a lot of work for Andy to do, as my courier and go-for, haven't I love?"

"Oh, you sure do, I wish I`d a fiver for every time I've been up and down those stairs in Warrender Park Road. But och, the view from up there is the great reward, and the way Archie and Marissa had the whole flat done up for us as a wedding present was braw. Quite a change from what I now see as that poky wee place I had in Peebles. Sold that, and Lizzie sold her flat too, so that gave us almost enough to buy the new place, without any mortgage. Oh, and I got a wee bit of money when my Aunt Senga died a couple of years ago. So that`ll keep the wolf from the door meantime."

"Sounds like a good outcome all around then. You`ll be able to afford a new pair of climbing boots, so we can get back out in the hills again," urged Ronald, hopefully.

"Yeah, the big escapade wore the last pair right into the ground. If you look over there, in that direction, you can just make out a load of ruined brick buildings," Andy pointed, "That's one of the other assets we hope to get something positive from. It's not a thing of beauty, as the remains of a World War Two depot of some kind, and there`s a bunker or two as well. The possible house-building site once it's cleared. And it's far enough from the Dower house not to be intrusive."

Lunch over, the bags were packed, and Lizzie described the route back. "I`ll show you where this daft bugger Andy nearly got himself killed the other day. Let's see what you make of it, Ronald, as something with a bit of potential. Andy says it is ripe for renovation. Don't you, my love."

"I do indeed, and it is," Andy led the way back down a slightly different route.

Re-entering the woodland by a wicket gate, they started to note and remark on the many different types of trees.

"There must have been an arborealist in the family a while back. Some exotic and non-native trees here. Although they are very grand, I do prefer the native species, rowan, pine, oak, silver birch, and the like. Somehow, native trees have much greater significance. Being more in tune with them is amazingly enriching. Perhaps it's the ultimate link we need with our landscapes. My god, I`m getting serious here."

"Well, I don't think either of us would disagree for one second, Lizzie," Ronald added with enthusiasm.

"Here are the decrepit remains of the stable buildings, and you can see where half the roof caved in. But if you allow your imagination a bit of free rein, you can visualise something nice being created here. The old stonework is a joy to look at."

As Andy said this, Ronald stepped forward and stretched his hand up to the top of the wall, where the roof had been. "There`s something here, guys. Let's see if I can get it." With the tips of his fingers, he managed to pull it clear, and it landed at his feet. An old key with a tag on it.

"Wow let's see what it is," Lizzie exclaimed, as she stepped forward to pick it up. Holding it up, so that the others could also see, she dusted the cobwebs off a big old iron key. Attached to it was what looked like a copper tag, with some writing on it. "It seems to say 5 Heriot Row, and there's a much smaller key also attached. This is as tantalising a mystery as that painting you recovered Andy."

After two more days of exploring, eating well, chatting, and sharing thoughts on how Spurryhillock could be revitalised as a more dynamic place, it was time to go.

"I've got a load of orders to meet back in Edinburgh, as my website has been busy, I see. You`ll have those stairs to run up and down a few times, my love. We`d best lock up here, and head back down the road, a little slower than you, Ronald, I've no doubt. Drive safely, and we`ll meet up again soon, I hope. We`ve got two curiosities to try and solve, well three, if you include the smaller key. I`ll start with Dad, to see if he has any ideas about the picture.

Before Andy and Lizzie departed though, they reminded themselves of their honeymoon, in an appropriate fashion. And as they then lay warmly together, reflected on the memory of it.

After the wonderful wedding, they had headed north to the Orkney Islands. A week of cliff walking, island hopping, wildlife watching, and special picnics, was only bettered by the greatest array of historic sites they`d ever imagined possible. Standing stones in the landscape especially captured their interest and sense of wonder. Endless waves on the surrounding shores somehow stirred the passion that they felt for each other.

It was a superb honeymoon, they had agreed. And on the ferry back to the mainland, Lizzie had enthused, "I feel some fine paintings to add to my collection coming out of this. All the ancient stones put our brief sojourn there into perspective and fill me with wonder and curiosity as to what the ancients' purposes were in erecting them."

"Profound meaning, of that I`m sure," Andy added.

As they were driving back down the road, Lizzie remarked, "So much seems to be happening in our lives these days Andy, my love. Events, changes, and responsibilities too, sometimes seem a bit of a jumble. I`m certainly not complaining, not for one second, indeed, I wouldn't have it any other way. I must pinch myself from time to time to try and keep track of it all and remind myself of the sequence of things; yes, the sequence of all the new happiness."

"As I wake some mornings, Lizzie, I find myself, wondering the same too. Where has our journey come from, and my goodness, where will it take us?"

5

Music was coming from Andy and Lizzie's flat. As they made their way up the stairs and entered the door, they were greeted with "Welcome home," by Marissa.

Then, a slightly more distant, "come in, come in," from Archie who was through in the kitchen. When you told us about the painting, we just had to come and see it. And the two of you, of course. We`ve got the kettle on. Is there anything else that needs to come up from the car?"

"Nothing that can`t wait," said Lizzie, as she carefully handed the painting to Archie.

He carried it over to the great bay window in the sitting room, held it up, and examined it, with a serious look on his face.

"So, you say you found this in the stable loft, Andy? Was there anything else there?"

"Yes, but I only glanced at it, as I was afraid that the rest of the roof might collapse on me. Looked like a load of old broken or rotten furniture. Why the painting survived at all, is a mystery. The frame was a bit rotten too, but Lizzie removed it before carefully cleaning the painting. Probably needs more attention, and she`s got what she`ll need to do that, here."

"I haven't a clue who this fine young man is. I suppose it must have come out of the big house before it was abandoned to the dry rot. What's this box he`s holding? Looks like he`s in tweeds. What era would you say it is, Lizzie?"

"Reckoned it was probably late Edwardian, so perhaps a bit before the first world war. Does that correspond with anyone in the family at that time, Dad?"

"Hard to say at this stage. Unfortunately, my mother, dumped a whole load of family papers and photos, when I was a boy. And her untimely death just broke much of the family thread. Should have asked my father more, but he just wasn't interested in that, indeed it was he, that let Spurryhillock go to the dogs. What a mystery, but we`ll investigate, I`m sure. Now, what about that key that you said you have?"

Again, Archie studied it closely, whilst standing by the window. "Now this is strange, but a bit more hopeful. Because I believe that the family was in Heriot Row, until about nineteen hundred, give or take a decade, and then moved to Grange, where we are now. So there`s a remote chance that this is the main key to the Heriot Row house. Though why it would be left at Spurryhillock, is anybody's guess. The smaller key could be anything."

With one mystery almost solved, and two mysteries, left hanging in the air, they sat down for a cup of tea and a chat.

"We`d a lovely time up there, and of course, Ronald came and stayed a few days too. Our business plan has perhaps progressed a wee bit. But I have a load of orders I, we, need to start on tomorrow," said Lizzie. How`s Hermione, Malcolm, and the girls?"

"All fine," Marissa said eagerly. The girls are a bit anxious about the exams, but we know they`ll do fine. Just need to keep reassuring them. Malcolm's got one or two jobs making some furniture in elm, I believe. Think it's someone out in East Lothian that's placed the order. For a castle restoration, we are told."

"That's great to hear, quite a high-profile job then. What about Hermione? How`s her work with young people`s mental health and nature?" Asked Lizzie.

"Seems to be going well, oh, it's early days, but I think she`s enjoying it, and believe she`ll be very good at it too. She certainly has the right temperament. It sort of picks up on that job she had ages ago, working on a nature reserve. That was before she married, eh, that bizarre character called Jamie."

"What about you Mum, now that you`ve retired?"

"Well, I`m certainly not missing the bureaucracy that I`d tholed for years. So now I`m doing some voluntary admin and support for the Artists Association."

"Wow, that's a fine switch. I`ll keep in with you. Have you got any grants on the go?"

"Not that I know of. Sorry"

"Hermione and the gang are wanting to come up to Spurryhillock in a few weeks, which`ll be nice. We can tell the girls that the problems with the Wi-Fi have been fixed. So, in the meantime I need to, I mean we, need to get on with the orders and promotion. Don't we Andy?"

"Eh, yes, we do. You know how much I appreciate running up and down the stairs for you, my love."

In addition to being Lizzie`s general go-for, Andy had taken a part-time job in a project working with disadvantaged young people. Many could easily have been the clients in his old job working with young offenders, but he was done with that bureaucratic scenario. Instead, the project was in a charity, and his work largely focussed on taking the young people away for a short residential experience in a remote bothy up in the Highlands. Some of them had never even been out of Edinburgh before and couldn't imagine a place without street lighting at night. The highland glen was therefore an entirely new experience, and in that novel setting, with a carefully structured programme of activities, group-agreed rules, group

34

cooking, and a high level of interaction with the leaders, the process of transforming troubled young lives was kindled.

For Andy, this was a new chapter in his life. The flashbacks seemed worst at night. More real than mere dreams, he would know he was awake, and the thankfully brief experience of re-living one of the frightening episodes on the Seven Signs escapade would engulf him. In that flashback episode, he would imagine he saw, felt, or even heard the terror of it. He`d sweat profusely, and stare beyond the immediate night-time scene. Then he would get up and go and sit in the great bay window so that even in the relative dark, his attention was drawn away to the lights and the sound of the city night. And so distracted in this way, he`d become calm once more. In telling Lizzie the next morning, he remarked that he knew the flashbacks were diminishing in frequency. Oh, he knew that the outcome of the Seven Signs was positive, and he felt he`d honoured what The Spirit had entrusted him with.

That Jenny Anderson had obtained funding for a PhD study of the Wildness of the Watershed, and indeed now had a student in place, was an immensely worthwhile outcome; one which would collate existing evidence, garner more and present it in hard well-argued fact. Andy knew that in the fullness of time, this would possibly influence policy on land use and appreciation.

As a man with much humanity in his heart, Andy did reflect upon the two men who went to prison: and on their self-inflicted fate. Lives so needlessly wasted. Their trial had been a nightmare, both as a witness, and observer, but thankfully that was over and done with.

Andy had written to the current occupants of number five Heriot Row, to explain something of the mysterious discovery of the key. He`d invited an email reply, and it duly arrived in his inbox.

"How fascinating, we`ve never had a key for that big lock, perhaps your key is the very one. Please do arrange a suitable time to bring it along and let's see if it fits," came the reply from William MacGillivray.

In due course, Lizzie and Andy made their way across town to the Georgian splendour of Heriot Row, with the key safely in a small backpack. Standing in front of the big formal-looking front door, painted an appealing olive colour, Lizzie boldly pressed the bell. Minutes later, footsteps could be heard in the hall, getting closer, till the door swung open and revealed an elderly gentleman, who welcomed them.

"Come away in please, I`m William MacGillivray; you must be Lizzie and Andy. I`m so keen to see if the key fits, so let's test it while we are right here. I did take the precaution of putting some lubricant in earlier, as this lock may not have been active in a very long time. The key to the door, perhaps."

Slowly, Lizzie put the key in the lock. Gave it a wee wiggle or two. Then started to turn it. It seemed to be the right fit, but initially, it was very stiff. She took it back out again and could see some grains of rust sticking to it. Cleaning it off with a tissue, she reinserted it, and put a bit more twist into it. Slowly, it began to turn, stiffly, with quite a bit of resistance. Then suddenly, the bolt shot out the side of the door. It worked. The trio gathered around the door and gasped. Lizzie unlocked it and then locked it again. William did it a few times, and with a great big smile on his face. Then Andy took his turn. A little more lubricant was added, for good measure.

"Mildred will be so thrilled with this. We`ve always felt that the door, grand and all that it is, just wasn't complete. Oh, I guess we could have got a new lock or key made, but this is the original, I`d say. Do come through for a well-earned coffee and a bun to go with it."

The south-facing living room was to the left of the entrance hall, going in past a fine pair of Doric columns. The room was pure Georgian. Panelling in perfect order and symmetry, a fireplace that Robert Adam could so easily have designed, three large south-facing windows, shuttering, and matching doors, one to enter by and the other for a cupboard. The furniture was equally grand.

"So do you think your ancestors lived here, some time back, Lizzie?" How long ago, and where did they move to?"

"Well, we are not certain, because so many of our family papers have not survived. But I reckon they moved out sometime in the nineteen-twenties, or even earlier. They may have been here from the start around 1810 or so. They also had an estate up north. And moved from here to a house in the Grange area."

What did you say your family name in Lizzie?"

"It's Ferguson."

"Now that's interesting indeed. But before I tell you why can I ask, would you consider selling the key to me? We`d love to have it."

"Oh, this is the rightful place for it William, this is where it belongs, indeed it's your door that it would appear it was made for, so there is no question of selling it to you, you shall have it, as a gift from Andy and me."

"Well, I am most grateful, and I`m sure that Mildred will be thrilled too. Oh, it's probably a bit big for everyday use, but it can live in the lock, on the inside, as part of the very fabric of this house. Thank you most sincerely. We`ve lived here for over thirty years now, and it's wonderful to be able to make the place that wee bit more complete."

"Now here`s the intriguing thing I referred to. In one of the cellars out the front there, underneath the pavement, are several cellars. We can be reasonably certain that we own most of them, but there`s one that is a bit uncertain. The title deeds are not specific about it. So, we just leave it. But it's full of stuff that was here when we bought the house, looks like it's mostly old furniture and perhaps household goods. Near the front is a kind of leather cabin trunk, reasonably intact, and on the lid, it had the name Capt. Alexander Ferguson. So, now I`m wondering."

With that, they heard the front door open and the sound of footsteps in the hall. Another door opened, then closed, and a tall fine-looking lady with a warm smile entered. William did the introductions, and quickly told the story of the key.

"It's lovely to meet you both, Lizzie, and Andy. I hope you've been well looked after by William here. I`m fascinated with the story of the key, and how you came to have it. And my goodness, from what you say, a perfect fit too."

"I`ll go and make us all some coffee dear, while you get to know each other, and hear the story of the key, now our key."

In a babble of excited voices, the story was retold, including how the events of its discovery were the result of such a near-miss for Andy.

"I must say, this is all very intriguing. To somehow make this rather random connection like this, is quite extraordinary. We`d often wondered where the key had gone but had just given up on it, and now here it is. I`m thrilled and thank you so much."

William brought the coffee in and poured it. So, as they slowly drank it, there was more chat to be enjoyed.

Then Mildred took them by surprise and said, "you know I seem to remember reading something about someone just like you, who went on a great adventure, got into a bit of rather violent danger, and it all seemed to end with two guys going to prison for their misdeeds. Can I ask, was it you, Andy? And I`m sure you suffered a bit because of it too Lizzie? I liked the brief mention of the thing that started it all off, you're meeting with a very strange and mysterious character somewhere up north. Did he not have a message for you?"

"Ae, that's me." said Andy, a little taken aback.

"Oh, I hope you didn't mind my mentioning it?"

"No, not at all. It's led to some quite interesting events."

William interjected, "I was just telling them, before you came home dear, about the cabin trunk in the cellar. There`s the possibility that in fact, it belonged to a Capt. Alexander Ferguson, one of Lizzie`s ancestors. Because her family owned this house, probably before it was sub-divided, between about 1810 and the nineteen twenties. Can we go and look, folks?"

Mildred led the way, downstairs, along a corridor through what looked like a study room, and then with a clanking of security chains, unlocked a door that led out to an open paved area well below street level. A row of neatly painted doors on the far side seemed to present a choice of cellars, somehow under the pavement. Going to the left-hand one of these, she opened it and switched on a light within. Immediately in front, all was neat, but a low arched opening to the left led into a dark clutter.

"This is the cellar, that we are uncertain about ownership, perhaps because it's under access to the whole house, which is now of course subdivided to make two. Sorry, there`s no light in here, so I brought a torch, and a duster too. It's a bit cramped for all of us to get in," William advised.

Mildred and Andy stood back, to let Lizzie and William enter, as both had to duck the lower entrance height.

"Thankfully, the cabin trunk I was telling you about is near the front of this lot," as he shone the torch on it.

And there it sat, raised a little off the ground on some kind of invisible support. Ancient leather, with wooden slats along it, the handles at either end, were also of thicker leather, and a brass lock on a hinged bracket, hinted at its apparent antiquity.

"We`ve never had a key for it, so there it sits awaiting attention, curiosity, or even a new purpose. There`s the name on it, I was telling you about Lizzie. Could that be an ancestor of yours, I wonder? Anyway, I`m sure Mildred will agree, you are welcome to have it, as it can't sit there forever. When we eventually sell this place, I`m sure it will just go in a skip along with all the other contests of this cellar." William ran the duster along with the ancient, once-white lettering: Capt. Alexander Ferguson.

Standing back, Andy joined Lizzie to admire the now much-neglected artefact. Out of curiosity, Andy tried the lock bracket, but it held fast. He lifted one end and remarked that it seemed to be quite heavy. "Shall we say yes to William and Mildred`s kind offer? I'm fascinated."

"Of course, we should Andy, let's investigate how we can get it out of here, and perhaps take it over to Dad`s garage. Then we can see what's to be done with it."

Emerging into the bright daylight, Lizzie said enthusiastically, "We`d love to have it. This is very thoughtful of you."

"Well, it's more likely to be yours than ours, and it needs to go, as do the other contents of the cellar. But that's another matter, I`m sure," said Mildred.

40

"We walked over this morning, but we can investigate getting some helpful muscle, and a van. So, when that's organised, we`ll be back in touch to arrange a convenient time to uplift it, Mildred." Andy added.

Back in the sitting room, they sat down for more coffee and an eager exchange of life`s experiences.

When they got over to the Grange, Archie seemed busy mowing the lawn, and the sounds emerging from the workshop suggested that Malcolm was busy being creative, as he liked to call it.

"I'm sure there will be some lunch soon, just let me finish this please folks. The ladies are both out at their endeavours," Archie shouted as the mower revved up again.

A cloud of dust in the workshop suggested that Malcolm was indeed doing something to a piece of wood, on the electric workbench. Waiting till there was a lull, Andy, and Lizzie studied a large piece of elm, which no doubt had much promise to be some beautiful piece of furniture, once the craftsman had got going on it.

"Hello Malcolm," Lizzie yelled through the dust-filled place.

Switching off whatever piece of equipment he was using, he waved back. Stepping forward out of the engulfing dust, he removed his mask and goggles, and greeted them, "So lovely to see you guys. I won`t say welcome to this stour-filled place. Let's go into the house." With that, he led them into the modern house that had been built in the grounds of the old house and was home to himself, Hermione, Monique, and Charlotte. "Everyone else is out, but Archie will join us for some lunch when he`s done with the grass cutting. Takes quite a pride in that, he does."

"What are your lock-picking skills like Malcolm?" Lizzie asked, with a wide grin.

"Not quite sure, cos I don't indulge in that very much, but you know, I do like a challenge. What a strange question! Why do you ask? Well, I guess you must have a lock that is calling out to be picked."

Archie came in, having got rid of all the grass cuttings that had clung to his clothing and footwear.

"These two have just asked me a question that would suggest that I must have some felonious tendencies, Archie. What do you make of that?"

"Well, it rather depends, I`d say. If you need a lawyer, then I`m your man, Malcolm."

"Lock picking," Lizzie quickly interjected.

"Don`t tell me, you've locked yourselves out of your lovely flat?" Said, Malcolm. But let's get the lunch underway first, then you can explain all."

It wasn't too long before an opportunity came up, to explain what it was all about.

"We could do with your muscle and van Malcolm, to uplift the trunk. Could we bring it back here please Dad, as I don't fancy hauling it up to three flights of tenement stairs?"

"No problem," Archie assured.

"We`ll give William and Mildred a call while we are here, to arrange a suitable date," as Lizzie got out her phone. "Here`s a photo of the trunk and the name on it."

As she showed it around, she asked Archie, "does this name mean anything to you Dad?"

Looking at it carefully, he finally said, "Hm, I`d a great uncle Alex who died in the first world war. He would actually have inherited, as the older of the two, but my grandfather, also Archibald, was landed with everything. I'm not so sure his heart was in it, as things rather went to pot. I seem to recall it being said that Alex was in the Navy and died at sea. He had studied law, and it wasn't long after gaining all his qualifications and joining one of the big law firms, that he was called up. If my mother hadn't thrown out so much stuff, we`d perhaps be in a better position with this. But you say that the current owners of that property in Heriot Row want to give you the trunk. Perhaps once Malcolm has done with getting his felonious skills to work, we might know a bit better."

"Can't wait to see what's in the trunk. Oh, and we kept the smaller key." Lizzie blurted excitedly. "You are a bit of an amateur historian to Malcolm. You might like to get your teeth into this."

Malcolm got out his phone and diddled in a few details. He was briefly away in his world. Then, he stated with great authority, here he is. "Capt. Alexander Ferguson, RN, died at sea, on 22nd February 1917, Son of Mr Archibald Ferguson, W.S. and Mrs Matilda Ferguson, of Spurryhillock and Glenmaddy. That`s from the Commonwealth War Graves Commission site."

"Is that all we are to be able to know of him, I wonder?" Asked Lizzie.

"So far it is, and it's not much, is it, I do hope that more does emerge, as that's a rather sad summary of his life," Malcolm sighed.

"My goodness," Archie exclaimed. "Spurryhillock and Glenmaddy. Now that's a completely new one on me."

6.

Landing on the floor of Malcolm's workshop with a thump, the great old leather trunk conveyed intrigue to the family group standing around. Now in the brighter light, it showed more detail than had been evident in the cellar where it had languished, forgotten, for almost a century. The leather had become a very dark brown, almost black with age. It stood perhaps two feet high, almost two feet deep, and some four feet long. The corners were all severely scuffed, with what must have been a lot of rough handling, and two thick leather straps wrapped around it, their ends inserted into brass clips. There were also two leather loops to hold it firm front and back. The brass lock and bracket tantalisingly held the lid down.

"That's been designed for serious use," said Andy in a rather hushed tone.

"Sure has," added Malcolm, with a respect for the craftsmanship it demonstrated. "Well now, about lock picking. Let's put it up on this pair of trestles so I can get at it."

More arms than were needed, as they eagerly lifted it and turned it on its back, as Malcolm placed the trestles underneath. Checking it was secure, he shone a light at the lock.

"OK, soft wire brush first," as he confidently removed all cobwebs and dust. Then he got an air spray and inserted the nozzle as close as possible to the keyhole. With a short blast or two, a few more bits of dust and the remains of a dead spider flew out. Now we give it a skoosh of this stuff, and retire for a cup of tea, while the penetrating oil does its business. Give it time to get right in and soften any rust."

The eager, curious, group rather reluctantly went out and sat around a table in the garden; to wait. The late Capt. Alexander Ferguson R.N. had become the all-consuming focus of interest.

"I`m very reluctant to do anything that would damage the trunk, other than the innards of the lock if that proves necessary. The trunk may not be worth much in itself, but it's the contents, whatever they may be. It may be heavy, but I don't think it's just got a load of old bricks in it. Bound to be much more interesting, I`m sure."

"OK, stand back audience, I don't want you discovering too much about my secret lock-picking expertise. It might arouse suspicion on my CV." So, Malcolm rolled up his sleeves with a kind of professional flair. He`d assembled an array of bits of wire, small screwdrivers, and a bent nail or two. A pair of pliers completed his toolkit, he very much hoped.

Silence fell over the watching group, as Malcolm did a lot of raking around inside the lock. This way and that, pushing and pulling, prodding, listening, and then adding more lubricant. After what seemed like an eternity, he straightened, and pronounced, "something is happening."

Wiping his hands on a cloth, he gave it another blast from the air gun and waited. "I`m no expert on locks, but I think I`ve discovered how this one works or worked. One more purposeful squiggle around inside to go. Perhaps."

The sense of anticipation was almost unbearable, as the group shuffled on impatient feet, hardly daring to breathe.

Even Bramble seemed to be taking an interest in the proceedings, with one ear slightly up, and tail wagging eagerly.

The bent nail was clamped firmly in the pliers and urged into the keyhole. His knuckles white with the firmness of the grip, Malcolm turned it purposefully clockwise, back anticlockwise, and then clockwise once more with a real twist of his wrist. Something clicked, and magically, the brass lock popped open. A century or more of secrets awaited discovery.

"Not so sure this lock`ll be much use anymore, but it's open, and I haven't wrecked the outside of it. Have I?"

Slowly opening the lid, Lizzie pushed it back as its ancient hinges creaked. Heads came forward in anticipation.

"Let's be organised, Malcolm. Have you a table we can put things on, please Archie? I suggest that we carefully remove what's here, one item at a time and by just one of us?" Lizzie pronounced, with some authority.

Happy to oblige," offered Archie.

"Perhaps some photos as we go, please," Lizzie added.

There was some discussion about the apparent contents first, and the condition that most of it was in.

"You know, it's quite remarkable that it, whatever it is, has survived relatively intact all this time. No sign of infestation. Very little effect of water or dampness. A little probably natural decay, but a bit of a time capsule that is calling out for investigation. OK, folks, I`ll start lifting these contents out, one at a time. Can we place them on the table, please? We can then produce an inventory in due course."

Everyone was impatient but knew that this must be done properly and with dignity.

So, clothing and uniforms were placed in one pile. Books in another. Documents in the third. And on through apparent academic material, and so on. Stretching right down to the bottom of the almost empty trunk, Archie carefully lifted out a strong wooden box, with some letters and numbers on it, starting BLB.

"Oh, my God," she exclaimed. "Is this not the very box that's in the painting of the young man? If it is, we are almost at the point of proving who he is, what he did, though we already know when he died."

46

"This is beyond my wildest dreams. It was almost worth getting half-killed by a collapsing roof, to get all this. You are going to be busy with your research Malcolm. But now we must get into that box folks."

"Here`s a shot in the dark, you know that other wee key that was attached to the bigger one for Heriot Row, do you think, possibly," as she trailed off. "Where did we leave it?"

"We didn't leave it anywhere. Abracadabra. Here it is," as Andy pulled it out of his pocket. "Malcolm, would you once again, do the honours, please?"

Going through the same process, but on a smaller scale, he inserted lubricant, gave it a blast of air, cleaned the key, and then much to everyone's chagrin said, "now we need to wait a wee bit, please. Could we have more tea?"

"Oh Ok," Lizzie ventured, the frustration visible on her face and in her tone.

The group retreated once more to the garden. Nervously or impatiently drank their tea. Finally, after what seemed like another eternity, Malcolm looked at his watch and said, "OK, now is the moment of truth folks."

Malcolm brought the box out into the garden this time, laid it on the table, and duly inserted the key. A perfect fit. After some internal click, he was able to open the lid.

Other things got somewhat neglected, in the week since the opening of the box.

The call went out from Archie, to assemble in their dining room on the coming Tuesday morning at ten o`clock; notebooks and pens were provided. Coffee on arrival.

Archie was seated regally at the head of the table in his big oak chair with the armrests on it. "Come away in Malcolm, grab a coffee from the pot on the sideboard, and pick a seat." The same warm greeting was extended to Lizzie and Andy, as they arrived just a few minutes later.

"Have you all got coffee and a biscuit? Good morning, all, I declare this meeting of the Ferguson research group, is now in session. You all know the areas of investigation that you were assigned, but I`ll recap on that for you. Lizzie, you were on the bundles of papers and maps I gave you when I handed Spurryhillock to Andy and yourself. Malcolm, you are on the contents of the box. Andy, you said you`d look at official records, like Scotland`s People and other stuff in Register House. Whilst I agreed to delve into current laws on land ownership and access as they may affect us today. Who`d like to start?"

Andy immediately ventured to summarise his findings. "So, I've now constructed what I would call the main line of the Ferguson family history, from today, going back to about sixteen hundred. That's nine generations that I could be fairly certain about, as gleaned from Scotland`s People. Some more recent stuff is not available because of the hundred-year rule, so I`ve picked a few brains within the family, on that. Here are copies for each of you, which I've printed out. Most of the records were from Edinburgh and Midlothian, but also some from the parish of Springbraes, where Spurryhillock is located. I've still to look at the mysterious Maddyburn. I`d say that the family chart I've just given you all, should be regarded as background material. But it certainly confirms Archie`s assertion that the main line of business was in banking of some sort or another. There are two or three wills that I've ordered up, and I rather expect them to be in legalese. What's also missing at this stage are the family details of the wives of the main line, and information about burial and gravestones. Think I've made good progress in the short time I had to do this. Oh, and I'm sure you`ll all be disappointed to know that I haven't found any criminals or obvious scallywags, yet. But given Scotland`s often troubled history, we`ll surely discover a dark shadow somewhere, in due course. Any questions?"

"Thanks, Andy, I think we`ll leave the questions till later, so who`s next?

"OK, I`ll share what I've found folks." Malcolm offered.

"On you go, I believe you`ve had quite a challenge."

"Yes, I have rather, but what a truly fascinating bundle of papers in that box. It's clear from it, that it was a distinct set of papers that Alex assembled while he was studying law, and in the brief time from that before he was called up. Had he survived, I think he would have taken it all a bit further. For reasons that only he knew, he seems to have focussed largely on two things, Glen Maddy and common land. From what I can gather, he was trying to get into an area there, that was either neglected or deliberately suppressed.

Anyway, Glen Maddy, which was some way north and west of Spurryhillock, in a parish called Lochhead, had been in Ferguson ownership from around sixteen fifty or earlier, until about eighteen twenty. Then it was sold to the Brigham family, they were from somewhere in Lancashire. During the Ferguson period, it was confiscated following the first Jacobite rising of seventeen fifteen. Though it was returned to what I`ll call our ownership sometime later. Alex did pose the question, from this, about our religious roots and Jacobite sympathies. But that matter does not seem to have been concluded.

Needless to say, I've been poring over his old handwritten notes and extracts from a few books of the time. Fortunately, I've got good eyesight, or I did before I started this quest.

He seems to have uncovered some serious questions about the way the Fergusons commandeered the substantial area of common land around a

49

feature called the Darach Stane. I`ll say more about that in a minute. He seems to be saying that from his research that the common land issue was legally unsatisfactory. But it went unchallenged, and when the land was sold to the Brighams, it just got accepted as fact. Alex was not happy about this chapter in the family history, and he`d dug as deep as he could, to prove that he was onto something.

He then went on to look at the Darach Stane. This was at the heart of the common land. It's marked on some early maps as being the site of a particular upright stone. He identified that it was removed by Rev. Ebenezer Snoddy in the seventeen fifties, who regarded it as a token of evil heathenism. So, he had its power for local people destroyed, as he vowed, by placing it face down in Glen Maddy kirk. The location was very deliberate, as he put it beneath the communion table, and had a bold cross inscribed on the new face of it, facing upwards. I should add that it looks like the Darach Stane had a large collection of acorns carved on it. Darach means oak, in Gaelic. The symbolism of oak and acorns surely shines through here, and Alex seemed to be excited by this.

I have a lot more work to do on these papers. Why they were in a British Linen Bank safe deposit box, is very strange. But whoever put together all the contents of the trunk, clearly felt that it was all a tribute to Alex following his death in the first world war. Or perhaps, the sad gesture of putting his life`s work to bed.

Anyway, that's as far as I`ve got folks, I`m sure there will be more to follow."

"Thanks for that, Malcolm. Well, you've certainly come up with something that takes us in a new direction altogether, probably more questions than answers right enough. More than just intriguing. Do you mind if we move on folks, for now, Lizzie, it must be your turn?"

"OK, that one is hard to follow, but here goes. The bundle of papers and maps that I have, is more comprehensive than I`d thought, at first. There`s probably enough material in there, to write a reasonable history of Spurryhillock from about eighteen hundred, or thereabouts. If there are title deeds, I guess they must be with your old office, Dad?"

"Oh, that could be so. Need to chase them up, if I can, because a copy would be very useful. I need to formalise the transfer of the estate to Andy and yourself, for tax reasons, if nothing else, anyway."

"From what I've got, there`s quite a lot about Spurryhillock house: description, probable date, possible architect, domestic staff, possible requisition during the last war, but it was reckoned to be too far gone by then, a few pictures, and a lovely description of a house party in about nineteen hundred.

"There`s a lot about the estate, mainly in map format. So, one map shows the land use and tenants, in about eighteen ninety. Another shows information about trees in different parts of the estate, though the date of that is less clear. Yet another map shows the landholding when it was a bit bigger, so it seems that the now neighbouring farm of Sunny Braes was part of it all and sold in about nineteen twenty-eight; for tax reasons, we are told. There are two military bases if that's the right word, but only one of which I was aware of. The sizeable army depot on the edge of the estate, most of which as we know is a ruin. But the papers show that it was returned to us after the war. The second is a nineteen-sixties cold war bunker. We`ll need to see if we can find that, and what the position of ownership is, as the site was acquired by the Ministry of Defence in nineteen sixty-one. It's a small site, I think. There`s some stuff about fencing grants on the higher ground in about nineteen seventy-three. And finally, there is a survey report under the Ancient Monuments Act of nineteen thirteen, dated a few years later, in which they seemed to be considering scheduling the top of Spurryhillock itself. But that appears to have been abandoned, for some reason.

So, there you have a summary of my document delving, folks. Oh, one final thing, I found a curious reference or note written at the top of one document. Not sure which one, but it was like a kind of aide memoir, that he would come back to. But it seems he never did as far as I can tell."

"Hurry up and tell us what it is," Marissa exclaimed impatiently.

"OK, well it's a short note that just reads, `Aikenhead Papers, Harold Ferguson of Spurryhillock, Slavery, 1756`. I`m not sure what on earth that can be about. But it does have a sinister ring to it, that we might not be so comfortable with. It's for another day though, as we've got quite enough to be getting along with already."

"Thanks, Lizzie dear, some of that I knew about, but since I'd never gone through those papers as thoroughly as you have, there's much I wasn't aware of. More to Spurryhillock than meets the eye. From what the three of you have discovered, there may well be some legal matter that I`ll need to explore further. That trunk and the box have been a kind of pandora's box for us, especially regarding that Glen Maddy Estate. Common land is a very difficult one to prove now, but it's become a significant contemporary issue, nonetheless. The Land Reform Act I think, two thousand and three here in Scotland, defines our rights and responsibilities, rather well. Some cases have refined this in many useful ways, depending on whether you are an owner or a user. The Scottish Land Fund throws some light on the circumstance under which land and or buildings can become a public asset and be acquired as such. So, I guess my role will be ongoing, depending upon what we want to do with all the information that we now have, and may accumulate as we dig deeper. Thank you, Pandora.

Let's have a break, for some more coffee and cake."

52

This was enjoyed, sitting in the sunshine in Archie and Marissa`s garden.

"How`s that elm construction you were working on Malcolm?" asked Lizzie, with a genuine interest in it. "The grain and colour of that wood are exquisite. And you seem to have your very own way of approaching it, working with it."

"Thanks, Lizzie, it's all progressing, but it's slow. A dining table and six chairs plus one, is a big commission. I just hope that all the noise I am making in the workshop doesn't disturb the neighbours or cause any complaints. I`m sure they aren't used to woodworking like this, here in the Grange."

Archie chipped in, "Don't worry too much about that. I`ll let you into a wee secret, I had a word with all the immediate neighbours a few months ago and asked them nicely to please bear with us. I was quite open about how happy you have made Hermione and the girls, after all, that they have been through. I don't mind saying, in this company, that you have transformed their lives. So, the least I could do was to informally smooth the way for you to be here and work here."

"That's very kind and thoughtful of you Archie, thank you, thank you."

"I estimate another three months of work on this commission. It depends upon the wood, and how I`m able to be guided by it, for each piece of every part. If it was straight pine, it would have been finished ages ago. And I can see myself being kept busy well into the future, as there`s a likely job coming up, for at least two substantial oak doors for a sort of nature retreat project down in the Borders. The person I've been dealing with there was quite specific that the doors need to convey an invitation for people to feel the life in the wood, as she put it. I`m also talking to a few others who like myself, work largely solo. There`s an idea to form a cooperative of some kind to help us source genuine native timber. But that's only an idea so far."

53

"Andy and I are working our way through the backlog of orders I've got. Want to get them all finished before you guys all come up to Spurryhillock. This trunk and box project is holding us back a bit, but my goodness it's fascinating. And I suspect we are only scraping the surface so far."

"Let's give it another half an hour, so we can work out what the priorities are now folks. This morning has fair stirred the collective imagination, I'd say," Archie said in a formal tone.

"I`ll start once more," said Andy. "What I`m working on as the family tree is an essential backdrop to the bigger picture. I`ll set the parameters as sixteen hundred to two thousand unless anything else crops up. We`ll know, perhaps a bit later, as I must include Monique and Charlotte. I`d like to add some information about wives, as that's a bit lacking so far. Another full day in Register House, with the structure I've already got to build on, should do it Not quite sure when the wills will be available, or indeed what they will throw up if anything. So, I'm going to be busy. As well as running up and down the stairs for Lizzie, of course."

I`d like to pull together the Spurryhillock story, at least in outline. With the family tree sitting beside it, we`ll have a much fuller picture of what the estate was all about."

"The Darach Stane fascinates me," said Malcolm. No doubt other things will spring from that. But the stone is the oldest part of my saga, and probably very symbolic. Now if we could but find it, folks, how fulfilling would that be? First, we`d need to find Maddyburn kirk though."

"It's the story of Alex that fascinated me," said Archie. He was Lizzie`s great uncle, after all, and he seemed to be almost airbrushed out of the family consciousness. Now that seems truly unjust. I want to put the record straight and give a good account of his life if I possibly can. I`ll keep on top of the legal matters we`ve already touched upon, of course, but Alex is my man. Why has he just been packed up in a trunk, forgotten, and left where his fate could have been the second death, in a skip? He knew he was onto something, clearly put a lot of effort into it, was way ahead of his time on this, before the war then left it all hanging.

"We each have our areas of focus or interest, but do you know what? I have a feeling already that Malcolm's Glen Maddy and the Darach Stane may emerge as the biggest of the lot. We know so little, but what we do know is truly tantalising. It may even be bigger than one family, this family's ancestral story. We are on the cusp of something profound."

"We need everyone's input on this, coming at it from different angles, but it will largely home in on where Glen Maddy fits into the picture, all of the tension tied up in the common land issue, and of course, ancient stone, now lost, which scared the bejesus out of the church, or at least one overzealous man of the cloth.

"How does this all sound? What timescale are we now working with folks? When shall we four meet again, and where?

"Let's crack on with it. A week from now," Malcolm boldly proposed.

"Agreed," came the reply, in unison.

7.

The following weekend, Lizzie and Hermione had business to attend to, but of a very different nature.

It was with a heavy heart, that Lizzie drove down into the Borders countryside. She was on a mission to visit Jamie`s parents who lived just outside Kelso. They were now old and frail, and their lives had fallen apart; they had no one else.

Hermione had completely switched off from Jamie`s suicide while he was in prison; life had moved on for her but for David and Margaret Scott, it had stood still. It was agreed that Lizzie would take this much-needed business forward, so Hermione waited anxiously at home to hear of the outcome, later in the day.

As Lizzie drew up in front of their pink sandstone and whin cottage in the scattered village, taking a deep breath, she got out of the car. The cottage door opened; a care-marked old man came out to meet her.

"Thank you for coming down, on behalf of your sister, I imagine, Lizzie, and it is lovely to see you. The kettle`s on, and Margaret is in the conservatory at the back. Oh, but it's been such a hard struggle for us, and we miss the girls so much."

"I know it has David, I know, and my heart goes out to you both. I`ve some photos of Monique and Charlotte, and a short video of them chattering about their school, I think. It's on my phone for you to see."

Entering the cottage did bring back a few memories for Lizzie, but they made her shudder. She remembered the handsome young man that Jamie had been, his confident but slightly stuffy manner, and what he later became too. Yes, she shuddered coldly at that thought, but went on through to the conservatory where Margaret was sitting, huddled in a shawl, despite the bright sunshine.

"Hello Margaret, how are you doing?" she said, as that was the best she could muster under the circumstances.

"Oh, I've been better dear, but we get by somehow. The roses that David still tends as best he can, are a nice touch of colour around the place. It's nice of you to come all this way to see us. Perhaps you`ll bring the girls to see us sometime? Can you pour the tea, please David?"

"Here are some flowers and a few wee things I've brought for you both. I do wish I`d been able to come and see you sooner. You do look like you are bearing up."

An awkward silence descended, as David poured the tea, and Lizzie took a seat.

"Since we got rid of the car, it's quite difficult to get around, but there is a bus at the road end a couple of times a day. Oh, and there`s the school bus too, but that's far too noisy for us, and it takes a funny route around every farm between here and Kelso. Don't know how long we can go on living here. A kind friend in the village helps to get us the few messages that we need."

"I`m sure Lizzie doesn't want to hear of all our domestic arrangements, dear. We`d love to have news about the girls. I'm sure they are getting bigger, and hopefully doing well at school."

"Here are a few photos of them for you, I framed them up, so you can put them on display."

"Oh my," exclaimed Margaret, clearly almost in tears.

Each of them held a picture and gasped. It was David`s turn to offer a sad comment, "these are all we have got now, all we have in life."

Lizzie struggled at this, to think of some way of trying to move this situation forward. She knew it would be difficult, but this sorrow was all-consuming.

"Can I suggest that during the summer holidays, I`ll bring the girls down for a day, and we could meet up at one of the country house gardens, which also has things to do?"

"How could we get there," Margaret asked, her voice trailing off.

"I`d come and collect you, and we`d meet together for a few hours. If that works, as I`m sure it would, we could do it again sometime."

This proposal seemed to lift their spirits a bit, much to Lizzie`s relief.

"The photos are gorgeous, the girls are gorgeous, we`ll add them to the wee collection we have on the sitting room wall," said Margaret, sounding a bit more hopeful. "How they appear to have grown. Tell us more about them please."

"Well, Hermione has taken them both riding today. After a lot of discussions, that's what they both finally agreed on. I'm sure they`ll have a great day out." She then spoke for some time about each of the girls, to bring Margaret and David up to date, and to re-establish some sense of connection.

"Hermione`s now got a wonderful job in a young people`s mental health project. It's with a charity. Connecting young people with nature." But they seemed less interested in hearing much about this. "Oh, I've brought a hammer and some picture hooks. Would you like me to put the pictures up on your wall for you?"

"That would be a great help, thank you. David`s not quite as practical, or should I say, able, as he used to be. We`ll treasure these photos."

With a bit of discussion, it was decided where the photos should go.

"Must have plenty of light on them," said, David.

So, with a bit of tapping of the hammer, they were put in place and admired.

"Now I have that video for you to see," as Lizzie got her phone out.

They took it, in turn, to study it closely, with Margaret having it first. It was just a short video about nothing in particular. Just two sisters chatting animatedly about school. By the time she handed it over to David, tears were running down her careworn face.

"Oh, I`m sorry to be making a show like this, but that video of the girls is really special. Isn't it, David?"

"It most certainly is. I wish we could see it every day now. But we don't have any of this kind of equipment to see it on." He sighed. "I fear that technology is beyond us at our age."

"Tell you what, have you any neighbour or friend that I could send it to, and they could let you see it from time to time?"

"Gosh, is it possible to do that?" Asked Margaret.

"Yes, it is, indeed. We`d need their agreement of course. Could you give them a call just now, and we`ll see if we can get this set up for you?"

"Mrs Heriot, Jean Heriot, who kindly helps with our shopping and things, would probably oblige. I`ll give her a phone now, while you are here, and you could explain better than me," Margaret replied.

The phone call was duly made, and Lizzie had the opportunity to speak to Jean, explaining the request that they had. She immediately said she`d be delighted to help Margaret and David in this way. "They do speak of their grandchildren quite often, so anything that helps them to have a better link is bound to be good. Yes, glad to be of help. I`ll give you my mobile number."

As soon as she received it and put it on her contacts list, she texted Jean to say a big thank you.

By the time Lizzie was getting ready to go, she noticed a change in Margaret and David. There seemed to be a flicker of hope in them, which had certainly not been evident when she`d arrived. Whether it was just the chat about the girls, having the photos, or having a better means of keeping in touch, it seemed to have lightened their mood. With due promises to keep in touch, and arrange the day visit in the summer holidays, farewells were exchanged, and she was on her way home once more.

Greatly relieved that she`d been able to give these poor old souls a glimmer of hope, and even a wee sense of purpose, she was also greatly pleased that it had been possible to do all this, without any mention of Jamie. Perhaps Margaret and David had the measure of him anyway, or just didn't want to go there, but either way, it made the drive up the road a much more positive experience.

Her day had been of value.

While all this had been happening, Hermione and the girls had had a wonderful day riding at the stables just south of Edinburgh. The skills they`d learned when they were younger, soon came back, and any initial nervousness was allayed by the instructor. Hermione had decided to enter into the spirit of the event, by riding too. It had been a good number of years since she`d been in the saddle but was determined that the girls should not see her anxiety. With just the three of them, the instructor was able to give good attention to each and pitch her advice accordingly.

"Look at me," yelled Monique as she got into a canter, after their lunch break. "This is fantastic, thank you for organising this. I can ride a pony once more. Could we do it again sometime?"

"Oh please, please," yelled Charlotte, as she too upped her pace.

"Pay attention to what you are doing girls. Less of this excited chatter." Snapped the instructor. "If you don't focus on what you are doing, you may well end up in A & E, with a broken bone or two. These ponies are perfectly capable of turfing you off. They don't like this shouting."

"Oh, sorry Miss," said Monique. "We didn't mean to cause a problem."

"Ok, just focus on what you are doing, and you can show all the excitement that you want when we are finished. You are doing well, Hermione. You`ll catch up with your girls soon enough. Though you might feel a bit stiff in the morning."

With another hour or so of activity, it was clear that the girls were getting a bit tired, so the instructor reckoned that it would be better for them to stop when the going was good, rather than wear them out altogether.

"Right folks, I think you've all done magnificently well; so impressed with your effort. I do believe you've enjoyed yourselves, and it's clear to me that you have indeed been riding before. Perhaps you`ll do it again. Would you like that?"

All nodded eagerly.

We`ll ride into the yard and do what needs to be done with the saddlery and ponies so that they`ll be ready for someone else tomorrow."

There was much-excited chatter in the car on the way home, with even more when they got into the house, and found Lizzie waiting to greet them.

After dinner, and the girls had gone to bed, exhausted but very happy, Lizzie and Hermione were able to sit and chat over a glass of wine, to compare notes.

"I know it's expensive, but I`ll gladly take the girls riding again," Hermione said. "How enthusiastic I`ll be about getting in the saddle again, may depend on what state I'm in tomorrow morning."

"I`m really grateful to you for taking them. They seem to have had a blast. No doubt Mum and Dad would chip into the cost if there`s a repeat of this."

Lizzie then outlined her day, and the value it seemed to have been for David and Margaret. "And we`ve now got an arrangement in place, with a friend of theirs to send occasional videos of the girls. It cut me to the quick when I heard them say, that Charlotte and Monique are all they`ve got. If Jamie were here, I`d have given him a good kicking."

Hermione raised her glass in agreement.

8.

When the quartet reassembled it had become a quintet, for Andy had invited Ronald to the ranks.

"I do hope this is OK folks, but Ronald has expressed an interest in this, his investigative skills are second to none, and an extra pair of hands or set of wheels will be most useful."

"Fine by me," said Archie at the head to the table. "A warm welcome to you Ronald. Have you got a coffee?"

"I have thanks Archie and thank you all for making me so welcome. Hope I can contribute something useful to this intriguing story."

"Pretty sure you will, indeed, you already have. From what I`ve heard about you, and read of your work in sundry national publications, you`ll take us places the rest of us just couldn't get to. We make a great team here, with such a fine variety of skills and interests. I'm going to crank up the pace a bit though, folks. We need to reach some conclusions and clear courses of action. Five minutes each, this morning, to summarise your areas of investigation, please. I've even brought a timer clock from the kitchen."

This sudden news took everyone aback. Even though they all knew that Archie could be quite demanding if it suited him.

Malcolm quickly stepped in. "Of course, you are right Archie, we should crack on a bit, but when you hear my input, you`ll quickly see that Glen Maddy which has rather taken us by surprise, cries out for further investigation, perhaps even action."

In the brief silence that followed, it was evident that the others had also been pursuing their intriguing areas of interest too. They wondered how this could all be rushed through in just five minutes apiece.

"Sorry to be sounding like I`m cracking the whip folks, but sometimes it does help to sharpen the pace. If we can each be disciplined to start with, then once that is shared, we can pull out of it what we feel would merit the most effort just now. That's not to say that anything you've done will get neglected in the longer term. Are you all OK with this approach, please?

"Fine, I`ll go first once more." Andy ventured. "Here`s the core family tree from about sixteen hundred, as you`ve seen an outline of before." He switched on the projector and focused on the big screen he`d erected at the far end of the table from Archie. It lit up. A clear flow chart down the generations drew everyone`s immediate attention. "I`ll just leave this up, as a constant backstory to pretty much everything else we`ll be hearing about. Don`t need to say much at this stage, as it's probably ninety-nine per cent accurate, all taken from official records. Pre sixteen hundred it gets much more difficult for us, as the relevant parish records don't seem to have survived. As you can see, I`ve avoided the temptation of adding much information about siblings and whom they married. If I'd done that, it would have quickly become utterly confusing, with the generations overlapping; a veritable forest, never mind a tree. Unless there are any questions, I`ll just leave this up for you."

"Thanks, Andy, very clear and succinct. Puts much of our discussion on solid ground, I`d say. Malcolm, can you please go next," as Archie set the clock.

"OK, I owe a large part of this to Alex`s research, which we found in the box. His military record will probably be available, but the request for that needs to come from the relevant senior descendant. Here are seven points.

One. Glen Maddy near Lochhead village or burgh, is probably the older of the two Ferguson landholdings.

Two. Fergusons were Jacobite, probably catholic, and all their property was part of the Forfeited Estates after the first Rising in 1715. Subsequently reinstated, as we know, though.

Three. In the confusion, when it was forfeited, the York Buildings Company, as what I`d call a government lackey, conveniently took control of the common land. How legal that was is debatable, and there is no charter to prove it one way or the other. But many local rights over that land were removed, or simply disappeared. When Glen Maddy was sold to the Brighams any reference to the common land seems to have evaporated. The local burgh council minutes do refer to the common land when the original Burgh charter was made in sixteen seventy-something.

Four. At the heart of the land, was the Darach Stane, still revered by the local people as a symbol of their natural world stretching back many hundreds of years, an enduring beacon of ancient harmony with the source and what we`d now call, the sustainability of life.

Five. As we know, the Rev Ebeneezer Snoddy was having none of this heathen stuff on his watch and had it removed, captured, and ignominiously dumped face down in a Christian kirk with the communion table placed definitively on top of it.

Six. That kirk was Maddyburn Kirk the remains of which are now beneath the waters of Birklinn Reservoir, created by the hydro company in about nineteen thirty-eight. Though that of course post-dates Alex`s efforts.

I`m nearly there folks. Seven. Alex was set to prove three things; that the ownership of the common land was at best, dubious; that a part of Glen Maddy still belongs to the Fergusons, and that the Darach Stane should be back where it belonged. Oops, six minutes. I rest my case."

Pregnant silence ensued.

"Ah, thanks Malcolm, I rather think that Alex has sharpened the focus of our mission. Quick coffee break, then it's you, Lizzie on Spurryhillock."

"Here goes then." She dived in.

There are three things I most urgently want to pursue:

First. Where is, or are, the second military remains? We could take the girls on a treasure hunt for it when we are up there on holiday. Oh, and what is it, or was it?

Second. I want every picture of the house as it was, that we can lay our hands on. I`d like to do a big photo interpretation of it. Oh, and it's described as being by, or in the style of early William Burn. It's been neglected in the gallery of great Scottish buildings, perhaps. And allied to this, how could the Fergusons have afforded such a big grand mansion?

Third. Does the summit of Spurryhillock need to be revisited and surveyed, for its potential archaeological interest?

Oh, and a fourth, coming from Malcolm`s amazing discoveries, how and when did we acquire Spurryhillock, if Glen Maddy appears to pre-date it?

That's me for now. Plenty to be getting on with. Eh, Malcolm, why were you diddling with your phone just now, that's very rude of you?"

"Sorry folks, I`ll come back to it, but I may have found something worthwhile, to add to my story."

"Thanks, Lizzie, a lot of unfinished business there. While you folk have been so busy, I`ve not made much headway with Alex, I confess. Well, that's not quite true, as I've found a few books of his. He was a very bright lad, Dux of his school, and as we know from the material that Lizzie now has, got a very good degree, from Edinburgh University. Two of his books, school prizes, caught my interest. The first was a beautifully illustrated book on native flora and fauna in Scotland, and the second was a slightly more obscure, tome on the symbolism of landscapes in ancient stone monuments. Although that's been superseded by numerous studies and publications in the interim, it shows us something of his interests, other than law. His National Trust membership card had been used as a marker.

Ronald looked up from his phone, and announced, "I've been following everything that's been said folks, and I know you are onto something exciting, tantalising even, as the newcomer, you've certainly fired my enthusiasm. I know it was very rude of me, but I texted a good friend of mine, who lives up near Birklinn Reservoir, and asked him if he could tell me what it's like these days. He quickly got back to me to tell me that he drives past it frequently. The water level is exceptionally low right now, perhaps for maintenance work on the dam or tunnels, and as you drive past it from the upper end, you can see the old road that was submerged when the dam was built, is now visible. It's still got tarmac on it, he says and seems to wind gently down the valley towards that dam. Doesn't know quite how far though. Says you can see the remains of something quite far down when you look across from the new road.

Could that be the remains of Maddyburn village or even the kirk?"

"You're forgiven, for playing around on your phone Ronald, even if it was bad manners. I think you should get back to your friend and thank him."

"Sure thing. Oh, my goodness, here's another text from him, with a couple of photos. He says he was passing this morning anyway when I texted him. So, he stopped, zoomed as best he could at these remains, I was telling you about, and he`s in no doubt that it is the lower walls of at least one ruined building." And so, saying, his phone with the pictures on it was duly handed around. "I`ll share them with you all, in due course."

9.

After the journey north, that final drive up the winding track to Spurryhillock always created a wonderful sense of anticipation, for Lizzie especially. The real start to so many childhood holidays, craning her head this way and that, to see when the house would finally come into view. Sometimes, in her imagination, she had seen a smiling housekeeper coming out to greet them, or a keeper standing sentinel, at the green door. But as the car pulled up at the door, reality kicked in, and the excitement of all the delights that this magical place had to offer an inquisitive or adventurous child welled up within her. She couldn't wait to get out and explore again.

Even if the excitement was more restrained now, she loved to be able to share that passion for the place with her beloved Andy. They`d arranged to come up a couple of days earlier than the rest of the family, to open up the house, light a log fire, let the birdsong in, and make love in whatever room, or at whatever time they fancied. Their house, for two days. Then all the noise and chatter, laughter, fun, and fine food would begin. And more.

Unloading the car and carrying everything into the house seemed like a fine part of the house party, as Marissa had grandly called the gathering. Some thought had gone into who should provide what. Ronald had been invited to join them too, and since the house would be full, he`d volunteered that he would be fine and could make himself very comfortable semi-camping in the floored attic, nearer to the dawn chorus.

The week was indeed filled with the joys of activity and adventure. Bramble joined in much of this, ending each action-packed day with her normally neat black coat, covered in bits of vegetation and splatters of mud. She seemed to enjoy the attention she received, as she was brushed clean once more. Licking eagerly and wagging her fine feathered tail.

One night, Lizzie took the girls camping at the top of Spurryhillock, near the big stones. They cooked and ate together, laughed a lot, and talked about everything and nothing, in the warm evening light. Recalling the riding they`d done, the idea of going for a trek seemed to appeal to them. Lizzie agreed that she felt sure this could be arranged soon. As the light faded into the moonless night, countless stars emerged to form that vast spectacle of the night dome; breath taking, captivating, and almost beyond anything that the girl's imagination could comprehend, as they sat there in wonder.

The cherry picker which Andy had obtained, enabled them to safely dismantle what remained, of the roof of the stables. Slates were salvaged for future re-use, whenever possible, and worm-eaten timbers removed, with plans for a grand bonfire on their last night. Looking down on what remained in the stable loft, it was clear, that most of the old furniture and domestic clutter, was beyond salvation, so much of it too was cautiously hauled out, for the bonfire.

"The wellheads and gables will need to be stabilised this year, if possible," Malcolm advised. "But if your plans for creating a couple of self-catering units there, can come to fruition, it will be a great asset to the place. Might be nice to clear a few trees and open up the front of it a bit though."

With Archie`s curiosity about the second of the military facilities, needing to be satisfied, a morning was set aside for a search party. It was decided that the girls should take a lead in this, with the others on the flanks of the road at one side and following the burn on the other. This would be for the first sweep. But since they didn't know what they were looking for, there was a bit of mystery added to the quest. The girls were kitted out with cams jackets and trousers, to look the part, and equipped with whistles too. Bramble would act as the mascot. Their brief was to search for anything that didn't look natural, in concrete or brick. On finding anything, their instructions were to give three long blasts on the whistles every minute or so until the others located them. On no account were they to try and enter any construction they found.

Giggles and squeals echoed down through the forest, as the safari set off on its quasi-military quest. Lizzie and Monique made their way down the track from the house to the road, watching anxiously but tempered with excitement, to where the girls were most likely to be. The men chose the rougher route following close to the burn, whilst acknowledging it was unlikely that they'd find anything amongst the tangle of fallen branches, brambles, and rocks. The woodland here was a real mixture, and the sunshine fell in dappled pools of green light.

Marissa had stayed behind, to set in some young plants she had for the border that ran along the front of the house, and around the sides. With climbing roses and clematis on trellises fixed to the walls, it looked every bit like a mini country garden.

In the woodland, there were sounds of breaking branches, jungle bashing, and birdsong echoing off trunk and bough, as the mission progressed with a sense of both fun and purpose. The gentle movement of water in the burn gave back the rippling light from above, whilst every so often a squawking pheasant crossed the ranks unannounced before disappearing once more into the greenery.

This sylvan scene was suddenly interrupted by the distant sounds of a whistle; three short blasts, as instructed. The sounds of Bramble barking helped to identify the direction for the adults to go to see what had been discovered. Lizzie and Hermione made haste, to see that the girls were all right, as much as anything else, having fixed on the general source of the alarm. Picking their way through the vegetation as they left the safety of the road, Hermione called out "Monique, Charlotte," at the top of her voice. It too came back as a fainter filtered echo. The men quickened their pace as they battled through the dense vegetation, and over many an obstacle.

Meanwhile, the girls lay in a heap of arms, legs, and uncontrollable laughter, as they tumbled down the small slope from whatever it was that had caused them to whistle in the first place. Bramble joined in the apparent hilarity, with yet more barking.

Hermione and Lizzie got to them first, their alarm at what they discovered was soon quelled by the continued sound of loud merriment and sporadic chattering coming from Monique and Charlotte still rolling around in the long grass. Helping them to their feet, Hermione asked with some concern still evident, "Oh girls, are you hurt, are you OK? We thought that some disaster had happened to you."

Before they could answer, the men appeared, and on also checking that the girls were indeed OK, Archie proclaimed, "well this must be it, whatever it is because it is certainly not a natural part of the woodland here."

Archie was quick to quell Bramble`s noisy excitement and made a fuss of her as if to thank her for the part she had played. She responded, by licking his hand enthusiastically.

They all clambered up the bank that the girls had just rolled down and looked at three concrete shafts coming up out of the ground, each one bigger than the other, two with the remains of wooden ventilation grilles on one side. The largest of them, about two and a half feet high, had a square manhole cover on top, but it was hard to examine closely as a fallen tree lay right across it. "Well, this is a surprise, and a mystery," said Archie, surveying the discovery. "And it seems to have the remains of a fence around it too. Oh, and there's what looks like it might have been an access track from the road, going off in roughly the right direction."

After a ponderous silence, it was Malcolm who spoke first. "Do you know what I think that is?" Everyone turned to look at him and await his pronouncement.

"It looks like one of these nineteen-sixties cold war bunkers. Hundreds of them were constructed all over the country to provide a safe place for monitoring the effects of nuclear attacks. Yea, that's what it is, and we are standing on top of a concrete room which that shaft there, leads down into. Some of these come up for sale from time to time, and most have reverted to the original landowner. So, Andy and Lizzie, you are the proud owners of a legacy of the cold war."

"It's going to take a chainsaw first to enable us to examine it," said Lizzie. But now we know what it almost certainly is, and where."

"And many, many thanks to Charlotte, Monique, and Bramble for making the great discovery for us. You've done a great job girls. Great explorers, the two of you. And you seem none the worse for your tumble. You've earned yourselves some extra cake when we get home and tell Marissa. Why did I never know this was here, I wonder? Until now that is."

"I wonder if there`s one of these on Glenmaddy, if so many of them were built, as you say, Malcolm?" Monique added with both humour and curiosity."

"Oh no disrespect to this discovery here folks, but perhaps Glenmaddy will hold many more profound secrets for us to discover. And share," said Malcolm, with a twinkle of assured confidence.

One evening, over dinner, Malcolm mentioned "Oh, there`s one thing amongst Alex`s papers, that I forgot to mention. It seemed a bit different from all the rest and quite difficult to read. Perhaps it had suffered worse, than the rest during a century in that box. Going back to it now, it does catch my interest though. It's a single sheet, handwritten, like the rest, of course. Simply headed, The Six Stages of Nature`s Fulfilment from Celtic Mythology, and in brackets after that, the word female. We know so little about Alex, that every snippet we can get, does throw a bit more light on his personality or interests. After all the much more legal stuff, and the case he was surely building there before war put a stop to it, something about mythology and mention of the word female, is surely a bit different?"

"Do go on please," said Archie. "It's so frustrating that I, know almost nothing about this great uncle of Lizzie`s. He certainly deserves much better than that. But for the war, he`d have inherited, and the outcome for all of us would have been so very different."

"Thanks, but all he then goes on to say are the six words: death, seed, loss, display, humanity, and rebirth. That's it. It's not unique of course, because much mythology includes these themes or sequences. Sometimes expressed in slightly different ways of course. What are we to make of it, folks? Do we make anything of it, or is it just random thoughts of a young man a bit more than a hundred years ago?"

"The fact that it's in amongst all the Glen Maddy papers is not by chance, I'd say," said Marissa. "I vote we add it to the depth of mysteries we are trying to unravel here. I hope this isn't the wee bit of wine I've had with my dinner talking, but could it be, that there`s a message for us hidden in it? Let's hope so."

Later that evening, over wine and a crackling log fire, the conversation ranged over everything they'd discovered, some that had probably yet to be so, and a myriad of other things too. With the curtains and windows open, bats could be seen flitting across the sky at dusk; diving, swooping and darting in great wide arcs. A pheasant squawked.

Ronald announced that his friends up north had now both located and visited the remains of Maddyburn kirk, by parking at the head of the reservoir, and walking down the old road. A strange experience, they said, as the mass of the dam loomed ever higher in front of them. "They've sent me a few photos, of course, and these make out the walls of the rectangular

73

building with one semi-circular end, to a height of about eighteen inches only. Around it, a few stones protruded through the silt, and on an investigation, these turned out to be gravestones. They said this was some hundred and fifty yards from the road, possibly a bit less. All is covered with a layer of mainly sand and dried mud, to a depth of perhaps six inches. Without a spade, they were unable to excavate much, but with their walking poles, they were able to discern a particular large flat stone some three feet by two feet, roughly where they expected the communion table or altar to have been. And on pushing away some of the silt, there appeared to be a simple cross carved on it. They took a photo of this too, and then covered it up.

Is this the Darach Stane, or part of it, which Rev. Snoddy had so ignominiously cast down and believed he`d commandeered for God?"

Ronald shared all the photos with everyone, and silence fell over the group as they all studied them closely.

"Please thank your friends for doing all this for us. I feel a seriously well-equipped work party coming on, as soon as is practical. That stone must come out of there. Though quite how, and what we`ll then do with it, I don't know?" Andy pondered aloud.

After everyone else had gone to bed, Lizzie devised a way to be with her mother only. Ostensibly just to tidy up a bit, she used the opportunity to speak quietly and personally.

"What is it dear? I sense that you have something that you want to say?"

"Well, yes there is, Mum. Though I should tell you sooner or later. It's a bit sad, but Andy and I are getting over it now"

"Getting over what?" asked Marissa with a bit of alarm in her voice.

Here goes, thought Lizzie, so taking a deep breath, she cautiously said, "just over two months ago, I wasn't feeling too great, because I was pregnant. But it sadly all ended in a miscarriage. I was at home at the time, and Andy was around. So, he helped me, and we got medical advice over the phone, because of Covid restrictions, but I got a quick appointment at out of hours, and we headed for the Infirmary. Miscarriage was confirmed, and the necessary treatment was administered. Then we went home again. I just lay low for a few days. Feeling very sad, we both were, as we do so want to have a baby, and of course, the clocks ticking". She tailed off.

"Oh Lizzie, I`m so truly sorry. It will have come as a bitter blow to both of you. How are you feeling now though?"

"Andy has been magnificent. Loving, caring, gentle; he`s seen me through this. We are determined to try again, Mum."

"That's so good to hear. And you know that your dad and I are here too if there`s anything you want."

"Thanks, Mum, but I`d rather just keep it between you and me for now, please."

"Of course. As you wish."

Then Marissa said something that took Lizzie by surprise. "You probably didn't know this, but before I had Monique and yourself, I`d had two miscarriages, about eighteen months apart. We`d almost given up when I fell pregnant again, and Monique was the result. A smooth, if anxious pregnancy, and a very healthy baby at the end of it. A couple of years later, a repeat performance, and you, my lovely, healthy, lively Lizzie, are the result. Couldn't have asked for more. I do tell you this, not to diminish how you are and how you feel after what you've gone through, cos that's very real. But only to offer some reassurance to you, from my own experience."

"Oh, thank you, Mum, for your kind and understanding words. I do feel so much better now I've told you. And what you've told me does give a bit of hope. Thank you."

Over another cup of tea, they chatted and drew strangely closer because of all that they were discussing.

10.

Archie applied a few of his investigative skills to try and track down more of what had happened to the Darach Stane. He consulted old books on antiquities, tracts on myths and legends, and such hints from local lore. Together, they pointed to the outline of a sad chapter in history, driven by the church's corruption, or obsessions, at the time.

Rev. Ebeneezer Snoddy, it would appear, was part of that zealous fanatical cabal within the church, which seemed to see bad in pretty much everything. He wanted to stamp out what he saw as the ungodly and didn't care about the human consequences; it was God's work, after all, he had pronounced. Seeing the Darach Stane standing there on that moor as he passed so often, bold, popular, more than just symbolical, heathen, and representing something that he could not see as being even the smallest part of God`s creation, as he saw it all laid out in his Book of Genesis, was just too much for him. It had to go.

So, the old books that Archie consulted, told him that one Sunday, from the pulpit, he ordered all the able men in the church to assemble two days hence, and come prepared to deal with the Darrach Stane once and for all. It would be condemned, smitten, broken, and turned to do only God's work.

Many of the men were most unhappy with the task that the dour minister had handed down for them, from the pulpit. But the church held sway in these parts, and the minister would visit damnation on them and their families if they did not obey. So, they turned up at the appointed hour, with bars and shovels, ponies, a sledge or two, and some rope. With Snoddy looking on in the belief that he was doing God's will, the men set about the stone, or the Stane, as they much preferred to call it. Digging around about it, they found it to be well rooted into the ground. "Those that erected this," they complained, out of earshot of Snoddy, "intended it to be permanent."

After many hours of digging and removing the submerged wedge stones around it, they finally had it loosened from the place it had been for many hundreds of years; a thousand years or more, probably. It was unceremoniously yoked to the ponies, hauled out of the ground, and dragged onto a sledge. Just as it was being lashed down, it split, with the top becoming detached from the lower. The men cowered in shock and fear, as they took this to be a message from the ancient powers that they still nurtured some respect for; ancient powers that put nature and man on at least an equal footing. A belief that was very much at odds with Snoddy`s doom-laden thundering of a Sunday, in which man had dominion over everything else. Other than God himself.

He chose to leave the base to rot upon this moor, and only take the evil top half of it to Maddyburn Kirk. There we will sink the heathen symbol, faceless in the dirt where it belongs. "Straighten your backs men and get what the Almighty has decreed from The Book, done before nightfall," Snoddy had ordered.

"Well, what can we say about Snoddy?" Asked Andy, in a critical tone. "He may have believed he was right, but it must have taken some kind of warped conviction for him to do what he did and treat the men in such a miserable way."

"It's almost impossible to believe that a man of God would do that. I seem to recall the phrase God is love, being bandied about when I was at Sunday School," Lizzie added.

Like a scene from a cloak and dagger movie, five dark-clad figures disgorged from a black van at the head of Birklinn Reservoir, under cover of night. Each bore a muffled head torch. A four-wheeled barrow came next, and in it were loaded an assortment of spades, mattocks, some short scaffolding planks, cut-down lengths of scaffolding pole, a long stout fence post, some rope, and a hand brush. Each item was accounted for and assigned a clear purpose in his surreptitious nocturnal mission.

Ronald and his friend Angus set off down the old road, almost at a trot; the advance party. Andy and Lizzie followed, towing the barrow and its load, at a more measured pace, holding the handle between them. Malcolm had been detailed as the driver, so it fell to him to keep the van out of sight of the main road. It was a well-known fact that there was always a regular lookout for poachers in that area.

The advance party got to the goal in just over half an hour and texted Lizzie to say that they had made it. Keeping as low as possible, and careful not to shine their head torches in the direction of the main road, they carried out a thorough survey of the silted remains of Maddy Burn Kirk and marked the area that would have to be cleared first. That done, Andy and Lizzie joined them, leaving the barrow on the old road. With the rapidly assembled site meeting, tasks and tools were assigned, and everyone got busy. Within some twenty minutes, the large flat stone with the cross on it had been cleared of silt, and an area of about six inches wide around it too. They quickly decided to remove the smaller adjoining floor stones at either end first and then those on the side furthest from the road.

Getting started on this was the most difficult part of it, so it took a fair bit of levering with the mattock to do this.

"Hey guys, I`m sweating like a pig," Lizzie exclaimed. "Don't think I was quite prepared for what seems like breaking rocks in this way."

"Yeah, but we`d rather you didn't break them, we want to be able to put them back after we are done with this," Angus added quickly.

"Don`t worry, I`ll be as careful as I can."

By removing a few inches more of the gravel and mud around the three sides they were able to see the thickness of the stone, and clear just enough beneath it to lever in the fence post. With a carefully placed rock as a fulcrum, the stone was released from its long slumber, and eased up far enough to get a couple of the planks pushed underneath it. Levering, it forwards a bit further, it was almost clear of the place that Snoddy had insisted on its being dumped all those years ago.

"Right, we need to somehow, carefully, turn it over so that we are moving it on Snoddy`s upper face. There should be some carving on the hidden face. Carving that gave the stone its full symbolism and meaning, perhaps," said Ronald."

This was, as they found, the most difficult part of the whole job. Using two of the other scaffolding planks, they levered the other side up, using sheer strength, body weight, balance, and a lot of heaving and grunting under a moonlit night. Once upright, though on its side, they reversed the process, but of course, as Andy added, "now we have a bit of gravity on our side." Scaffolding planks were then used to lower it as gently as possible, whilst placing short lengths of scaffolding tube between the layers of planks, to act as rollers.

"Man alive, this must be how the Egyptians moved such huge blocks of stone as they did. Thank you, Pharoah," Lizzie exclaimed.

Standing around, to catch their breath, each shone their light on what was now the upper face of the stone. Ronald had got the brush from the barrow and set about cleaning the surface. As he did so, the beautiful carving of a large collection of acorns became clear. Gasps of delight filled the air, as their hearts pounded with excitement. They stared in wonder at what they had unearthed.

It was Angus who broke the silence: "I confess that I did nurture a few doubts about this exercise folks, though I lacked nothing in intrigue. But here it is, The Darach Stane, or most of it, dare I say it, we`ve achieved something wonderful."

"We have indeed," said Lizzie. "Though the jobs are not quite finished yet, we have to get it out of here without getting caught."

With that, they all sprang into action once more, in what seemed like a choreographed manoeuvre. The barrow was hauled over from the road, a ramp was created with the planks, to get the stone on board. It was tied down. Planks were laid ahead, like tracks for the barrow to run on. The stones that had been around the Darach Stane were replaced. The silt was used to fill every crevice between them and then scattered liberally all over the site, with only a dull hollow where the Darach Stane had been. Slowly and carefully, the barrow was wheeled over to the old road. Planks and all the tools were loaded securely. Malcolm was texted to give a progress report, and a photo of the Stane was sent to him too, as if proof was needed.

They took it in turn, working in pairs to haul the heavily laden barrow up the old road, always mindful of the need to avoid shining torches anywhere in the direction of the new road. Occasional cars glided past in the night, oblivious to what was going on down in the reservoir. By the time they got about halfway, the light was beginning to lift in the east, marking the horizon now. So, torches were all extinguished, and further text to Malcolm. By the time they could just make out the head of the Reservoir, where the new road diverged from the old, vehicle lights showed as the van was reversed into position. Without any pause for a ceremony, planks were once again used as a ramp. The barrow and its priceless load were wheeled aboard, and wedges jammed on either side of the wheels. A quick check that nothing had been left behind as evidence, and they were on their way.

Angus had kindly agreed to provide safe, secret storage of the Stane, pending any decisions, on what to do next.

"That, my friends, has been a very good night's work." Said Malcolm, with triumph in his voice.

11.

There was a brief lull in activity. Andy had two four-day residentials as part of his work. Ronald had several urgent pieces of work to tackle for a national publication. Malcolm was desperate to get ahead with the elm commission. Lizzie still had a backlog of orders to deal with and wanted to spend some time updating her website. Hermione wanted to spend more time with Monique and Charlette because they had important schoolwork to do before the start of the term. She also wanted to discuss the idea of producing a video or two for David and Margaret but realised this had to be done sensitively. Marissa felt that the garden had been a bit neglected of late, and needed her attention, to smarten it up. Meanwhile, Archie had some pressing legal matters with one if the charities he gave so freely of his time and commitment. Everyone was busy.

But at least once every week or so, there is one family meal together, usually in the big house. Lizzie and Andy did feel that it must be their turn to host it soon, so a date was set, in this case; a Saturday early evening meal. Supplies were purchased, followed by more running up the stairs for Andy. The two of them had given a lot of thought to the menu and drinks, and somehow achieved something new, which would probably go down well with everyone, no easy task.

A table big enough was created in the bow windowed sitting room, and enough chairs were also gathered. Cutlery, glasses, and dishes were all commandeered from wherever. Lizzie proudly announced as everyone arrived, that the theme was The Darach Stane. Now that set everyone thinking. Already, a very large photo painting of the Stane in its imagined fifteenth-century setting dominated the big wall, with special lighting on it to bring out the mixture of the fulness of nature it so deserved. Plenty of drama in it too. She`d produced some specially printed serviettes with the acorns as the central image. Each course had a name, like an acorn pate, Darach pottage, and sweet skylark trifle. It all went down very well and was much appreciated, sprinkled with laughter and fine chat that included everyone.

After the meal, the girls chose to sit apart and do their own thing, they were happy. Somehow, the conversation turned to the subject of volunteering. It was probably Archie who set it off in his inimitable way. It ranged through the many ways in which everyone around the table is, or was doing something whether out of kindness, interest, or even passion, for an organisation of one sort or another. It all added up to a fine contribution to the wider community. Opinions and comments came in thick and fast.

Marissa said quite openly, "that as far as she was concerned, it is volunteering that makes the world go round. Take the voluntary effort out of community life, and the whole lot would collapse like a house of cards. Where would our entire culture be then?" she asked.

"I see it as the finest measure of our civilisation here," Malcolm boldly ventured. "We need it everywhere, and we've got it everywhere. Throughout every stratum of society, rich and poor, of all ages, and all abilities. Everywhere."

Andy came next, with, "I see it in every sport, at every level, people just being useful, investing their skills and knowledge, to make good things happen. Of course, there would be virtually no youth or children's activity without a whole army of volunteers. I call them the salt of the earth."

"Now what of the arts?" asked Hermione. "Music of every sort, literature, dance, theatre, oh, and everything historic too. Urban and rural, for all ages, and as we've heard abilities too. Almost every manifestation of it has volunteers right at the heart of it."

"Just thinks of what comes out of campaigning by people with conviction and if you'll pardon the phrase, have the balls to do something about it?" Lizzie added with passion in her voice. "Even those who take the time to comment on planning and civic matters. Some would call it democracy, others, that it's just the busybodies at work, but underneath all that, it's pure volunteering for a positive purpose."

Finally, it was Archie`s turn to wade in. "What puzzles and troubles me somewhat, are those who could or should be doing something for people other than themselves. Those who just can't be bothered do actually receive all the benefits from those who volunteer around them. I've tested this question out on several people over the years, and they just sweep it aside by saying they are too busy. Sometimes I asked people to help with something worthwhile, when I knew damn fine, they were not doing very much already, other than thinking of themselves, or at best, their own small, limited circle. Always the same reply, I`m too busy really. Couldn't give a toss, more like. These are the ones I`d like to be able to give a good shake, and at the very least say something like, get a grip and do your part in this community we all live in, benefit from, and enjoy, whether we recognise it or not. I rest my case."

"And well made too, Archie, if I may say," Andy replied. "It's strange that we should be discussing this subject. I mean it's not something we`d talk about much normally, we just get on with it. It happens, quietly, with no fuss. But we've all had something to say, each taking a different approach. Was it something you put in the food, m`love, that somehow got us going?"

"I wouldn't think so, Andy, my man. You helped to cook it, so you should know. But it is intriguing that right out of the blue, it somehow dominates the dinner table chat for half an hour. I`d like to think that it is a two-way street, volunteering, I mean. Oh, many people don't even call it that they just do it, it's what they do. But there's a kind of fulfilment for us in it, even if we don't seek that out at all."

"Yes, how right you are, Lizzie, and I`d take it a wee bit further, I think it's the measure of who or what we are as individuals. Gosh this is getting quite serious," said Marissa. "It kind of begs the question, are people who don't volunteer for anything, don`t do anything for anyone other than themselves or their immediate family, somehow lesser people? Well, they are certainly less fulfilled. And as Archie says, they are not playing their part. Who said something about it making the world go round? Oh yes, it was me. Well, it does, it's both the power that drives the community we live in, and it certainly oils the machinery of almost all human endeavour. Whew! I too rest my case."

"There are all sorts of ways in which children and young people are encouraged to see the value of this and it's no longer seen as just a moral thing that the church taught once. And from my experience, we see it throughout, even in the poorest parts of the community. So, what might be seen as the middle-class image of it, just doesn't hold." Said Hermione, eagerly.

"Yeah, there are some people who are just so up themselves that they don't get it. Oops sorry folks, that must have been the drink talking a bit, with that rather sloppy language," Andy seemed to confess. "But there's certainly a load of truth in it. More drink anyone? Can I refill glasses?"

"Not if it makes us reckless in what we say," quipped Malcolm. "But you are so right, and yes, a refill would be lovely thanks."

As glasses were being refilled, it was Marissa who rounded off the subject of volunteering but with real conviction. "You know, I`d go so far as to say, that those who do not volunteer in some practical way, who refuse to get their hands dirty, metaphorically, of course, are just freewheeling on the rest of us. They are a silent, pernicious burden on all the goodwill that surrounds them."

"Whew, follow that," exclaimed Lizzie. "But you are so, so right."

The wine was duly passed around, with the flow of more chatter and laughter, which was only interrupted when Monique appeared through from the kitchen. "When are we going home, mummy, I`m a bit tired?"

"Yes dear, very soon, it is getting late. We won't be long, I promise."

As they were going out of the door, Archie added an aside that, "for everything they'd shared so enthusiastically about volunteers, as much could be said all over again about the place of charities in the community. Remove them, and there is nothing."

And with that, they were gone, down the winding stairs.

12.

The intensity of close family, whilst a happy thing to have, caused Lizzie and Andy to seek a break together for a few days.

"Yeah, a few days camping in the Highlands is what we need," said Lizzie. "I have an idea, why don't we go up to Glenmaddy and explore thereabouts? That'd be nice for us, and it's an area we don't know too well yet. Wild camping of course. Bit of walking. And yes, I will have my camera."

"OK, well we`ll need to get organised then. Food, equipment, a map or two, and drive to somewhere it's fine to park, yet be away for two or three days."

The next twenty-four hours were hectic, putting it all together, but with their usual efficiency in these things. And then they were off. Just the two of them together, no one else to think about, no project deadlines or work, just the beckoning wide open spaces to enjoy.

In a small, scattered village just off the main road, they found a suitable place to park. It was overlooked by a couple of cottages, but not intrusive for either of them. Boots on, their rucksacks were swung over one shoulder first, then the other. Straps adjusted and clipped in place. Walking poles adjusted and grasped firmly. Car locked.

"I just love the silent ritual of doing this. It's a mixture of knowing what must be done, in what order, final adjustments, and the sense of eager anticipation," said Andy.

"Yes, me too. And knowing that it's just too bad if anything has been forgotten, cos our world is on our feet and our backs, for the duration. All we`ll need to add as we go is water and fresh air. It's quite magical."

Together, they consulted the map, and agreed on a route up a wee path away from the village and following close to a burn in its gorge. Through hazel, birch, and rowan woods, by banks of wildflowers, and serenaded by echoing birdsong, a cuckoo mocked their upwards journey, in what seemed like light-hearted humour.

"It's so easy in a place like this, to feel an engagement with nature, a connection, I'd even call it synergy. Seems to touch who and what we are, deeply I`d say," said Lizzie happily, as she stopped briefly to tighten her boot lace.

"Steady now, you are getting right into the serious stuff here. But you are spot on, my love, spot on. Fits my mood to perfection. I`d add that the whole experience is a journey through and among, not anywhere. It's the now, that is so precious. And the sounds from the flow of the burn are a murmur of agreement too."

As the woodland thinned on the higher ground on either side of the burn, trees became sparser, and more open areas changed the terrain underfoot, the path having veered off to the right. Early bell heather gave a real blast of colours from pink right through to purple, and a new aroma filled the air.

"Let's give it another twenty minutes, and then look for a good spot to set up the tent, Lizzie love. We`ll need the water supply from the burn here, as well."

This route steepened a bit, and they had to pick their way with care. But even that experience was a pleasure, knowing that each gentle footfall was their adjustment to what nature had provided for them. Lizzie led the way. In time, the curve of the slope eased onto a more level area. "Perfect for camping somewhere hereabouts," said Andy cheerfully.

The invisible skylark poured its music all around as an apparent blessing on their venture.

While Andy busied himself finding the best spot to pitch their tent, Lizzie had taken their stove out of the rucksack, got some water from the burn, and proceeded to brew up the anticipated mugs of tea.

Five minutes later she went over to Andy, who`d laid the bits of the tent out on a nice flat grassy area, and said, "tea`s up, my love."

Sitting side by side on a big, rounded boulder, they slowly drank that tea, enjoyed some flapjack that Andy had made, and looked at the map of the area they were in.

"When I compared this modern OS map with some of the much earlier ones that Alex had drawn on, and two rather more recent ones, it was clear that this has had the name Darach Muir at one time, though that's a bit out of kilter with its present condition. Darach implies that it was once synonymous with oak trees, whilst Muir does suggest a wide-open area, which it certainly is now. The deer grazing amongst other things has made certain of that. Without measuring it exactly, I`d nonetheless reckon it's over five square kilometres, that's almost thirteen hundred acres, perhaps more. Gently rounded, and there are not too many contour lines on it. But when we get up to the highest point, to the site of the Darach Stane, we`ll see extensive views over the lands beyond. I'd be interested to know what settlements this would have included in pre-clearance days."

"Didn't Alex identify that it was common land at one time, Andy?"

"He sure did, although not specifically about the extent of the common land, it's fair to assume that it covered much of what perhaps later became known as the Muir. If we`d a Gaelic scholar here, then perhaps we`d get some clues of land use on it, as in the names of burns that drain off it, or places of summer grazing. I don't see any shielings marked on the map, but that doesn't mean that none existed. They've just not been identified archaeologically yet."

"Now that we have the Darach Stane," Lizzie chipped in. "We have evidence in stone and carving of the place of the oak tree in some ancient culture. Perhaps when we are confident enough to do it, we`ll get some experts in such stones and carvings to have a go at dating it. Now that would be interesting to know."

"Why did you say we need to be confident my love, we've got it safely hidden away for now?"

"Well, the circumstances under which we got it were a bit unusual, and we don't know the status of what's left of the Kirk that we got it from, even if it's normal under a hundred feet of water. My god, it could be a scheduled Ancient Monument for all we know. And digging around on them is an offence, I`m told."

"Yeah, you are right, we do need to clarify that, as well as imagine what the Hydro people would make of it. I can visualise the Health and Safety people there, being a bit perplexed. There is probably a load of bylaws which we have breached too. Though one thing is certain, as soon as the Reservoir refills, which it surely will this coming winter, there will be no way of putting the Stane back, now will there? Talking of Ancient Monuments, I`d a look at the site of the Darach Stane up there at the top, and it is scheduled. Several hundred square yards of it, all around the highest bit. Though oddly there's a twin summit if I can call it that, very close to the main one, which is not scheduled."

"That's both limiting, on what we can do, and very strange about the second summit. More questions than answers, I fear, Andy. But anyway, I didn't bring a spade. Did you?"

"I knew there was something I'd forgotten. So now I've been rumbled."

Chatting, laughing, cooking, eating, and just being together in this wild place, was a joy. Well, towards dusk they revelled in all that it gave them, as the light, warm breeze was just enough to keep the midges away. At last crawling into the tent, which Andy had pitched with his usual skill, Lizzie asked casually, "did you read the spec for this tent, you know, what it`s most suitable for?"

"Eh, not really. I would have automatically assumed that if it said anything, it would be for camping."

"Oh, no doubt about that, but what about lovemaking? You know, a kind of love nest?"

"Rather doubt if that would be stated on the spec, but there`s only one way to find out."

Following a leisurely breakfast, the happy couple packed away all the camping gear and equipment, checked over the site, and once more swung their rucksacks on their backs. They set off on an agreed wide arc, that would take them around near the southern rim of the Muir. In the occasional peat hag that they found, there were the remains of old tree roots jutting out from the edges.

"I knew it, clear evidence of ancient forest with this bog oak, as it's so often called. Let's take a small bit and see if we can find someone who can either date it for us or even identify the species of a tree when we get home." And so saying, Andy picked up a piece lying in the bottom of the peat hag and fixed it onto the outside of his rucksack.

A little further around, they found a few humps and hollows that looked a bit different from the surrounding terrain. Lizzie photographed them, whilst making the maximum use of light and shadow from the sun. "The sun is too high in the sky just now, so not enough contrast, but hey, we can only do what we can do. There`s so little difference in elevation from the surrounding Muir, and the vegetation confuses it a bit too."

They counted seven of these vaguely rectangular formations, with rounded corners. Andy paced them all out, and they agreed that the common size was about seven feet by fourteen feet. "They seem to run along the side of the slope here. And look, over there is the start of a small burn starting to make its way close by. So, if this was a summer sheiling, as seems most likely, its location here, beside the burn, is not by chance. I`ll mark its location lightly on the map, so we've some record of it, as well as your photos too, my love."

The lack of any collection of stones suggested to them that whatever the structures had been, they were probably low-level turf walled and heather thatched. "These would indeed only be suitable for summer use," said Lizzie. "I`m sure if we went further down the hill, we`d find the sad evidence of pre-clearance settlement. That's a bit challenging for me Andy because it begs the question as to what hand my ancestors may have had in any clearance activity here. In saying it would take a lot more research to come to any conclusion on that, I`m not ducking the question, honestly, I am not. Although Alex was primarily concerned about other legal matters, I wonder if he had any thoughts on this. We`ll most likely never know. And it may sound crazy to say this, but I wish he was here now, to see what we are starting to make of his unwitting, tantalising legacy."

"Whatever, we know we can't rewrite history, but we sure can learn from it, indeed, we must learn from it. That is at least a useful outcome."

Andy and Lizzie felt a mixture of elation and sorrow, with what they had discovered, what they had in truth, just touched upon. So, they walked on in thoughtful silence for a while, before stopping for lunch.

"It's so tantalising, isn't it, that what looks today, like just a big expanse of apparently empty treeless Muir, around a small hill, has at various times been covered in scrub woodland, including oak, and also the location of long-lost human activity too," said Lizzie. "The strongest piece of evidence we have is the Stane, and that tells me that the ancient humans here or hereabouts not only had harmony with nature because they knew she sustained them. Yes, I think nature is feminine. And from that, they had icons from nature that they respected greatly, they worshipped. Of course, that is the very thing that Snoddy was bent on eradicating all signs of. He was certain of the first chapter of Genesis, which says something like "Let them have dominion ... Fill the earth and subdue it and have dominion over it."

"Wow, your Sunday School lessons have stuck Lizzie. But you`re right, that's what Snoddy was all about. The wonderful thing is though, that we are now learning a different creed, or re-learning a very old one, in which we are on a par with nature, and must live in harmony with it. I`d elevate nature, and feel we must be guided by it."

"We can`t see into the future, but we now have the means to predict a lot of things, Andy. Not you and I particularly, but society generally. I`ll stick my neck out here though and say that if we accept the femininity of nature, then wisdom and practicality will surely follow. Let nature have dominion over us, for a change. We`ll sure as hell be the better for it."

"Remind me never to fall out with you, my love," Andy retorted in a light-hearted vein. "But I too know that you are right. So very right."

"You`ll also be delighted to hear Andy, that I think young people are taking more of a lead in some of this. Many of them are showing fresh vision. I guess they are less encumbered by ideas that are long past their sell-by. Whether older people believe they are wiser, like it or not, younger people feel empowered to just tell it how it is."

"It's so good to be away together like this Lizzie, and philosophise a bit, as well as have the experience."

Walking hand in hand was not very practical in the rougher terrain, but in their hearts, that's exactly what they were doing.

Further round on the arc their route was taking, they came across another likely candidate for sheilings designation. The same kind of location, and the same characteristics, though slightly harder to make it out. Andy marked the location on the map, and Lizzie did her best to get some photos.

Continuing, they found more tree roots sticking out of a peat hag. One was an almost complete base of a trunk and seven or eight main roots radiating from it. A stark remnant of what had been when that layer of peat was formed.

The next historic structure was a much more recent circular sheep pen, in quite a good condition.

"Although this is a thing of fine craftsmanship by some drystone wall builders, I see it primarily as a monument to the clearances, and the arrival of the sheep in large numbers," Andy said, with a note of resignation in his voice. "That took time, skill, and a lot of effort to build, as there's not a lot of stone around here. That investment had to be worth it. Your ancestors, I wonder."

"Oh, no doubt," she said, her voice trailing away, and shaking her head.

"Anyway, I`d like us to get plenty of water from the next flowing burn, and then make our way to the top of the hill, where if all goes well, we`ll camp for the night. Camping at the site of the Darach Stane does appeal to me. And the weather is still looking fair for it too," said Andy.

After about half an hour, they came to a suitable burn and filled every water container that they had. They also took the chance to have a very good drink themselves, in the mid-afternoon heat. After a wee rest during which they took in the landscape character, felt at one with it, and allowed themselves time to just listen and smell, without chatting. Each in their pace with nature, it was a rich experience, they agreed as they chatted later.

Ascent to the top of Darach hill was a fine stroll, with the views widening almost at every step. Short heather, not yet in full bloom, mosses, and lichens on the few areas of exposed peat. A stone here and there. Bright yellow tormentil flourished almost everywhere and seemed to sprinkle cheerful sunbursts on every surface. With a long flowering season, they are often regarded as every walker or climber`s companion. It is a such convivial company with stars of bright colour.

At the top, rucksacks were quickly removed, and the happy pair just took in as much of the view as they could. They tried to identify familiar mountains on the horizon. This gave a real sense of place in the wider landscapes. Some had been climbed, whilst others awaited that challenge. River valley and lochs abounded, and a hint at a village or two amongst all this, added to the story of people in the countryside. Before they could sit down and relax enough, they felt bound to find the exact spot where the Darach Stane had been so brutally hauled out of the ground and casually broken. They walked to the highest point but agreed that since it was the largest solid rock on the surface, there would have been no way of digging a hole to insert it in. So, they walked around in a kind of spiral, hoping to find evidence of a hollow or softer ground. After two or three ever-widening circuits, they found a place that looked likely. It was south-facing, a hollow, with a stone bluff behind it to give greater rigidity.

There was indeed a distinct hollow, perhaps a foot or so deeper, where the ground had been disturbed, and a few rocks lay around half overgrown with vegetation. Nothing else on the whole summit looked even half as likely as this. Lizzie took many photos, to record the scene.

On looking from this vantage point there was a temptation to believe that the Darach Stane had been facing directly at both the midday sun, and at a faraway mountain with a prominent, distinctive shape. All this directly above the smaller second summit of this hill.

On recognising this, they concluded it was probably not by chance, and much more research would be needed to check on any other possible seasonal or other alignments.

"Of course much has changed over the centuries, millennia even, not the basic landform, because that goes back to the last ice age. But vegetation, tree cover, and any other heathen monuments that may have been given the Snoddy treatment. So, we are not looking at the vista as it was when the Darach Stane was erected," Lizzie advised. "Let's take a look at the second summit Andy. Does it hold any secrets, I wonder?"

It was about fifty yards south of the main summit, and only about a foot lower in height.

When they got there, it was Andy who spoke first. "In a strange way, the character of this is quite different. Less rocky, with softer ground and vegetation. A few rocks were scattered about two or three feet from the gently rounded summit. Another hollow almost at the summit suggested some form of human activity at some time, but what?

"Although I haven`t a clue as to what it is, this place is of significance to the whole story too," Lizzie added.

More photos were taken, as yet another valuable record.

Just as they were about to conclude this survey, Lizzie yelled across to Andy, "my God, come over here and look at this stone here, it's off to the side, as if of no importance. But I believe it may just be the missing half of our Darach Stane.

With that, what more fitting more special, and more rewarding place could here be for the second camp? Right beside the original site of the Darach

Stane, with all its incredible symbolism. A symbolism that was originally not some representation of anything monumental worshipping the past, but a living, dynamic symbolism that was alive in the people hereabouts. And to find the lower half of it lying there in the heather, where Snoddy had so disrespectfully cast it aside, was even more special. To cap it all, there remained the question of the second top. It was significant, but in what way? Only more research would begin to answer that.

Andy pitched the tent right between the two tops, where a flat grassy area seemed to call out, camp here.

The well-rehearsed camp routine fell into place, so naturally, Andy and Lizzie were as one in it.

Chat after the meal, once more carried them into the half-light of dusk. They'd seen that landscape near and far, change as their perspectives adjusted to it. finally, only the line of the horizon marked the boundary between land and sky. Time to turn in.

Another leisurely breakfast for the contented couple the next day. Looking at the map once more, they decided upon an arc like the previous day but running nearer the northern boundary.

"Surely this will take us closer to the road, which can't be too different from the route it followed in Snoddy`s time?" asked Lizzy. "We can`t seem to get away from the shadow of that man."

"It will, but let's not be deflected by that. Let's enjoy the Muir as we find it, and you can always have your camera at the ready."

"Oh yes, talking of that, I'd like a load of photos from here, before the sun gets too high in the sky." So, Lizzie spent fully half an hour on this mission, while Andy lay back on the heather and tormentil, and dozed contentedly.

"Right, let's go," she announced suddenly, and that rapidly brought Andy out of his dwam.

"Oh, yeah, ok yeah. I must have been away with it there. Sure, lets go."

With rucksacks hoisted once more, and walking poles at the ready, they descended close to where their ascent had been the previous day, to complete the circumnavigation. The going was easy, but the ancient landscape and people's interaction with it then were in their minds.

"I imagine that they had many uses for oak in those days, so it would have been valuable to them. They would have used it sparingly, I`m sure," said Lizzie thoughtfully. "That oak is so slow growing, would have added to its special place in their culture, surely. And as the seed, the acorn is a potent symbol of the cycle of life. No wonder they held it with more than just respect."

"Indeed, you are right. I was just thinking of common land, and its place in the history of land use, rights, and abuse. T`would probably be a good idea to read up more on it and re-read all that Alex had to say about it, and this piece of land we are standing on. I'm intrigued by what he said about the legal ownership being dubious, or questionable. How did that slip through the net into doubt? Does it mean anything today? The doubt, I mean. And where might it sit alongside the rapidly growing community ownership initiatives movement? And if we stir this up in any way, what might the consequences be? I have a feeling that this is unfinished business, and Alex has given us the means to change things. Perhaps."

"I`m not sure I want any battles or violent controversy here Andy, my boy, just look what happened when, albeit very unwittingly, you stirred up a few hornet's nests. My god, you are lucky to be alive. Mind you, the big thing now is community empowerment of one sort or another, and that's most certainly a different dynamic. It has the political blessing from Holyrood, no less, though perhaps in a distorted way. Lochhead, the nearest local community to here probably hasn't a clue about Darach Muir."

"That might change when the story of the rediscovery of the Stane gets out, as it surely will. And finding the missing part of it is going to be like a catalyst. Ooops, Lizzie, I have noted what you said earlier about the controversy. Honest, I have."

"Just as well, we have a new major role to play in deciding what to do with Spurryhillock and creating the means to realise whatever plan we come up with. And then there`s my business and your job to consider. At least we don't have to do anything at all about the flat for many years to come. It's just perfect, Daddy did such a truly wonderful job there. Well, the tradesman did, he`s not into DIY at all."

13.

Angus messaged everyone in the Stane recovery team, plus Archie, with a much-anticipated update on what he`d done with it, in his care.

"When I got home after our highly unusual, probably nefarious, nocturnal adventure, I got some rest first. Then, I unloaded it, still on the barrow, from the back of the van. Using the planks as support to keep it up off the ground, I set about cleaning it. It occurred to me that your Rev. Snoddy character had no regard whatever for the acorns, though at least he does not seem to have damaged them much, I didn't feel that I should cause any damage to his cross on the other side. It is, after all, part of the story of the Stane, albeit not the more precious to us. I carefully pressure-washed the Stane, and the full beauty of the acorn carving came out very well. There may even be a hint of a few oak leaf shapes around the edge of the acorns. Though they are a bit indistinct. So here are a few photos of the Stane, taken in what I hope is the best light.

I've also cleaned and photographed the broken end, as you can see. So, if by some miracle another bit of the Stane ever does turn up, you`ll know what you are trying to match it against.

Quite a mission this, and I`ve just heard on the grapevine that the maintenance work on the reservoir dam is now finished, so the water levels will be rising again, pretty soon."

Each received the message and photos with a sense of excitement and gratitude to Angus. A few messages between them expressed a real sense of impatience to see the Stane anew. But it was Lizzie who, in thanking Angus for all he had done and sharing it, added, "well, as it so happens, I think Andy and I have located the other half. Here`s a photo of it."

With that, the airwaves were buzzing.

"We must retrieve it," Archie volunteered. "Do you think the two broken ends are any kind of match," he added with a tone of impatience.

"Steady now Archie, it's far too early to say with any degree of certainty. But there does seem to be some similarity. We must remember that the two bits of stone have been in very different places, and climates, for many years. If you guys can give me a good indication of the location of that stone, I`ll find a mate up here, who can help me, and we`ll take the ATV, which also has a hoist on it, over the Muir one evening, and retrieve it for you. Taking an ATV over the Muir briefly, won't attract much attention."

"That would be wonderful Angus, very much appreciated, and thank you," came Archie`s swift response.

As everyone, went about their business over the next few days, there was as always, a lot of catching up to do.

Archie wanted to perfect the appearance of his lawn, noting that the man they paid to tend the garden, could do the rest.

Marissa was busy with her voluntary work, which gave her such a real sense of purpose, being valued, she often said.

The elm furniture that Malcolm was making, was nearing completion, and he`d had one planned viewing of it from the family that had commissioned it. With a few suggestions about minor details, they had seemed well pleased with what they saw and felt about it.

Spending a lot of time outdoors with the young people in her caseload was not without its challenges, but Hermione loved the job she had and could see the slow but steady progress, the benefits, that each was gaining from it. Not a quick fix, she had been heard to say, but a great way to make a wee difference to troubled young lives.

Ronald had been away on various journalistic ventures, so he`d been a bit out of the loop locally.

The stairs up to their flat, and back down again, were as ever a familiar challenge to Andy, especially when laden. But Lizzie`s order book never seemed to dry up, indeed it must have been growing steadily, as she sought to keep up with demand.

And when he was not running up and down the stairs, Andy was away with groups of young people to the bothy. He always came back exhausted because it was a full-on responsibility for the leaders. Some of the young people needed intensive support, at any time of the day or night. But a full washing machine after his return was, he felt, just one of the good measures of the value of the work.

Right out of the blue, there was a phone call from Dr Robertson, the owner of the house on Heriot Row. "Hello, is that Andy?"

"Yes, indeed it is, how are you getting along?" Andy replied somewhat curiously.

"Oh, we are fine thank you, so kind of you to ask. I do need to tell you, however, that we are intending to move to a more convenient house over in Fife, to be a bit nearer the grandchildren. So, we were wondering if you would want to go through the stuff in that cellar before we just have it cleared?"

"I would thank you yes, Dr Robertson," Andy responded. "After the great discoveries we made in that trunk, it would be good to see what else might be there in the cellar. I`ll tell you what, we`ll clear it for you if you like. I imagine most of it will just need to be dumped, but you never know."

"That's very kind of you. No desperate hurry, but can I leave it with you?"

"Yes, that's fine, I`ll be in touch."

David and Margaret had been somehow just getting on with their difficult lives, down in the Borders. One day led on to the next, in what to them seemed like an interminable sadness. One day, however, when their neighbour Jean called with a bag of groceries from the supermarket, she seemed even more cheerful than her normal positive manner. "I've got a wee treat here for you folks. No, it's nothing you could eat, I think it's much more exciting than that. Here, let's sit around at the table for this."

When they were seated, Jean got out her phone and opened a file on it. "Right, here we go, I've got a wee video of young Monique and Charlotte for you to look at. I`m sure you`ll like it. Their aunt Lizzie sent it as she promised she`d do."

David and Margaret sat in rapt silence, as they watched the video, not just once, but three times. "Oh my, they look so lovely, so much bigger, so eager, and they seem to be speaking directly to us, David," as tears rolled down her cheeks. "This is such a joy to see, Jean, don't you agree David?"

Almost unable to speak, as he choked back the tears too, all he could say was "wonderful, truly wonderful."

"Thank you, Jean, it's been a real pleasure to see and hear the girls once more. Oh, you've brought them back into our lives."

"It's a pleasure, and it's been no trouble at all. Lizzie did the work and made it happen. I feel I've just been the Postie, for this. Your two grandchildren are delightful and so chatty. I've never met them of course, but here they are for you both, courtesy of my phone. I believe that their aunt Lizzie, is going to bring them down soon, for the day, and you`ll all go to one of the big house gardens. That'll be a treat for you, and I`ll probably arrange with Lizzie to take the two of you there, and then collect you home later."

"Oh, we don't want to be any trouble to you, couldn't we get a bus or something?" said Margaret.

"Honestly, it will be no bother to me at all, I`ll be so pleased to help a wee bit. So please don't give it another thought now."

"Well, if you say so Jean, you are so kind."

They watched the video once more, and it was as if a sunbeam had suddenly shone into the room.

As she drove the short distance home, Jean felt content. Her little effort had given these two poor old souls a glimmer of hope and lifted their spirits. Kindness costs nothing, she concluded, as she stepped outside her own wee cottage.

14.

No summer would be complete for Lizzie and Andy, without several expeditions of one sort or another; they must have felt another coming on. After dinner one evening, they sat down at the kitchen table with some maps, to stir their spirit of adventure, and focus on their shared love of wild places.

Lizzie picked up a sheet, and exclaimed, "It has to be railway to railway this time, Andy my boy."

"OK, what sheet have you there then, my love, that has got you going, so?"

"It's Sheet 42," she said, as she glanced at the top left-hand corner. The one that covers Loch Ossian through to Dalwhinnie, and beyond."

"Ah yes, I can picture the landscape, are you suggesting a start at Corrour Station, or perhaps finishing there?"

"I`d say start there, it's ever so slightly off this map, but most of Loch Ossian is here," she pointed.

"So, since you are our route finder for this venture, where would you suggest we go from there?"

"Well first, I`d say, let's cycle it, and wild camp. We`d have to be self-sufficient, cos there are no shops within miles of where I`m going to suggest we go."

"That's fine love, I can do self-sufficient. If you can guarantee nobody will attack us," Andy said with a wry smile.

"Well, I can't promise that, but I'd say the chances of that happening up there on those tracks, are less than point zero, zero of one per cent. The madmen were locked up, so the wild places are safe once more."

"Whew, that's a relief, but you know I was only kidding, love?"

"Yes, I could see that mischievous twinkle in your eye. We`d take the train to Corrour, cycle around the north side of Loch Ossian, and then continue out, to the north to the bottom end of Loch Laggan. From there, with various ups and downs, we`d come out at Dalwhinnie, and get the train home. How does that sound, Andy?"

"Fine by me, let's make it three days or so, and get cracking with the planning."

So, the next day, Andy was down at Waverley to book tickets, especially for the bikes. "Always a bloody nightmare is that part of it," he muttered to himself, as he anxiously waited in the queue at the ticket desk. After what seemed like an eternity, in which the ticket clerk tried all sorts of different combinations, dates, and other unseen variables, on the system, the printer finally spewed out the necessary bike tickets first. Without them, he knew they`d be running the risk of being stranded at some station, with no way of getting their bikes on board. Then when that necessity was complete, he got the tickets for Lizzie and himself. And was able to march back up the ramp, out into the open air, clutching the tickets for a great wild adventure, each of them on two wheels.

Meanwhile, Lizzie had organised the food they`d need, giving it a lot of care to ensure there would be enough, but not too much. "Everything is down to weight," she muttered to herself, as she collected the last of it from a specialist shop. That evening, they tended to their bikes and sorted out the equipment they`d need. "Checklists are the way to do this," he advised Lizzie.

"Eh, yes, I`d kind of worked that out. If you forget anything, there`s no going back to get it once you set off."

Just two days later, they were on an early train to Glasgow to pick up the West Highland Line at Queen Street. The day had started with some rain, but by the time they were rattling across Rannoch Moor, the sky cleared, and the sun came out. As they reached Rannoch Station, Lizzie could see a shadow of anxiety on Andy`s face. "Was this where you got shot by that madman called Jock?"

"It most certainly was Lizzie," as he shuddered at the thought of it. "There`s the very gate I clambered over and fell in a heap, as the train was coming into the station. Oh my God, but the memory of it is awful."

"Don't worry, that was a while back now, my love, you are safe with me. And look, as the doors are opening, there`s no gun-wielding apparition of a man glaring at you through the windows. Just a quiet, lazy wee station with a café, after the sun, has come out." As she squeezed his hand.

The train pulled away and she could feel him relax. But in no time, it was necessary to get organised to alight at Corrour. So, by the time, the train reached this, the highest mainline station in the UK, Andy and Lizzie were waiting ready at the door, with their bikes fully laden for the two-wheeled journey ahead. They let the walkers go first and then crossed the siding, to where a new house and café had been built just a few years ago.

"Only one thing for us to do Andy, let's press on, and get those wheels turning."

"Fine by me, my love."

As they set off along the track, the sound of wheels on gravel, blended beautifully with birdsong and a light breeze against the moorland vegetation. Ahead lay Loch Ossian and beyond that the long valley leading up to that nick on the horizon, the Bealach Dubh, with the great mass of Ben Alder to the right. Simultaneously, they both felt the wonder of being amongst the mountains, and their spirits soared with it.

Their route took them near Loch Ossian, then a sharp swing to the left, and down over a bridge, before a magical cycle through the woodland on the north side of the loch. It was obvious to them, that judging by the quality of the track, this estate was backed by plenty of investment. And so, created a cycling experience almost in a league of its own. At a clearing on the right, overlooking the loch, they stopped for a brew-up and sat in silence, as they soaked in the splendour of it all. After a while, Lizzie got out the map and started naming the mountains and hills they could see. She also pointed out the general direction of a number that were out of sight. Eventually, she said quietly, "We must get going again."

At the end of the loch, they could just see glimpses of the somewhat controversial new lodge, in glass and granite, on their right, before the road then headed north towards yet another sun-glinting loch. A few miles further on, the track crossed a bridge over a burn. They stopped. They looked around. Without uttering a word, they nodded to each other and started wheeling their bikes up the rough terrain beside the burn. Round a gentle bend above a small waterfall, a flattish grassy area opened in front of them. No words were necessary, they just lay their bikes down at the edge of it.

The campsite was perfect, just far enough away from the track to be a bit secluded, the never-ending sound of the water as it flowed by bank and boulder, and the high mountains enclosing the idyllic scene. As soon as the tent was up, once more without a word, they stripped off and were straight into the pool beside it. True, the water was cold, but immensely invigorating, refreshing, and filled their hearts with joy, as they lay back and let the sun do its magic too.

Packing up the campsite next morning, was a well-rehearsed routine so that everything had a place, and everything was in its place. A final check over the site, making sure that nothing was left, and they were off once more, heading north. That special sound of tyres on gravel was like music to them. Although the wind had got up a bit, it did not deter Andy and Lizzie at all, for they were buoyed along by the great romance of the night before, and the thought that they'd taken a step closer to the confidence that they'd spend the rest of their lives together. Following a steady climb up to the crest of the ridge that the track crossed, their route then took them down into a mixture of woodland, forest, and open areas. Views opened wide all around, and along the next valley, with mountains beyond, and lochs below. As the track weaved this way and that, so the vistas changed with it. A light overnight shower had just served to freshen the whole scene, and give that distinct tangy smell, after the rain.

The track descended to a few houses at the southwestern end of Loch Laggan before a right turn into a different estate. A mile or so of the flat track was then replaced by a steep zig-zag ascent eastwards to an intriguing high-level loch. On one side were the great slabs of the Ardverickie Wall, a great favourite amongst the serious climbing fraternity. On the opposite side, the mountains rose by ascending ridge and spur towards a clutch of popular high mountains. Whilst the near end of the loch was a truly breath-taking beach of golden sands. A beach within the mountains. There, Andy, and Lizzie once more needed no discussion, as their bikes were laid down, and regardless of who may or may not be in the area, into the loch they went. The water was a little warmer in the shallows than the burn of the previous evening, and so they lay, side by side, as it lapped around them. The sunshine kissed each point upon them, that it could catch, and so their bodies glowed. Though they knew that the glow was about the warmth of the sun filtered in ripples across their bodies.

When they felt they had had sufficient pleasure from this mountain-clasped experience, they moved up the beach to dry off, slowly. Once done, and re-clothed themselves, it was time for a brew-up. Tea and biscuits and time to take in the splendour of the scene. Once seen, never forgotten, they happily agreed together.

The track took them along the side of the loch, and onto the same, south side of the next loch. Then they entered the forest. Mostly commercial, with trees of all ages and stages, and a slightly confusing array of tracks, made it necessary for Lizzie to consult the map now and again. When they stopped briefly at a crossing, where advice from the map and decision-making was called for, Lizzie remarked confidently, "there is something very satisfying about making a good decision and finding out later that it was indeed the correct one."

"Eh, yes, I`ll take your word for it love. I'm only too happy to follow your route-finding skills."

As they approached the valley where they knew Ardverickie House was located on the Lochside way down at the bottom, they turned away from that, southwards, and higher into the hills. A substantial new mini-hydro structure filled the valley bottom. Not a pretty sight, they agreed but making very good use of a natural resource in as thoughtfully designed way, as possible. The track grew steadily rougher, suggesting to Andy that they must be nearing the edge of that estate, and then an extraordinary timber bridge structure loomed up ahead. Clearly well-designed in its day, and probably over-engineered too, it was beginning to look very sorry for itself. Some bits were rotten, others were missing, and a sign proclaimed that those using it, did so at their own risk. Andy and Lizzie stopped and surveyed the scene.

"It looks very dodgy to me, Andy, but as far as I can see, there is no alternative. This is a kind of Lady McBeth moment, methinks." Then, to their amazement, or delight, a small group of cyclists came along the track on the other side, towards the bridge. Almost without pausing the apparent leader just sailed across the thing, with only the rattle of a few loose planks to suggest that anything could be amiss. The rest followed. They all stopped for a chat with Andy and Lizzie, about the usual sort of things like "where have you come from, where are you heading for", and so on with

111

the pleasantries between fellow enthusiasts. When it came to the inevitable subject of the bridge, the leader of the group gave a potted history of it, and the difficulty of getting anyone to pay for the maintenance when it's near the junction or march, of two completely different estates.

"But what about its current safety?" asked Lizzie rather anxiously.

"Well, you've just seen this lot negotiate it without any mishap, so I`d say you two will be fine. Stick to the middle and keep going is the best bet. I've been doing this for years, with no problems. Yet."

It was the word yet, part of this, that undermined Lizzie's confidence.

"Tell you what," said Andy. I'll go first, and if I am ok, you can follow. How does that sound?"

"Oh, OK, I guess so, but do be careful. Remember, we just got married a couple of months ago and have a whole future in front of us."

"I promise to be careful and take the advice we`ve had from that guy to heart. So here goes."

Carefully positioning his bike at the start of the old wooden bridge, right in the middle, Andy moved steadily to get going. Sure enough, a few planks rattled a bit, but nothing moved in any alarming way. So, he increased his speed, focussed on staying right in the middle of the structure`s trackway, and with a few more planks rumbling somewhat, he was across, and safely on the grassy bank that led up to the far side of it. Andy stopped. "Hey, that was OK Lizzie, now you."

"I just can't do it, man, it looks so rotten and unstable. I`m frightened."

"OK, hang on, I`ll walk back over, and I can wheel your bike across. You can walk directly behind me. How does that sound, Lizzie dear?"

"Hmmm, well I guess so, I`ll give that a try, Andy."

So, Andy quickly walked back over the ancient structure and felt a few planks wobble a bit under his feet, but he got back across safely. Taking Lizzie`s bike in a firm grip on the centre of the handlebars and the seat, he started walking back across, with at least a sense of purpose. Lizzie followed closely behind and was visibly nervous. The same wobbling planks only heightened her fear, but she doggedly stuck to the place right behind the back wheel of her bicycle. In a matter of minutes, which had seemed like an hour, they were safe across together. So, an embrace seemed the most appropriate way of showing the great relief they felt. "Well done my love, you did it. I`m fair proud of you."

Eager to get away from that whole experience, Lizzie quickly said, "Let's get to Loch Pattack over there, and camp for the night."

"Yeah, that's a good plan. The track gets very neglected over the next mile or more, and we are at the outer extremity of Ardverickie Estate here. But if we take our time, we might get through, dry-shod."

So, they either cycled or walked, as the terrain dictated, and apart from a bit of mud, did indeed get through reasonably dry. A pair of well-built stone gate piers, one on either side of the road, but minus any actual gate, signalled the start of Ben Alder Estate. In no time at all, Lock Pattack was on their right, with nice flat grassy areas along the shore to choose from as a campsite. Wheeling their bikes down onto this and admiring the mountain views beyond the Loch. The huge bulk of Ben Alder once more filled the scene, with neighbouring hills adding to the true setting of that ever-popular mountain. Picking a spot that looked highly suitable, in no time, the tent was up, and dinner was being cooked on the stove. Andy and Lizzie made a great team when it came to the business of sorting out life on a wild camp. One task followed another, as if like clockwork. And so, they sat down on the grass, with the sound of ripples on the shore, to enjoy the food they agreed they`d earned.

"Well, I may have picked the route Andy, but I won't be in a hurry to come back this way again, because that bridge just scared the living daylights out of me."

"A bit of a challenge was that old wreck, but you did it, darling. You did it."

Lizzie and Andy slept well that night, sure of the happiness that they were together, enjoying most of the journey, and their sleeping bags snuggled up close.

The next morning, they woke to the sound of light rain drumming on the tent. "Do you know, I don't find that sound itself in any way depressing, in fact, quite the opposite because we feel snug and dry in here. That's a lovely feeling, almost in defiance of the sound of the rain. But it's the prospect of having to get out there and sort out breakfast and all the rest in the rain that I'm not so keen on," Andy said rather philosophically.

"I`m with you there. And the longer we can lie here and just listen to it from our relative comfort, the longer we can put off the inevitable. But sooner or later, I know, I'm going to need a pee, so this indulgence here, can`t last forever. I know that only too well. So, who`s first, to go for it?"

"Let's toss a coin if we can find one," Andy suggested.

Lizzie fumbled in her panier and found a five-pence piece. "OK, heads you are out the door first and tails it's me."

She tossed and when it landed, she sighed, "I seem to be the one to lead the way here."

Dealing with the business of ablutions, breakfast, striking camp, and packing up, was all accomplished with slick efficiency. Their outer waterproof clothing from head to toe did the trick very well, only the midges in their millions marred the precision with which everything was

114

tackled. In no time at all, it seemed though, they were ready to roll, not least because with a bit of movement they might escape the midges. It worked, well almost.

The route then took them to ever-improving estate tracks as they neared the environs of Ben Alder Lodge. Loch Ericht stretched out to left and right as the rapid descent brought them down to that level. With no dilly dally, they pressed on along towards Dalwhinnie. That familiar sound of wheels on gravel was their accompaniment, as the pedals turned. Up a gear, down a gear to accommodate the varying gradients, and the gentle twists and turns that the track took to get around or over a small hill or cross a bridge over a burn. The sign of traffic on the A9 road ahead long preceded any sound from the vehicles. But a blue train heading north tooted loudly, and the sound echoed down the Loch towards the happy couple.

Leaving the Loch behind, at the small north-eastern dam, they found that in no time they were sitting in the station`s small waiting room, slowly drying out a bit. Their affectionate chat was only interrupted by the sound of their train approaching the platform.

Loading their bikes onto the train, with the relevant tickets on display, seemed like a fitting conclusion to a great venture.

15.

Archie had now looked closely and critically at what he now very respectfully called the Alex Papers. Studying them in some detail, and in his mind, constructing the legal arguments or propositions that war had curtailed, he realised that there was indeed something in it all, regarding the common land on Glenmaddy. Discussing it with a former colleague over a dram in their Club, Archie said, "I think that given some of the more recent research on this whole matter, my grand-uncle Alex was ahead of his time. Nobody was particularly interested in it in those days."

"From what you say Archie and the way you've put it, there does seem to be something in it. Perhaps not entirely conclusive, but your Alex has done a thorough, objective, and well-constructed job, of showing that there is at the very least a grey area. That means several things, I`d say. The first is that your ancestors probably acted ultra vires, or outside the law, in laying claim to the common land. The matter is confused of course, by the period in which the estate was forfeited following the Jacobite rebellion. Because that introduces a third party, in the form of the York Buildings Company, and its role in acting on behalf of the British Government regarding the handling and disposal or otherwise, of the forfeited estates. Muddy waters indeed."

"I value your informal comment on this Geordie, because my mind is a bit rusty on land matters now, and I sometimes think I'm so immersed in this, that I can't see the wood for the trees, or I don't think I can anyway."

"It's a pleasure, and you know how I love to be able to get my teeth into something a bit historical. The fourth party in this is the Brighams, or whatever their name is, was. If their descendants are still the owners, then they will just be acting in good faith at what they've had handed down to them."

"As far as I've been able to discover Geordie, the ownership is now vested in some obscure offshore entity. But there is no record of a change of ownership anywhere, which is hardly surprising. Oh, there`s a lot more research that could be done on this, if we were of the mind to do it. Did I tell you about the Darach Stane, which is part of the story in some way?"

"No, please do, this sounds like another fascinating twist."

Archie then gave a brief and up-to-date account of this tale that could well have spanned millennia or two.

"My god man, your immediate family is not short on smedddum. What they've done takes a poke at both the legislative background to the Hydro schemes and the Ancient Monuments acts too. Depending upon what they plan to do with it, they may find that they have a brush with some wildlife habitat legislation. Oh, and removing the stone in the first place may upset more recent land access stuff. Whew, this lot is not for the faint-hearted."

"Yes, I rather feared that the route has been mined, legally. Or could potentially be a legal minefield, at least. And of course, the other side to this whole saga is now hugely popular, in the area of our relationship with nature. There`s a powerful groundswell of passion about that, and it has political clout too. So, a rediscovered, ancient emblem that, could very quickly mobilise the eco-spiritual and environmental troops, not to mention the archaeologists too. But do you know what Geordie, I`m loving this, wherever it leads, or whoever it pokes?"

Since Malcolm had the van, Archie asked him if he could clear out the cellar at the McGillivray property in Heriot Row. "Yes, that's fine. I`ll do that as soon as I can. Can you give me his phone number, please? Is everything just to go to the rubbish recycling place?"

"Most of it yes, I`m sure, but can you be on the lookout for any books or papers that may have survived? Oh, and any pictures too. You never know what we might yet retrieve for the history of the Fergusons, and Alex in particular."

"Just you leave it with me. And I`ll keep you posted on it."

In the middle of all this, rather surprisingly, the Business Plan for Spurryhillock was beginning to take shape. Lizzie and Andy had had all sorts of meetings with relevant officials and discussed their aspirations with the rest of the family. The Planning Officer they were dealing with by email up till now had the Anglo-Irish sounding name of Orla Wheelwright. Well perhaps it should be the other way round, as they pondered it, but Irish-Anglo just didn't` fit. They`d also looked into planning laws, and even tried to make something of the disposal of the former military estate. They investigated what sort of developments were taking place at the cutting edge of ecotourism provision and dabbled in the developing area of funding for agriculture, and contemporary land use. Listed building consent regulations had come into the equation, along with access to capital grant schemes for tourism development. It had been a mammoth task, and not yet complete.

They found Archie to be their best source of good counsel when they needed that objective critical eye. Though they found this ironic because, in the forty or so years in which he`d been at the helm on Spurryhillock, the one word that always seemed to come to mind was neglect. He'd seen the property as a bit of a liability, and lack of any great interest in it as an estate just made matters worse.

Andy and Lizzie had put together the first draft which they'd given to him about a week before and set up a meeting in Spurryhillock, to discuss it. This started with a drive around all that was reasonably accessible, in the ancient, unroadworthy land rover. With running commentary about what was where, rather than the detail of the plans, they took in everything that could be seen. They then retired to the dining room with its great oak table. Coffee and flapjack were served.

"The starting point is that we need to raise a bit of capital to kick things off," said Lizzie, optimistically. "And we may need partners for some elements of the plan. So not everything will be in our full control, but everything must be a money earner one way or another, and quickly. The house is sacrosanct in all of this of course.

The first thing to go, to raise capital would be the remains of the army camp, for new house building. That's derelict and just a liability, it's at the perimeter of the estate, out of sight, and nearest to the town, which is thankfully quite prosperous these days. More work to do on how best to carry this out, either as developers ourselves or by selling to a commercial developer. Along with that, the cold war bunker, and perhaps half an acre could go, but once again, more work to be done on that. The boathouse could be developed by someone, on a very long lease. And the stables likewise.

Camping pods and the likes are all the rage and require relatively little infrastructure, so that field beside the road a little further down from the access to the bunker, would be well suited to a camping pod site, for say a dozen of them. Whether to buy or lease in, would be for consideration."

Andy then took over, "I brought in a structural surveyor to look at the ruins of the old house, or castle. Without digging any holes, clambering all over it, or chopping down any trees to get a better look, she said that the basic structure of the walls would appear to sound. No major cracks or collapses, to contend with and no apparent subsidence. Its B Listed, of course. Internally it's been a bit of a hotchpotch of different periods of construction, even if externally it does look like a single entity. She said

119

that sometimes the interface between different periods of construction doesn't work very well structurally, but it seems to be OK here. So, her quick informal conclusion was that we have a sound shell of a building to work with."

"The woodland is in poor condition, but it needs to be viewed in the overall context of future land use, and any potential government or forestry support which may be available," Lizzie concluded. "What do you think, Dad?"

As he thoughtfully poured himself another coffee and passed the cafetiere around, he drew breath. "Even as the first draft, there`s a huge amount in it, you've put a lot of thought and care into it. I like that. I'm not a businessman as you know, but I like your approach. How many years will this plan take to be realised, do you think?"

"Seven is the minimum, Dad, possibly a bit more."

"That's a wise approach to take to it. The general sequence you've outlined is very practical, and prudent too. And your judgment on what can be disposed of fits the bill well. One major question does arise though, and we need to face up to it, sensitively. This is going to be pretty much a full-time job for someone, to manage it. Much of it is on-site. Now Lizzie dear, I know that both Andy and you are very keen to have a child, or indeed, children. Yes, your mother did tell me in the confidence of your sad loss, and I`m truly sorry about that, my heart goes out to both of you. When the time comes and you are successful, as I very much hope you will be, how`s that going to work out, with the flat in Edinburgh, and this place, and the plans for it? Oh, and your job, Archie, and your business, Lizzie, dear? I know you want to make this place at least pay for itself, but to do so, you may well be entering a new chapter in your lives altogether. A challenging one at that."

"Of course, we know that right now, we are in an unknown area Dad. The business plan may not stack up as we`ve hoped, jobs, babies perhaps, oh yes, it's all in the melting pot. But we are sure of one thing, we can't just leave Spurryhillock as it is, as the liability, we know you thought it was, for almost forty years Dad. Sorry for being so blunt about it."

After a slightly awkward silence, Archie responded, "yes, you are right of course. I let this place slip, and I know I've given you a potentially poisoned chalice. Mind you, it wasn't in great shape, when I was given responsibility for it all those years ago either. Well, the two of you have great spirit, wonderful initiative, and obvious determination. I can see that. I wouldn't have given you the place if I didn't believe in you.

So, I`ll be glad to do whatever I can to help you realise this plan for Spurryhillock, make it a nice place to be, and yes, keep it in the family for another generation or two. Let's work on it, and make it happen; somehow."

On their return to Edinburgh, Andy found there was a message for him on the voicemail from Professor Anderson. She sounded very eager to set up a meeting involving a potential PhD student for the watershed landscape's theme. This immediately kindled very mixed feelings for Andy. He was of course delighted that someone had picked up on it and showed real interest in the potential it offered for a major study of some kind. He felt strangely vindicated that all the passion he`d put into the venture was attracting serious interest in academia. No doubt, in the end, some in-depth research would prove the point that The Spirit had entrusted to him. It would also make all the terrifying experiences he`d endured a bit more worthwhile.

But that stirred up all sorts of memories that he wanted to put behind him. And strangely, life had moved on quite a bit in the interim. Life had moved on very significantly.

So, the message from Professor Anderson, had him facing in two directions suddenly, it seemed. He was still very focused on the recent meeting about Spurryhillock and highly motivated about what the outcome of that meant for him, and Lizzie, in this new chapter in life, as Archie had so cogently described it. Whereas the message was drawing him back to an earlier chapter, and all the difficult associations it reminded him of.

Andy knew however that the only way the watershed project, as he called it, would move ahead in any way, was if someone else took it up, or at least some aspect of it. The message, and a meeting from it, would perhaps herald the new chapter that it needed.

A meeting was therefore agreed upon and set up as requested, a couple of weeks hence, in one of the university seminar rooms. Not in a noisy café this time, Andy mused.

Malcolm reported back in due course, that he`d cleared the Heriot Row cellar, and most of it was indeed junk. "Disintegrating furniture, and the remains of domestic bric-a-brac."

"OK, very many thanks for doing this, really appreciated. Was there anything of any interest though? Andy asked.

Well, that's hard to say, but I did bring back a couple of crates of books and stuff that hadn't fallen apart. I've put them in the shed behind my house, beside the lawnmower."

"`Ta, we`ll investigate, in due course."

With a quick trawl online by Lizzie, for a suitable place to take Monique and Charlotte to meet with their grandparents, she soon identified Mellerstain House and gardens. Well, it was the gardens and café that caught her attention, and it wasn't too far from where David and Margaret lived. She phoned Jean first to get a suitable date for her, then David, and finally Mellerstain. From all this, a suitable date was fixed, before the end of the school holidays.

"Do you want to come, Hermione?" Lizzie asked rather cautiously.

"It's still a bit difficult really, I think. I feel so sorry for them, and I`m sure they are desperate to see the girls. It's been too long really, but as you know, I just couldn't bring myself to organise anything. Life`s so good now, with dearest Malcolm, that stirring up any memories of Jamie, is too raw for me. Oh, bless you, Lizzie, you seem to understand, and I'm so truly grateful to you for this."

"It's OK, Hermione, don't worry, I'm glad to do this, and you won't feel hurt when I say that the important part of the meeting is so that David and Margaret can see their grandchildren once more. I`m going to do another wee video of the girls for them before we go to Mellerstain, because the last one was such a success, or so Jean tells me, and I don't doubt it for one second. Jean`s a star. Could you discuss some of this with the girls please though? They need to have some understanding of how important this is for their ageing, lonely grandparents. They also need to be persuaded not to have their phones or tablets out when they are with David and Margaret. And you can reassure them that there will be no discussion, well not if I can help it, about Jamie."

"Yes of course I will, mind you, I think in their own ways they had the measure of him a long time ago, Do David and Margaret know about the new life I now have with Malcolm, though? That could be awkward."

"Yes, I made a point of mentioning it when I visited them, and although it touched a raw nerve, I think they understood. They certainly don't bear you any malice Hermione, you can be sure of that. Meeting the girls again will eclipse all of that, so don't worry."

"Thanks so much. Oh god, this does bring so much back you know. I've still to do something with Jamie's ashes. That's my awful responsibility.

I do occasionally wonder what his land agent clients made of him; he was a bit of an anachronism. Perhaps some of them liked him though. He did mention Sir Hector Melrose a few times, and I see he died last year. But the whole Jamie business gives me the shivers, just thinking of it."

16.

Angus had done some deer stalking in his time, including the business of taking the carcasses out, usually one at a time, on the back of a pony. This was a bit different though. He managed to borrow a suitable vehicle, trailer, and all-terrain vehicle for an evening; no questions asked. His mate Jock kindly agreed to accompany him on this apparently clandestine mission.

"This is the weirdest caper I've ever been on, and that's saying something, but going out to get a particular old stone from a particular place on the Muir, beats them all. Mind you in the greater scheme of things, of just how legal it is, it's probably on the much safer end of the spectrum. Though quite how we`d explain it to the cops if they should turn up is beyond me." Jock said with his usual fine humour.

"Yep, I`ll say it's unusual, my man, but it's not half as unusual as . ." And then the cut himself short, as he was sworn to secrecy about the rest of that nocturnal caper. "Hey man, life would be so dull without the odd thing that's a bit different from the norm."

So, stopping at a wider bit of the verge, where a very faint track left the road, heading out across the Muir, they reversed the whole vehicle and trailer a few yards along that track. With the ATV, then unloaded, they set off on this bumpy journey to find the highest point, which Andy had said would be almost a mile distant. Sure enough, it came into view, a pimple on the top of the Muir. They'd left the track by this stage, as it had veered east to some other unknown destination. Stopping at the summit, they got out, and Angus consulted his phone.

"You expecting a phone call or something, pal?" asked Jock.

"Nope, just looking for a photo somewhere on here. Ah, here it is. Give me a minute till I get my bearings. What we are looking for is a particular stone, larger than the rest roundabout here in the heather, somewhere beside the slight hollow between the two tops. My god, it's a bit devoid of clear features here."

"I'm getting more and more curious about this escapade, but I don't suppose you are going to tell me any more than you already have, which wasn't much. Mind you, you did say there`s a pint in it for me, so that`ll do fine?"

"All top-secret stuff, for now, I`m afraid, pal. Right the stone should be up to three feet long, slightly flat, and around two feet wide. Might be a bit heavier at one end. That's what we are looking for."

More searching followed, and furtively looking over towards where the vehicle was, they certainly didn't want to see any flashing blue lights drawing up beside it.

"Is this it, pal?" as Jock kicked a solid-looking stone a few yards away.

"Let's see, yes indeed it could be. I`ll just check the photo on my phone," said Angus. A couple of minutes elapsed, and then he said triumphantly, "yep, this is it. Let's get it loaded onto the ATV. We can slide it up the planks I've brought. Nae bother to the likes of us, man."

With the stone loaded after a bit of heaving and grunting, they bumped their way back over to the track, and across the Muir to the vehicle. All safely aboard again and with no trace of them having been there at all, they headed back to town.

"Right pal, where`s that pint you promised me?"

On returning the, no questions asked, ATV the next day, Angus laid the newly recovered stone end onto the main Darach Stane, and it was an almost perfect fit. He messaged everyone to tell them the good news and sent photos too.

17.

Putting the Darach Stane back together again, was the next challenge.

A string of messages, texts, and even a phone call or two ensued, in which several thoughts were exchanged as to how best to do this, some more fantastical than others. It was Archie who got the best suggestion, from a former client of his, who ran one of Edinburgh`s monumental mason companies. They met, in the Club of course, and over lunch discussed the problem at hand.

Walter was affable, cheery, and very keen to give his best advice. "This is, oddly enough, a problem that we come across quite regularly, though perhaps not with stones, or Stanes, of such provenance as this one you have. It's health and safety that drives this, yes, the dreaded H & S, Archie."

"Well, who would have believed it", chuckled Archie as he took a well-considered sip of the malt, they had by this time progressed to.

"Yes, it crops up in all the older cemeteries in the city in which a headstone has got broken and the family or descendants of whoever is in the lair, want to have it fixed, and eh, shall we say, they have the money to have this done. Or it may be that the entire stone has worked loose and needs to be reattached to the base. Following a tragic fatality or two in which children have been killed by a falling headstone whilst playing in a cemetery, the owners of the cemeteries, usually the Edinburgh Council, two new policies have been created. If a stone or part of it is loose, then it must be deliberately couped, as we say. That means taken down and laid flat. It's then the responsibility of the lair owner to have it fixed, or not, as the case may be."

"Good heavens Walter, there`s a lot more to this, than I'd ever have imagined."

"Oh, I'm not done yet, because now we get to the crunch about reattaching stones or bits of them. There's a clear protocol, and it doesn't depend on cement alone, or super glue either. All the bits that are going to be reattached must be taken back to our workshop for a start. The parts must be very securely fixed together with short lengths of stainless-steel rod drilled and resinned into both. Usually two rods per joint."

"Holes are drilled into each piece so that they line up very neatly, the quick-setting resin is then inserted into both holes on each side, and the rod is also pressed home. It's left to cure, and only then can it be returned to the cemetery for re-erection."

"Well, well, well," exclaimed Archie, whether in surprise or fuelled by the lovely malt they were getting tucked into. "This Darach Stane is going to be more of a challenge than I had imagined. Oh, I know it's not going to be in a cemetery, but we want the repair to be permanent, don't we?"

"Well, it must be done right, or it`ll no` work, or endure, Archie. Hey, this is lovely stuff we are drinking. Hmm, a very fine malt indeed. Here, tell you what, I've got a pal in our professional association who is based within reasonable travelling distance of where the bits of the Stane are. He owes me a big favour, as I occasionally remind him, at the Association dinners. I could ask him to reattach the two halves, but it would be up to your team to take it and erect it back where it belongs. He may not have the gear for that. But I can give some informal advice on that part of it. Informal, you understand?"

"This is more than I could ever have hoped for Walter. Very good of you. Can I leave it with you to contact your, eh, colleague please?"

"Of course, Archie, glad to be of help. I do recall when you kindly helped me with a legal problem when there was a big falling out in some family we were trying to deal with. It was almost down to fisticuffs, as one half of the family wanted a particular kind of stone, more traditional, as I recall, whilst the other half was hell-bent on something, eh, how should I put it, garish. Yes, garish, no other word for it. But you know the saying about piper and tune, so I`d to try and please both. And the owners of the cemetery wouldn't permit any action, until there was full agreement, in writing. Do you remember that case, Archie?"

"Oh, I do indeed. But as far as I can remember, I spoke to both halves of the family separately first, then got them all around a table together. Not quite sure how I did it, but there were no fisticuffs, and I achieved a kind of consensus, a compromise I suppose. Well, I was glad to have sorted that one out for you Walter."

"You did thanks, and the stone is still there in the cemetery for all to see and visit if they want to."

"Let's have a wee snifter for the road, my friend."

18.

Ronald returned from his investigative travels, which as he said, "Had mainly been about many years of political dithering's around the issue of Scotland's provision of National Parks. A lot of unfinished business there," he added.

As he met with Andy and Lizzie, they had a much-needed catch-up on all that had been happening and was in hand.

"You guys don't hang around, do you? I do take my hat off to you, for all this great progress."

"Thanks, Ronald," Lizzie replied. Eh, dare I ask what you have planned for the next week or two?"

"This sounds ominous. Eh, what did you have in mind? There may be a wee gap or two in my schedule," he chuckled.

Well, the Darach Stane is going to be reinstated in its rightful place, we've decided that. This may cause quite a bit of interest, support, and possibly controversy too. So, we need to try and get a handle on local opinion or even awareness on several things, but it needs to be done in such a way that it doesn't raise any expectations in the immediate future. You are good at sussing things out, Ronald."

"Hm, thanks for the compliment, guys. I wonder what's coming now?"

"Well, we know with a fair degree of certainty that the common land was appropriated in some way, not long after the Jacobite Rebellion, 1715 one. And we have a good idea of the rough extent of it too. The question here is what, if any, local knowledge or awareness is there of this? It's probably lurking somewhere in local lore or cultural tradition rather than fact. But you can never tell what some avid local historian may have unearthed. Alex was a bit more abstract, in that he was looking only at the legal position, as far as we know," said Lizzie.

"When it comes to the Darach Stane, we want to hear of what the locals know of it too, if anything," asked Andy. "We also want to bring the picture a bit more up-to-date, on issues like eco-spirituality and the local environmental lobby. Because that might tell us how ready the community could be for the Darach Stane."

"Not much then?" Malcolm quipped. "Yeah, there are a few mountains up there I want to climb too. I mean real mountains, with cairns at the top. Sure I`ll do what I can for you. I can see why you might want to know the lie of the land on these things. I think you might be in for some nasty surprises too, depending on how this pans out. You know a thing or two about vested interests Andy, now don't you just? But let's leave all that for another day."

Not wanting to be left out of all the fun, Marissa did a bit of research on the significance of oak in Scottish history and lore. She knew so well of a growing popular awareness of it today, of how much wildlife oak very often supported, or attracted; sustained, even. Birdlife, bug life, ferns, lichens and mosses, and a whole range of other living things, that loved an oak. Especially an old oak. She knew also that a lot of this awareness was ancient, too. Indeed, in days of yore, the oak was worshipped. And that almost God-like status, therefore, cropped up in imagery, poetry, fable, song, and saga. So, the oak is no ordinary tree, she mused, as she started her quest for the ancient symbolism it carried.

She quietly got on with her research and knew that when the time was right, she`d have a significant body of knowledge to demonstrate clearly, why the imagery on the Darach Stane, indeed, its very name, was of such

131

significance. A carving of a bunch of acorns, the very seed of future oak for another four hundred years perhaps, was surely iconic.

As Jean drove her car up to park at Mellerstain, she knew her two passengers were both excited and nervous. David and Margaret had fussed about it quite a lot during the previous week, with so many questions and not enough answers. Jean helped them to keep it in perspective, with her ever-cheerful, calm manner.

"Och, you`ll be fine," she said quite often whether on the phone or whilst visiting them. "That video of the girls we got last week was a treat. They are such lovely-looking girls, and well-mannered too. Oh, you`ll see so many changes in them, since you last saw them, of course, you will, but memories will come flooding back too, you know. You`ll have some lunch with them in the café, which will be nice, I`ve heard it's a lovely place to meet and chat, over some nice food. The girls can run about a bit outside, but there are nice benches or picnic tables you can sit with Lizzie, and the girls will pop back to you from time to time. Och yes, you`ll be fine."

And so, it was. It was fine. Lizzie managed the reunion very well, with care and sensitivity. Jean had gone off home, having agreed that Lizzie would phone her when it was time to collect them. Oh, there were different kinds of underlying nervousness of course. David and Margaret had forgotten how to relate easily to young people; they didn't know enough about the girls to make ready conversation. And for their part, the girls were not used to chatting with frail elderly people. But Lizzie`s natural talent for people overcame all of that, by gently leading the conversation, the questions, and at times hinting to Monique and Charlotte that they should tell their grandparents about something at school, or about their friends, their musical instruments, what they did last weekend, their house and how they have organised their bedrooms, and so much more. Slowly, what had been a rather one-way flow of information changed, as both David and Margaret seemed to warm to the special occasion and began to ask questions of the girls themselves.

As expected, the wide-open spaces beckoned now and again, for a bit of exploring, but little gifts were brought back each time, in the form of a few wildflowers. These gifts were more than just flowers though, they betokened youthful fun, warm hearts and despite all that had happened in the interim: affection.

The weather was kind to them, the setting seemed to be perfect, and Lizzie could see just how much David and Margaret were getting out of this occasion. They`d probably reflect on it for weeks to come. For their part, Monique and Charlotte had been exemplary; they had truly risen to it all, as fine young women, which they were fast becoming.

In due course though, it was obvious that David and Margaret were getting a bit tired, with the day being so very different from the norm for them.

Discreetly, Lizzie texted Jean to say in about half an hour would be fine, please. She found them all at the picnic table and quietly walked up so as not to interrupt. "Have you had a nice day folks? Oh, those are lovely flowers that you've brought together girls. How kind and thoughtful."

Margaret looked up, "Hello Jean, we've been having a lovely time. The flowers are gorgeous, so we`ll need to get them in water as soon as we get home. We are thrilled to have been able to get reacquainted with this fine pair. They've told us so much about themselves, and what busy lives they lead. Different times than when we were at school. Thank you for organising today."

"Will we go over to the car now?" They all rose slowly from the table.

The car was strangely quiet, as they drove the short distance home. So much to think about, Jean imagined.

133

And it was the same in the car with Lizzie. Not much chat, just a lot of thinking, and wondering. No doubt the questions will come later, she thought.

Questions, that may be difficult to deal with, but at least Hermione would be part of that scenario when it came.

19.

True to his word, Walter contacted his pal, who as he said, owed him a big favour. Within just a few days a chap by the name of Alistair was in touch and hooked up with Angus. The next day a truck appeared, all equipped with a hoist. webbing, ropes, and wedges. The two halves of the Stane were lifted aboard and secured. Just three days later the reunited Darach Stane was delivered back intact and in all its glory. The junction between the parts that had been separated two centuries earlier by Snoddy was almost invisible. It had all been cleaned too, so the acorns stood out with a freshness that had been concealed for a long long time. The very image, that had fired Snoddy with such righteous indignation, or so he thought.

Messages and texts from Angus to the gang, along with photos attached, stimulated a fair buzz of electronic replies. The airwaves were hot with excitement.

"As soon as we get some feedback from Malcolm, we`ll be able to put together a plan for reinstating the Darach Stane in its rightful place. We`ll also have a hint at what the local reaction might be," Lizzie messaged. "We could of course just erect it and leave it at that, a sort of low-profile approach."

In the dream that Andy said he believed he`d had, he saw a piper marching boldly in front of the ATV, which bore the Darach Stane towards reinstatement in its rightful place atop the Muir. There, a hole had been prepared, and as the gang gathered around, there were speeches as the base of the Stane was then gently lowered into what should be its proud position for another thousand years or more.

A dream, of course. The reality was different, but every bit as moving.

So much had gone into making this moment possible in the first place. A young man, who over a hundred years ago had had the vision to investigate something obscure, that had caught his interest. He`d been forensic in his research and constructed a sound case insofar as it went. Then that ghastly war had taken him away from his chosen task and finally taken him to the bottom of the Atlantic Ocean, along with all his comrades.

A succession of chance discoveries of that old painting, that key, a trunk, and a box, had all led his ancestors and friends to pick up where he had left off though. Some very unusual nocturnal goings-on in the bed of a dried-up reservoir, with a lot of hard physical effort. The random discovery of a missing piece, the skills of a monumental mason, and an amazing collection of goodwill, all combined to create this special occasion in which the ATV was indeed once more driven across the Muir with its precious load.

Instead of a piper at the helm though, there was a small group of people who carried forward the sequel to Alex`s vision a century ago, and bore the picks and shovels on their shoulders, to make the core part of it happen. Their deeds were obscured by the enveloping mist, and that constant drizzle failed to dampen their zeal in any way. A collection of rabbits that had been eagerly munching the vegetation, scattered and left the hilltop for temporary human intervention.

Andy and Lizzie marked out the extent of the Scheduled Monument area, using four pegs, one in each corner of the rectangle. "In a way, it's strange that the people who designated this area chose a rectangle like this to define the boundary," said Andy. "Probably not based on any detailed survey, but just creating a simple statement of the officially protected area. Can't imagine the sheep or deer would be too bothered about it, as they eat their way across the wee hilltop. And, weirdly, they excluded that other slightly lesser top. Ah well, the inspectors are not here to answer that question, so we`ll just use the opportunity this gives us to put the Stane there, without committing any offences under the Ancient Monuments Act, or whatever it's called.

Ok, gather around please folks, here`s the plan, oh and welcome to the top of Darach Muir. This is a special occasion as we roll back over two hundred years of wrongdoing and give our respects to over a thousand years of wisdom and the true place of nature in our lives."

"Well-spoken Andy," replied Marissa. "It's as if we are reclaiming nature`s place in the priority of things; nature`s dominion."

"We are, indeed, Marissa. Now the area that we can't touch because it's a Scheduled Ancient Monument, has been marked out by Lizzie with those four pegs. It seems almost certain that the Darach Stane stood almost at the highest point, but we can't put it there. For some reason this ever so slightly lesser top is not protected, so we can dig there. The base of the stone looks like it was set in the ground about two feet, and probably held firm with wedge stones all around it, before being backfilled with earth. We could have decided to set it in concrete, but that's too permanent, and not in the spirit of this at all."

"What do you mean, not permanent, man," exclaimed Malcolm, with some alarm. "I thought we had a millennium in mind."

"I predict that what we are doing will have an Ancient Monument`s Inspector out here pronto, to see what we've been up to. Who knows what course of official action that will be set in train? Malcolm here has very kindly been getting a handle on where the Darach Stane fits into local lore or even current awareness. And I think it's fair to say, that it does have a place in this. Am I right, Malcolm?"

"You are true, there`s a bit of reference to it in tradition and song, as a lost emblem in local culture. The character of Rev. Ebeneezer Snoddy hasn't been entirely forgotten either. There`s a thread emerging in the contemporary debate on common land too. So, you are quite right."

"This being so, could we imagine that perhaps, yes maybe, once the Stane is back here, there will be a local cry for it to be back right where it belongs, up there? That's not for us to do, but let's not do anything today, that would prevent it from being possible, at the will of the local people, should they so wish. Setting it in concrete would therefore not be a good plan."

"How right you are," said Archie. "How right you are. So where do you want us to dig?"

"There`s a sort of a wee hollow at the top over here, so let's get a hole just over two feet square, and two feet deep. Angus, could you supervise that, please?"

"Gladly, pal. Here`s a tarp that I want all the excavated soil to be put on, and stones kept to one side of it. As the senior, here Archie, could you cut the first sod please?"

"Wow, what an honour. As a gesture in this, Marissa dear, could you place your hand on top of mine on the spade, as I shove it into the ground? Oh, we must have a wee bit of ceremony here, so on a count of three please everyone."

The cry went up then with everyone joining in the countdown: "three, two, one", as the mist gently absorbed the eager human voices.

Angus organised a kind of shift system so that everyone would have a hand in this digging, keeping the sides of the hole straight, and collecting suitable wedge stones. It was surprisingly hard work. About a foot down, they came to a biggish stone, that proved very difficult to extract. So, it took a lot of digging around it without widening the hole any more than was absolutely necessary, and then levering it out, and putting it to one side.

Once it was out of the hole, the excavation got a bit easier again, and the two-foot depth was reached, almost down onto the bedrock. Angus thanked everyone for their effort and set about straightening the sides of the hole, removing the loosened soil by hand, from time to time. "Time for a tea break now, I think."

As everyone sat around where best they could find a nice perch, sandwiches, flapjack, and mugs of tea were handed around by Marissa.

"Ah, I am ready for this." Seemed to be the common thread in the chat.

Marissa had started to take an interest in the big stone that had caused such difficulty and then laid it to the side. Suddenly, she exclaimed, "my God, take a look at this."

Everyone jumped up and came over to where she had cleared the mud off most of it, and on one side there was a carving of an oak leaf appearing out of the dirt. "That's a lot more than we bargained for, raises all sorts of questions, and instantly makes this site a whole lot more significant," she added.

A kind of site meeting followed in which the focus was on what best to do now. Opinions, comments, and sundry proposals were all shared. It was Archie however that pulled it together though. "Look, OK, we have come up with something new, but time is limited for the key task of the day. We have not done anything especially illegal in digging that hole, even if the alleged owner of the land could object. I propose we press on and get the job done properly as intended. Take that stone away with us, and consider, its destiny later."

The nods of agreement indicated consent to this, so the tea break was continued, with an added source of interest to ponder upon.

When Angus was happy with the hole, he brought the ATV right up to it, put slings around the Darach Stane, attached these to the hoist, and carefully lifted the heavy load. "Which way do you wish the acorns to face?" he asked.

"I would propose south because we could easily get bogged down in a debate about symbolism here; the rising sun, or the setting sun. No, I propose south." Marissa said, with some authority.

"Right while I start lining it up for that, can someone please define south for me?"

"Here, I think my phone has a compass in it somewhere," Andy said quickly, as he got it out of his pocket.

"Lizzie, could you please go and stand about three feet on that side of the hole," he pointed. "I`ll line you up for a good southerly direction, and when the Stane is in the hole, you can tell Angus when he`s got it right. Then we can do the wedge stones around it."

So, Lizzie did as asked, Andy held his phone compass, and instructed her to left or right a bit until he was happy with her exact location. "Now please stay put."

"OK Angus, it's all yours." So, the Stane was slowly lowered and tilted more vertically as its base went down into the hole.

When the bottom of the base touched down, he said, "right, now I need to take the webbing off, and when that's done, we`ll need to manually manoeuvre it into place to line it up for Lizzie, get some packing stones in and get it plum. So, I need a couple of strong bodies, one on either side please."

Malcolm and Andy stepped forward, as Angus got down on his knees beside the Stane.

"Right then, let's get it more or less upright first." With some heaving and grunting, this was achieved. "Hold it there."

"Now Lizzie, I`ll rotate it a bit, and you can shout out when you think it's getting lined up." At which Angus got his arms around it and turned it. "Is that looking roughly correct, for now, Lizzie?"

"Quite good, but not there yet."

"OK, I'm going to adjust its position in the hole with this crowbar, so hold it steady you guys."

With that, he stood up, lifted the crowbar, and move the base position around a bit until he was happy that it was suitably centred. Putting the crowbar down, he got down on his knees and put some handfuls of smaller stones around the bottom. "Now Lizzie, let's be getting a good southerly orientation of this ancient Stane."

"OK, I want it turned a little bit clockwise."

Angus gestured what clockwise meant here, for the two Stane steadiers.

"Keep going clockwise, guys. A wee bit more. And stop," as she eyed it up. "That's good. Are you going to check it for plum, Angus?"

Reaching for the bead, as he called it, he advised the steadiers which way to go, very carefully. When he was happy, having moved around it quite a bit to achieve this, he said, "Right hold it there, while I get some wedges and packers in."

"Right, the rest of you, keep me supplied with lots of suitable stones now."

Angus then beavered away, putting stones in the hole evenly around the Stane, bashing them down with a mash hammer to get them tight, adding more stones, and more bashing. "How are you guys doing, Lizzie is it still true?"

Getting the affirmative that he needed, he continued with his task with a real sense of purpose. At about mid-level he put in a ring of larger stones

141

very firmly jammed between the Stane and the sides of the hole. Then continued as before, placing, adjusting, and bashing. Close to the top, another ring of larger stones, jammed in tightly, as before. "OK, you guys can all stand down now, your task is complete."

The last spread of stones on the surface, suitably firmed in together, tightly, some soil on top, and Angus finally stood, stretched, straightened his back, and admired the Darach Stane back in place, and very much as the ancients had first erected it, a thousand or more years ago.

"Just give me a minute to deal with this tarp and the tools please, and then we`ll all be ready to fully appreciate the fruits of today's labours, together." Carefully pulling the edges of the tarp together, and getting a loop of rope around it, he hoisted it aboard the ATV. The tools all followed. "Now please scatter these spare loose stones out onto the Muir," he asked.

So said, stones were being ceremoniously thrown in wide arcs over the heather, most disappearing amongst the vegetation.

"That's it done folks," Archie said proudly. "Your Darach Stane, our own Darach Stane, back pretty much where it belongs."

There were thanks and congratulations all around, as everyone admired it from all angles, and photographed it likewise.

It was Archie who broke the silence. "Thank you all for this, and especially Angus. Without your involvement and direction, I don't think we`d have got on very well. Delighted to have given you back your Darach Stane. Now before we go can we agree, low profile on this for now, and I've asked Malcolm to handle any press interest that may crop up. We`ll have to play it by ear, as to what might happen next. We can be very happy with what we've done, but we may have poked a hornet's nest too."

With no trace whatsoever left, as to who might have done it, The Darach Stane had quietly, anonymously reappeared out on the Muir, where sing the skylarks now. Or so it seemed.

20.

Two days later, Marissa answered a ring on the doorbell, back in the very respectable Grange area of Edinburgh. Two police officers were standing there, as she opened the door. "We are looking for Mr Archibald Fergusson, the registered owner of that vehicle there." One of them pointed toward his car sitting in the drive.

"Oh, he`s in the kitchen I think, you`d better come in, can you tell me why you are enquiring about this please?"

"No, we need to speak directly with Mr Ferguson. If you could take us to him, please."

Somewhat anxiously Marissa led the way through to the kitchen, as the Police followed her. "Sorry, the breakfast is not cleared up yet. Archie dear, these two Police officers wish to speak to you about your car, I believe."

"Good morning, I`m Archie Ferguson, what seems to be the issue with my car?"

"Can you please tell us where you were, presumably with your car two days ago?" asked the smaller of the two officers.

"Oh, yes, I was up north with my family. Why do you ask?"

"Can you be a bit more specific please, Sir?" Asked the taller of the two.

"We were just up for the day, mainly on minor roads well west of the Pitlochry area. We had a picnic, though the mist came down at one stage."

"It's been reported to us, by our colleagues up north, from an account by a member of the public, that your car was spotted parked for several hours along with others, on an unclassified road in that area. At or around that time, some activity which may or may not have been legal, took place on

144

the neighbouring moor. Can you confirm that you were involved in this activity, Sir?"

"I`ll neither confirm nor deny this, because you seem to be working from some very second-hand information, at best. And your apparent information about the location, is somewhat vague, to say the least. I`m a lawyer, so I will only proceed if you can provide a sounder basis for whatever is being alleged."

At this, the Police were somewhat taken aback. "Will you excuse us a minute please?" They went out into the hall to consult each other.

On returning, the taller of the two, said, "We have noted what you have said, Mr Ferguson, and you may hear further about this matter, in due course."

After they had left, Marissa turned to Archie, and said, "Well, we've been half rumbled, it would seem, but for what? Your comment about the hornets' nest may be correct, but all that's happening as far as I can see is that they are buzzing around a bit."

"Yes, that's a good analysis dear, they are fishing, but their gear is not up to the mark for it. Yet. I`ll have a word with Malcolm and Angus first, I think. I'm not unduly worried, as it rather depends on who's made a report about what, where, and when, and what hard evidence they may have produced if any. Two and two may not necessarily make four unless they are more strongly connected."

In the pub that evening, Angus was just enjoying a beer or two with some friends, when he overheard a conversation at the neighbouring table. His ears pricked up when the word Darach Stane came across above the wider babble of voices. The chat came and went a bit, because of where he was sitting with his back to the group, but he knew that two of that group were stalkers, sometimes gamekeepers and occasional poachers too. He heard the words `mysteriously appeared`, `ancient tradition`, and `growing interest`. Then it all became indistinct. Deciding that he wouldn't make any approach to the group, he did wonder how best to play this. There was obviously some gossip about it going around.

As luck would have it, the next day, he was walking along the village street from the local shop, when one of the guys from the previous night came along the other way. Neither seemed to be in any hurry. "Hello mate," Angus greeted him warmly. "How're tricks?"

"Hello, pal, not bad at all. Escaped the Covies thing so far, but the wife`s very worried about it though, probably on account of her mother, who's quite frail now."

"Yeah, that is a worry, isn't it? What's happening around and about? Any gossip I'm missing?"

"Oh, you know damn fine I don't gossip. Too many other things to be doing. That cold spell that we had in the spring is not going to be good for the game this year. Still having to feed the pheasants, and that's a costly business."

"Sure is, but your boss can surely afford it," said Angus.

"He can be such a grumpy old bugger at times though. Anyway, how's the craic with you?"

"Aye, fine really. Been reading a great book recently about local lore, just generally, not here in particular. Picked it up in a charity shop."

"Oh yeah, and what's it saying," Angus asked. "Though I guess the main thing is we should never dismiss it altogether, we should be proud of it, as it tells us something about the road that got us to where we are now."

"My god, you can be a serious guy at times. But yes, I`d agree with the general drift of that. Someone was chatting about a thing called the Darach

Stane in the pub last night. Bit of a mystery if I heard him right. Didn't want to appear to be smart, but I like what he was saying. Old, he said ancient, and mystery; sounded intriguing. But then we were disturbed when Mick fell over at the bar; pissed he was."

"Yeah, I saw that cos I was in the bar last night myself. Poor old guy, he`s never been the same since his wife died."

"Oh yes, so you were, in the bar I mean. Anyway, need to be getting on. Stay safe."

"And you too pal."

In the calm that they hoped would follow all the excitement of replanting the Darach Stane, Andy and Lizzie took the opportunity to escape to Spurryhillock, primarily to work up and design their business plan.

"Spurryhillock is not going to reorganise or develop itself." Lizzie had said rather impatiently.

Although it wasn't costing too much, the rent from the farm was almost paying for running the house, but no more than that. "It's not doing anything." She`d added.

When they arrived, their first, and very enjoyable, task, was to do a big walk around all the key locations, buildings, ruins, woodland, and farmland too. It was raining quite heavily, and although they were both well equipped for this, they didn't dilly dally, as the wind was clearly getting up too. They saw what they had to see though.

Back at the house, there was a note from the tenant which awaited them, in which he said he was thinking of relinquishing the tenancy. So, this news did hurry things along a bit with a sense of urgency. "We needn't panic,

147

just yet, as there will always be a demand for grazing and wintering upland stock," Andy said reassuringly.

They took notes as they went, and Lizzie had her camera at the ready.

The initial division of labour was Andy would work up the text, and the bones of the document, and Lizzie would do the design. She would make an otherwise rather dry, factual document vibrant, giving it `real sex appeal`, as she put it. "We need that to be able to wow any potential grant funders, partners, financiers, and the tourism whiz kids."

On day one, Lizzie assembled any photos that might be useful, and where necessary called upon photoshop to give them some punch. She took to the same graphic design she`d used on her website and developed a concept of what it might look like. For his part, Andy employed his writing skills to put a bit of buzz into the overall concept, description, history, potential, and current fiscal regimes. He had to cover each entity on the estate: house, `castle`, stables, cottage ruins, boathouse, farm and farm buildings, agriculture, woodland, the military remains, even an old quarry he`d come across, and potential community benefit of involvement too. Lizzie added the visual images, of those that merited it, as they might appear. They were, they joked, producing a sales brochure. But not selling the place, but rather wanting to sell the concept.

To help them get a bit of objective view on it, they`d invited Malcolm for the last day or so and asked him to go over it with a very critical eye, "No holds barred" they said. His previous job in a marketing and business planning agency was, they reckoned, going to give him a real insight, and punchy advice to offer.

By the end of day one, it was beginning to take shape. The overall aim, key actions, individual components, time plan, budget estimates, flow charts, and so on right through to the finished article. All of this dressed in smart clothes to give Lizzie`s amazing imagery. Malcolm arrived that evening, so they enjoyed a lovely evening together, meal, malt, and blazing log fire. "Hey, very good to see you Malcolm, thank you muchly for coming. Relax and enjoy.

"It was worth it just to come and be with you lovely people; all so convivial. Tomorrow may be a bit more challenging. My pencil is sharpened!"

True to his word, after breakfast, Malcolm said "Right, let's get down to business, please. I've got my laptop, so if I can log in to your Wi-fi systems, you can send me what you have."

Andy gave him the card with the relevant login codes from the back of the house modem, and Malcolm duly got into the system. Opening the relevant file that Lizzie had sent him, he spent over an hour poring over it, with a few exclamation noises from time to time. They had no way of knowing how to interpret these. It was a frustrating wait.

Eventually, the silence was broken. "Firstly, I like the look of what you are proposing, and it makes it easy to read. It's as if you are walking me into the estate, in a kind of guided tour, introducing the overall purpose and aims, and each feature that you think should be developed. Yes, I like it a lot. Now, I know you've done your homework, but you wisely haven't cluttered up the narrative with all the background material. That's great insofar as it goes. But you need to show where the information comes from, which person, agency, a bit of legislation, and so on. To do this, I'd suggest a simple reference in the form of a reduced-sized number, and then an addendum or appendix at the back to show the source. Not too much info in that, but just show that you didn't get it out of the air. Are you OK with that?"

They agreed it made good sense.

"Secondly then, currently, community benefit is all-important, especially when it comes to seeking any form of public funding. So, you might like to beef that up a bit; infer that it's not you two who will benefit, but Joe Public. And of course, to that, you can add the benefits in terms of health and wellbeing. Yes, you have a little of that, but don't be modest about this, this place could transform people's lives, or set them on a path to feeling better about themselves. Are you OK with that too, guys?

Good, I know this is giving you more work, but you need to achieve it in the minimum number of extra words. Imagine I`m an official in a public funding agency, and you want me to read it, enjoy it, and see all the right contemporary concepts in there. So finally, for now, you need to beef up the economic benefits for this part of Scotland. Somehow quantify the income that will come to this area each year, or better still, over five years. Don't bullshit that one, get it as good and as accurate as you can.

If you can weave all that lot into it, without altering the lovely design, or making it much bulkier. Oh, I nearly forgot, website and social media. But you know all about that Lizzie. Set them up and get them live as soon as you possibly can."

"Many thanks, Malcolm we are so grateful to you for this. We've clearly still got work to do on this, so we`ll give that a real blast tomorrow before we go home. You`ll please have some lunch with us now?" Lizzie invited.

21.

The autumn night had been a wild one, as Lizzie and Andy were all too aware. Living in a top-floor tenement in Bruntsfield, they`d heard the slates on the roof rattle, and the wind doing its very best to test the new glazing for flaws. It found some, and it whistled. When they did get up, after a somewhat sleepless night, and looked out of the window, there was a scene of carnage from the few precious trees, with bits of branches all over the place, slates, and what looked like a chimney pot in pieces in the middle of the cobbled road; a car swerved round it. A wheelie bin or two had been in transit. On the pavement opposite, a young man was walking or attempting to walk in the remnants of the gale.

"I rather think that someone will need to check the roof for any damage, later in the day," Lizzie remarked, as she surveyed the scene outside. "The disadvantage of living on the top floor is that the effects of any damage will appear here first, then we have the task of convincing the others that there is a common problem, and it may cost them their share to put it right."

"Ah, but on a good day, the views and sunshine are nice, as I recall," Andy added, to try and put a bit of a positive spin on things. Mind you, I`d have an uneasy feeling sometime in the night. It had nothing to do with the roof I'm glad to say, but more to do with the lack of any evident response to the Darach Stane. Oh, I know your dad had a visit from the Police, but nothing seems to have come of that, thankfully. And yes, Angus said he`d wheedled out a bit of local chat up-by, but that's all, as far as we know. It's a bit uncanny, don't you think, my love?"

"I'm a bit disappointed, as I thought, hoped, people would notice, and word would get around. After all our effort, it's a bit of a damp squib.

The time came around again for Andy to set off on one of the usual residential events in Glen Treig Bothy with a group of young people. Located in a small glen near the head of Loch Treig, the bothy had all the requirements for the activities they`d be involved in, ready to hand, with remoteness, a big loch, mountains big and small, crags, and plenty of room for both conservation and gardening too. It was ideal, and Andy knew that an experience there, had changed many troubled young lives, by providing a turning point for them.

Andy usually walked across town with his own rucksack on his back, to the converted warehouse that was base. With a spring in his step, this journey was always a pleasure, as it was for him, part of the build-up to something worthwhile. At the base, there was the hustle and bustle of getting everything and everyone ready for departure in the minibus. The long journey was a bit tedious, involving driving, a train, walking, and of course carrying-in everything that would be needed for the five-day venture. This tended to generate a few complaints, every time, without fail. Some of the young people had never been out of Edinburgh much, other than to the bothy in the Borders, used for shorter ventures. The charity that ran these experiences and programmes, had over thirty years of expertise behind it, in providing something both challenging and effective for young people who above all, needed change. Change, away from offending, poverty, drugs, alcohol, and all sorts of mental health problems. This is what Andy especially liked about his involvement, he knew he was helping to make a difference, where it was needed. Small salary, big on satisfaction.

As the last part of the rough track curves down, and the length of Loch Treig opens out to the right, the mountains close in, providing shelter for the lodge and outbuildings. Crossing the bridge over the main feed river to the Loch is like a final transition into the start of that new world, which will be home for the next week. A world of discovery for these young people, discovery and challenge, discovery and confidence, discovery, and new personal insights, that are hopefully that much-needed turning point for everyone. Andy knew only too well, the responsibility that he shared with the other staff and volunteers, to create a safe environment, and make it all happen.

At the bothy, a former stalker's cottage, and byre, the opening up process started the minute they arrived. Unbolting the shutters over the windows, to let daylight and fresh air enter. Getting the fire lit, and a brew on the go as quickly as possible. Flushing out the dormant simple water supply, to ensure that what came out of the tap would be pure and clear, even if a little peat flavoured. The stacking of food in the cupboard in an organised way. Allocating bunks and sleeping quarters. Putting mugs on the big communal table. Everyone had been trained for this, and with a bit of support, fulfilled their role systematically. Within little over half an hour, there was a pot of freshly brewed tea, at the ready.

A tried and tested induction then started, which was aimed at leaving Edinburgh life far behind, and beginning to embrace something completely new. No electricity, no Wi-Fi or phone signal, just mile upon mile of the semi-natural world. The first sessions, for the remainder of that day, were focused on enabling everyone to begin to get to know each other. Through a series of games, gentle activities, and discussion that was aimed at enabling everyone to say a little bit about themselves and feel safe in doing so. The focus would then move on, to domestic matters like cooking, cleaning, and keeping the bothy functioning for this new community. Establishing the rules for behaviour came next, with the young people setting their own standards. The first time Andy took part in this exercise, he was surprised by how strict the young people were in setting their own rules for behaviour. He couldn't imagine a group of adults being so severe on themselves, and he reckoned they would be more complicated, with various caveats to cover the unforeseen or human foibles. The young people on the other hand saw things in a much more

153

black-and-white picture. Though Andy had then surmised that sticking to these rules would be a different business. Time would tell.

On the Wednesday afternoon of that week, most of the staff and volunteers had some time off, because the young people were away on a conservation project further up the glen, with a partner organisation. Don, who was one of the volunteers asked Andy if he`d like to do some rock climbing on a crag nearby. This rather took Andy by surprise. Rock climbing was not his thing, and indeed he tended to avoid it if he could. But Don persisted.

"Oh well, nothing else to do than man up a bit here." Andy thought to himself. He`d confidence in Don, as he had the ticket necessary for this level of rock climbing, and they had all the equipment for it.

"OK, let's do it," Andy said, as boldly as he could. Let's get the gear. Do you have a particular route in mind?"

"Yeah, don't know what it's called, but it's on a crag just over there, I`ve done it with some young people before. It's got some fixed belays on it too."

As they set off, sharing the load between them, Don led the way, striding out over the rough terrain. As they went, a thought occurred to Andy, that he somehow had met Don before. The more he thought about it the less clear it became though. So, he shrugged his shoulders and pressed on. At the foot of the crag, with everything laid out on the heather at their feet, they sat down briefly to admire the view and discuss the progress of the week so far. Or so Andy thought.

"You don't recognise me, do you, pal?" Don enquired, with a tone in his voice, that Andy couldn`t quite make out.

"Well other than here with this project, no, I don't think I do, Don. Why, do you recognise me from somewhere?"

"Oh yes, I sure do."

"You should have said earlier."

"Ah well you see, I didn't know whether you'd want to be reminded of it or not, pal."

"Reminded of what?"

"OK, here goes then. A day about two or more years ago in a social work office in Young Street, back in Edinburgh, where you created a big scene. Though you probably didn't know it, because you were gone out the door before anyone could do anything."

This sent a shiver down Andy`s back, the likes of which he hadn't felt for some time. "Eh, do tell me more," he said nervously.

"OK, I was a young person on a kind of supervision order for all the bad things I`d been doing. But I guess that was better than going to prison. So, I`d an appointment to meet you, as my social worker, or whatever they called you then. I was sitting quietly in the waiting area, when it seemed like there was one hell of a commotion in your office, with you doing a lot of shouting. Then a sound of something breaking. The door was ever so slightly ajar, but you must have made a call on your mobile, and all I could hear was something about `opposite the World`s End`. Then you stormed out, almost ran down the corridor to the back door, and slammed it so hard that the glass in it almost exploded. Do you remember that?"

"I do rather, yes."

"Well, I was left in the waiting area for ages, as staff were rushing about trying to make sense of what had happened. I found it to be quite an entertainment, as it would have been our third or fourth meeting, perhaps. Then a woman that I imagined was one of the seniors appeared on the scene and instructed everyone to leave the glass that was now spread all

155

along the corridor. She shouted, that they should close the corridor with tape or cones, call some specialist firm to clear it all up, and board up the door. She announced that it was a health and safety scene."

By this time Andy didn't know how to feel, or what to make of it. "I do hope that someone did attend to you, Don?"

"Eventually, someone must have remembered that I`d been signed-in, for my appointment with you, so another colleague of yours appeared, and she announced that she`d now been assigned to supervise me. So that was the end of you, and she took me into the meeting room. Well, it wasn't entirely the end of you, because as I had more meetings with her, I started to compare the two of you. I'm like that, with my kind of background. All these well-meaning professionals lined up to sort me out."

"We`d a job to do, Don," Andy replied, as he gathered his thoughts.

"Of course, you do, or did. A nice secure professional job, that needed the likes of me, for it to exist at all. You probably don't remember anything about me, as I`d be a load of notes on a screen. I came from one of the poorest, roughest areas in the city. That's what shaped me. And I still bear a lot of anger about that, even though I`m now doing something worthwhile. I keep my anger in check most of the time, but my god, it's still there. It can boil over at times. I call the area I grew up in, Edinburgh`s Disgrace. That's got nothing to do with that load of columns up on Calton Hill, that I heard of later. Edinburgh`s a divided city, and just one of the abysmal statistics is male life expectancy. I know that sounds very serious stuff coming from me, having left school aged fifteen. But after your departure, something did happen, that turned me around a bit."

"What was that."

"The lassie that followed you, was something else. A bit posh, and cold, I had her down as coming from Barnton, or Trinity perhaps, with no deep

156

understanding of my background. But as you say, she`d a job to do. I got the feeling that she did want to find something that might move me on a bit, Andy. I wasn't so sure about you on that score, pal."

"I`d hoped I was beginning to make a start." As Andy tried to redeem his image in this very unexpected discussion, out in the middle of nowhere.

"Oh, perhaps you did. I guess that in the brief time you had me on your files, I did actually keep out of trouble. Or possibly, I just didn't get caught. Anyway Pauline, yes, that was her name, did get me hooked up with this charity outfit, and that began to make a difference, for the first time in my life. So, they got me involved in this kind of residential, they seemed to believe in me, and they gave me a wee bit of responsibility along the way. They listened to me in a way that nobody had ever done before. They trained me in low-level hill walking and convinced me I could get a leadership qualification. I did that first, and then they got me going on the rock-climbing stuff, so I was assessed on that, a few months ago. And there are other plans too."

"Well, I`m so glad you have got all this out of it. As you probably gathered, I went through a crisis, and it's only now that I can say I`m over it, Don."

"Guess so, but let's get some climbing in here, pal."

Don started by getting us into our slings, then took the rope, and announced, "I'll take this up and put it through the belay, which is just out of site, above that lip."

So, fixing the end, to the back of his sling to keep his hands free, he set off up the crag, with what seemed to Andy, like ease and confidence. He disappeared out of sight, and Andy felt quite alone. Especially after all he had just heard.

"Below," came the cry from Don. "Now get a hold of one end of the rope, as I showed you, and do not let go. Have you that done now?"

"Yes," Andy shouted as loud as he could and heard his voice echo off the surrounding crags and hills.

With that, Don came abseiling down, slightly to the right of the lip and overhang, his feet bouncing off the rock, like a nimble ballet dancer. As he landed, his next comment, put Andy in a cold sweat, but there was no going back now.

"The tables are turned now, pal, I`m the qualified gaffer."

With that, he fixed the end of the rope to Andy`s sling with what seemed like a very complicated, knot, but he did it with such confidence and skill.

"Right pal, are you ready? You are going to go up the same route that I took. There are plenty of holds. Just take your time, and remember, three points of contact at any time. Always focus on what you are doing, and don't waste time by looking down. It's up, that you want to go, not down. I`ll stand back a bit so I can see you, and when you have touched the belay, give me a shout and you can abseil back down the way you went up. Keep a bit to the right though. Off you go then."

Andy approached the base of the crag with a bit of trepidation, but he knew he must somehow do it. Not just because of the current scenario with Don, but also because he knew he`d be more useful to everyone if he could climb, a bit, at least. So, he surveyed the rock, in front of him, to each side, and above. He sketched out, in his mind, the route he thought he would take. Not necessarily with the detail of every move, but enough to give him the sense of purpose he knew he needed. So, by hand and foot, testing each hold as he went, for reassurance, if nothing else, he slowly moved upwards. Don seemed to be keeping the tension on the rope, as he climbed. There could be no stopping, or not for any length of time because he knew that if he did, he`d be stuck. What Don had done so easily and with speed, was taking Andy an eternity, or so he thought. The sweat was now beginning to trickle down his face, and he had to somehow get it out of his eyes, using whichever hand was free, between moves. His stomach was churning too. But he stiffened his resolve by telling himself to get a grip, both literally and metaphorically. If Don, his former client, and tearaway could do it, so could Andy Borthwick. In the briefest of flashbacks, he remembered some of the terrifying encounters he`d had on his big venture, and survived, well more or less.

Drawing level with the rim above the overhang, which he glanced left at, he knew that the belay must be getting a bit nearer. Surely, he would see it soon. Please God, he would glimpse it before much longer. Sure enough, as he picked yet more well-chosen holds, he inched closer and closer to where the rope ran through a stainless-steel ring, bolted into the rock, just above him. Whether he`d ever do this again he neither knew nor cared. Just get me to that ring he pleaded within. The rope was at least still being held taut, to Andy`s immense relief. He touched the ring.

"That's me at the top, preparing to come down," Andy yelled.

"OK, remember what I said, lean back, feet well apart, and keep to the right a bit. When you are ready."

Andy adjusted his position as best he could dare, and slowly started shuffling his feet down the rock face. His hands clasped the knot and rope, till his knuckles turned white. All was going well, and he was just past the rim when one foot slipped, and he swung free into the hollow below the overhang. Panic. Oh God, the very thing he feared most. Although Don held the rope firm, Andy just dangled there, swinging from side to side, at a hideous angle.

"Get me safely down from here, Don," Andy yelled into the empty hollow, his words coming back to him from the rock face.

"Now you are in a pickle, pal. Remember, I`m the gaffer. And I'm just having one of my fits of anger, with the way life has been for me and

159

growing up in such a shit environment. Also anger at all the criminal inequality in Edinburgh. Man alive, I'm raging." Don bellowed.

"Look, I understand how you feel, man, but this is no time for philosophising about inequality. Just get me down out of here safely. Please."

"Not so fast, I`m the one holding the rope now. Your future, your destiny is in my hands, pal."

"For fuck sakes be sensible about this Don. Sure, you have the rope. But to let me fall is not going to help you or your future one little bit. I'd be dead, this organisation would be in the dock, and you`d be up the creek. So do the decent thing, pal."

"Well, I'm not a vindictive sort really, but to have you dangling there does give me a wee buzz. You see you represent a lot of wrong things, you may not know it, but you do. We need radical change, not platitudes wrapped up in professional patter."

"I'm sure we do Don. That's one of the reasons I got out of it, believe it or not. Feel I'm ten times more use to this charity than I did before. I want you to believe me. Now, can you for heaven`s sakes let me down from here, and I`m sure we can chew the fat later. We`ll find that we are not a million miles apart."

"You can never be where I`ve been, or understand it, feel it, properly. But now that I've said what I have, and I think you've listened, I don't feel quite so angry, and I`ll spare you any more agony."

Andy found himself, drenched in sweat, being lowered to the solid ground at the base of the crag. Where he lay, in utter silence, incredulous at what had just happened. Meanwhile, Don busied himself with coiling up the rope, and removing his harness, while he too remained silent.

It took Andy to find the courage to break that silence between them, with "You are an insufferable and irresponsible bastard Don and deserve to get locked up for that. But I do understand just about enough of your circumstances, to know where you were coming from. We must resolve this between us before we leave this place."

"OK, I guess we do, or the rest of this residential is going to be ruined by my actions here. Now that I've had a few minutes to think about it, I realise that what I did was a bit dodgy, sorry about that. I sometimes get a bit carried away, and when I realised who you were, for sure, that combination just blew it for me."

"Na, no, it was much worse than that, Don, you nearly killed me. Do you realise that?"

"Oh, I had a firm grip on the rope at all times, there were just things I had to say."

"Not at that time, you didn't. There`s a time and a place for everything, and you picked the wrong time. I don't know what the training for a rock climb leader involves, but I`m willing to bet that it always has something about the safety and welfare of participants. Yes, always, not just when the fancy takes you. I did a long placement in your area, when I was training, and believe it or not, I took the ghastly circumstances of many young people there to heart. How any young person could emerge from that, unscathed was beyond my comprehension. But resorting to the almost criminal behaviour that you have just done, sure as hell will not fix it. It just deepens the divide, as you called it. "I'm alive, thank God, and I do admire the way you have begun to turn your life around, and indeed make something of it, don't throw that all away in an act of reckless anger, pal."

"Oh, I'm sure you are right, but do you understand why anger might boil over at times?"

"Yes and no. Anger like that is always dangerous and might lead to a very nasty outcome for you. An outcome that in the greater scheme of things, you do not deserve. And yes, I know enough about your area to know that anyone who manages to get a little bit away from it and stand back, would be feeling a rage. Of course, things should be different, on almost every front there. But working towards solutions will be more productive in the end, I`d say. We missed our chance of a revolution here in this country, about a hundred years ago."

"I saw you as just another well-meaning middle-class professional, sent to put sticking plaster over the cracks. And you failed me, by doing a bunk. What am I to make of that?"

"Making assumptions is always a bad idea Don. Ok, I came from a different place than you. My parents both worked hard in poorly paid jobs in a rural area. The working conditions for my dad were awful – digging ditches, and planting trees. He would come home at the end of each day, plastered in mud. I was the first person in my family, ever, to get into higher education. And I had one or two serious brushes with the law and tragedy myself. We are not a million miles apart. So don't make assumptions based on completely inadequate information. And don't threaten to kill them, on that pathetic basis either."

"My search for justice goes on Andy, and I can't help that. Sometimes I lash out because that's what injustice causes. I know it's reckless, and probably not very productive, but at times, I just feel I must do something, or I'll go stone mad. I`m sorry you were on the receiving end today. That was wrong of me. You do seem to have a bit of understanding and humanity in you after all, could I impose on you, even after this, and ask you to help me with my anger?"

"Not sure that I`d be the best person to do that after this escapade here. You need to find an aggressive outlet, to ensure that something like this never happens again to any other poor sod. And I will have a think about who may be able to help you. I`ll be discreet about it, though."

With that, they set off back towards the bothy in pensive silence.

22.

An article in the national press about a new book on common land historically and today attracted quite a bit of interest in the correspondence pages the next day, and beyond. One of the correspondents was from the community relating to the Darach Muir area, and she seemed to have somehow picked up on the local connection. Though not referring to the Darach Stane, she voiced a bit of invective about the apparent land grab all those years ago.

Then all went quiet again for a day or three.

However, Ronald had heard on his journalistic grapevine that some members of an environmental organisation in the area, had spotted the Darach Stane, and were planning a group visit to it the following Sunday. What, he wondered, might be the outcome of that?

Word must somehow have got to the Factor of the Glenmaddy Estate, who had, in turn, contacted the relevant officer in Scottish Land & Estates, who as it happened was in the same climbing fraternity as Malcolm. Ear to the ground, he had of course heard of these mumblings.

Then two weeks later, a convoy of very puzzled and suspicious members of Scottish Gamekeepers rumbled up in their respective estate vehicles, to survey the scene.

Hot on the heels of that, Historic Environment Scotland rolled up with a rapidly created sign to the effect that the site of the Darach Stane was a Scheduled Ancient Monument, and that it would be an offence to excavate or deface it in any way. This was firmly concreted into the ground on the road ward perimeter of the scheduled site. Angus confessed that he had discreetly tipped them the wink.

Attached to the minutes of the previous meeting of the local association of the National Trust for Scotland being circulated to all members, was a notice of a specially organised forthcoming meeting, entitled The Symbolism of the Darach Stane in Ancient Times and Today. Guest speaker to be announced.

A message to all from Malcolm read simply, "The cat is out of the bag."

This set the airwaves abuzz, as he had imagined it would. It was therefore agreed to have a meeting over coffee in Lizzie and Andy`s flat, the following Sunday afternoon. Time to take stock of the developing situation.

"We`ll need some flapjack and Dundee cake to mark the occasion, and fuel our grey cells," Archie advised. I`ll organise that."

As each of these various local organisations met, or the interests of one kind or another did their business, mostly independently of each other, a flurry of activity ensued. They were all coming at it from different angles, pursuing their motivation. Some were very sympathetic, whilst others were hostile.

"It's amazing how one stone can generate such widely differing responses," Andy commented to Lizzie one morning.

"True, but we should not be surprised, because we've got everything from heavily vested interests, right through to those that feel that the Darach Stane confirms their strongest passions. I`m working on a piece right now that attempts to express the diversity, the passion, the drama of the place, and at the heart of what I would now call the beloved Darach Stane. Not sure when it will be finished. And anyway, no sooner will it be complete, than it may have been superseded by further events."

The Factor of Glenmaddy had of course been in contact with the owner of the estate, who had understandably expressed some alarm at what had happened, and more especially what the implications might be. Lawyers were consulted, and the advice was that some action would need to be taken, and soon. But what that action might be, was exercising the legal minds and that of their client too. They knew that they couldn't pin this on anyone in particular because there was no evidence to prove who had done the deed of erecting the Darach Stane, which was now protected under the Ancient Monuments Acts. "Dammit, they've gone and put an emergency order on over half a hectare at the top of the hill," the Factor had fumed.

All sorts of case law was consulted, to see if there was any useful precedent that could be utilised in any way. It wasn't looking good though. New access laws would make it almost impossible to prevent public access, which had been growing considerably. That in turn it was reported, was creating parking problems. The local authority was adamant that there was no money for any road improvements or restrictions and voiced great concern about who would enforce any restrictions anyway. It was all going around in circles.

The issue of common land had been raised, and while the legal minds thought they had that one sewn up reasonably well, there was a nagging doubt. They had independently consulted the same sources as Alexander Ferguson all those years ago, and came to the same conclusions, even if they didn't know that they were replicating his efforts. That conclusion was that there was probably a hole in the absolute title to the land, probably either due to some sloppy work by the York Buildings Company, or some shrewd sleight of hand by those acting for the first Brighams. Though it could equally have been those acting for the Fergusons before they sold up. "My God it's a mess," the Factor fumed yet again.

"I'd always believed that title to land would be watertight. It would seem that I was wrong about that," the owner sighed. "Whatever we do, it must succeed. This is costing me money."

A week later, the lawyers came back with a proposal, well two proposals. At this point, the owner groaned even more loudly.

"The first option would be to make it as difficult as possible to gain access to Darach Muir. To do this we`d suggest the erection of two miles of fence on either side of the road, and as close to the road as is possible bearing in mind the relevant Public Highways regulations. In addition, we would advocate the excavation of a one-metre-deep ditch very close to the fence and immediately on the Muir-ward side of it. This would certainly be largely effective against most potential visitors. There is one possible obstacle however and that is that the track you have referred to, as could be deemed a longstanding public footpath, and therefore, this would be deemed in breach of the public access legislation. So that's a bit of a problem.

The second is that we take out a kind of blanket interdict against any local residents who may seek to claim common land rights on the Muir and exercise them in any way. How effective this could be is at this stage hard to say, and it does run the risk of implying that there may be common land there in the first place. Though Scottish Land and Estates would take a keen interest in supporting this, I imagine, for fear of precedent being established somehow. We could define local residents as either all Council Taxpayers in that community and, or those on the voters' roll. Both are well defined."

"Christ man, either option is heavy-handed, costly, or risks provoking public ire," the owner retorted. "Or indeed, all of the above. We`ve always sought to maintain a low-profile positive interaction with the local community; poachers notwithstanding, of course."

"Yes, I`m aware of all this, but with respect, you asked for our advice, and I would suggest that these are the only two options that are open to you, Sir."

"If we take the interdict course, how public would that be? Or how would it be served?"

"A small notice in the two major national newspapers would I think suffice. I can let you know the wording of it before we post it if you like. A Sherriff Court order would suffice, rather than going to the Court of Session."

"Very well, can you proceed with that please?"

This decision presented the Factor with a ghastly dilemma. He was himself part of that local community. Perhaps he should have declared an interest, at the meeting? Oh God, he thought, it's perfectly comfortable to be dealing with the day-to-day business of rents, fences, grants, and fly-tipping, but to be in any way party to serving an indiscriminate notice like this on his neighbours, and indeed, on himself too, was more than he could bear. On the few occasions when he had been so stressed or vexed in that past, he always confided in his wife. She was after all an active member of several community interests.

23.

Eager to get the Spurryhillock business plan finished, Andy and Lizzie had cosseted themselves away in their top-floor flat, with a metaphorical Do Not Disturb sign hovering above.

"This has been dragging on a wee bit too long Andy love, so we must get it into print. Then we can see how best to drive forward all that the estate so desperately needs. We`ll have a limited number printed in hard copy, and as many as could ever be needed in digital format."

So, with a concerted effort over the best part of two days, they did minor but prudent refinements, redrafts, design tweaking, and much discussion, and by the end of that intensive exercise, they had the document they wanted. The following day, Lizzie took it to her favourite printer and obtained twenty copies. These she carried home to Andy with a real sense of pride and achievement.

They then sat down in a slightly more relaxed mode, with a coffee, and made an action list for the ensuing three months. That done, they took a copy round to Archie and delivered another to Malcolm.

Archie retreated into his study to pore over it critically. Emerging after about half an hour, in which they had been chatting with Marissa, and showing her a copy too, he was clutching his well-read copy and smiling.

"You guys have done an amazing job on this, highly professional, with plenty of vision, well-argued, and attractive to read. Yes, a good read, but with a real punch in it. I`m delighted to see sound plans for the place, as I know I neglected Spurryhillock. True, a lovely place for us to go on holiday to, but the gradual decline over the years was depressing. That neglect was brought home to me when you had the roof of the stable collapse on you. Now that was a wake-up call. Mind you, just look what`s come out of it about both my uncle Alex and the Darach Stane. Anyways, thank you for doing this plan, I now feel that you guys will do something wonderful with Spurryhillock. Not just for us, but for a much wider public benefit. I do like that."

"So do I folks. I want it to be able to start generating an income, which has been so lacking over the years. Archie did his best, I know that. And I was so worried when you nearly got killed by that roof, Andy. That brought it home to me how perilous the place is, both physically and financially. If I can please add a personal request, I'll be even happier," Marissa asked.

"What's that, Mum?

"I love to be a kind of maître-d when we have a houseful of people. That's a real joy to me, so I hope that can continue?"

"Of course, you will Mum, and we love it when you are at the helm there. It helps bring the place alive, and we all do appreciate it."

"That`s lovely to hear and thank you." Now if there was just the patter of tiny feet too, Marissa thought to herself.

"As you know I love to tend the wee bit of garden around the house too, so I`d want to continue to do that. It's rather special for me. As you know my dear mother`s ashes are scattered in there, at her request."

"That garden is your garden mummy, and so it shall remain, we promise you that. And we love to see it too."

"One final thing is my special bench up at the wee loch is also very precious to me. I go there for the calm and beauty of the place, and yes, to think too. So, we must keep the bench for me please."

"Well, we are not going to put a plaque on it, just yet, but it is indeed your bench, and so it shall remain, Marissa," Archie added fondly.

"This will all be wonderful, and you know that if there is anything that you think I could do to help this plan along, I'll gladly do so. All you must do is ask. Though I know that it's very much your show dears."

"Thanks, Mum, you never know, you may get a request yet. And thank you for your support, we are glad of it.

"The one thing I can probably usefully do," said Archie, "is to help with any formal paperwork, any legal stuff of course, and record keeping. Though I'm sure you`ll develop your own financial systems for this business. But you`ve got me behind you all the way, of that you can be sure."

"Thanks, Dad, we`ll certainly call on your services. Although we all have that big unknown of the Darach Stane lurking around, which can or could be time-consuming, we`ll want to make some real headway on the plan over the next three months. So well into the winter, I`d say. Andy and I have drawn up a priority action plan for this. Some of this is about refining what we can or can't do. And what we will need to do to move some of the big things forward, like planning permission, or dealing with any planning constraints. There`s some documentation that we need to find, like the stuff about the return of the former military facilities to the estate. And we need to get our heads around new agricultural policies, land use, and subsidies."

"We`ll need to start to line up an architect. And since we need an injection of capital, we need to know how we are going to do that, with potential housing development." Andy added in a serious tone.

"I thought you`d trained as a social worker Andy, not a developer," Marissa said with a smile.

"Steep learning curve for both of us Mum."

24.

Word seemed to have got out that the estate was planning to serve an unprecedented interdict of some kind on all the residents in the community. This was the one big new topic of conversation in bar and byre, and by every local organisation.

All was not of course quite so positive everywhere, or in every quarter of the village of Lochhead. A group of men, standing around chatting outside the local general hardware shop, seemed to have a different perspective on things.

" I just can't see what all the fuss is about," said one, as he moved his cap further back on his head. "For gods sakes, it's just a stone, an old lump of a stone from what I hear. Why go to all the bother of digging it up from where it's been for hundreds of years, and doing nobody any harm there? Daft waste of energy, I`d say."

"Man alive, Wattie, how right you are," another replied. "As if that wasn't daft enough, they then go and dig a hole out there on the Muir, to re-erect it, or something. They`ll be worshipping it next if I'm not mistaken. Mark my words, boys."

"Aye, Jock, you've got it there all right. A crazy caper by moonlight, from what I've heard. We`ll have a bunch of chanting hippies in our village next. That's all we need."

"The Muir was fine the way it was; a hare for the pot when the keeper is well out of sight, and we`d all be happy. Now they've stuck this carved thing in the middle of it. It`s no` right, no right at all, boys."

There was however a regular stream of people visiting the Darach Stane, and it rapidly gained a kind of iconic status. Unsurprisingly, it also generated a flurry of interest and curiosity about the common land matter. One astute resident who liked to read more than just the news in his copy of The Herald of a morning had spotted a notice by some legal firm representing Glenmaddy Estate of the intention to obtain an interdict.

The History and Amenity Society appointed a subcommittee to investigate thoroughly both the common land and Darach Stane traditions and background. With two avid and well-versed historians, and a retired lawyer at the helm of this group, they got into both topics with a vengeance.

Angus naturally decided to keep well clear of the issues and hoped that the use of that need-to-know ATV would not have come to anyone's attention.

An informal collection of people who were largely into eco-spiritual enrichment visited the Darach Stane with rapt enthusiasm. For here in their backyard, as it were, was an ancient emblem that encapsulated much of the theme they had been exploring together of late. That it stretched away back into some undefined period in history thrilled them. It seemed to be confirming that the oak was at the very heart of the beliefs of that culture; they understood in some profound way, along with the sun and water, what sustained their living landscape in all its fullness. They also knew it could be an even greater fullness if only a lack of true political will and vested interests could be sorted out.

In addition to the pending interdict by the estate, several other interests were acting in response.

When the health and safety department of the hydro company heard of what had happened, they sent a man and a digger to excavate a huge trench across the access to the old road and extend some distance on either side of it. They also sent some other men with bollards and concrete to prevent any further incursion. Though in due course, this action was called into question, as it was discovered that there didn't seem to be any official legal order formally closing the old road as a public highway. Most remiss.

To add to that, the Highways Department of the local authority was at a bit of a loss to know what to do about the obvious increase in parking on that narrow unclassified road. There was no budget to do anything new, so it was agreed to keep an eye on the situation.

One individual who regarded himself as an authority on what he called the true highland history since the union of the crowns, and especially the times of the clearances onwards, picked up the issue of common land with a passion. Although some people locally, did think he went on about things overmuch, they also respected his almost encyclopaedic knowledge. His opinion was not to be taken lightly, they acknowledged. His keen interest in what he suspected was going on here, with the plans for an interdict, sent him into a frenzy, and he shared all he got. Or believed he was getting.

Even the Women's Institute took an interest in the possible implications of it all because they often had their annual summer picnic up on the Muir. Would that be prevented in future, they fretted.

Back in Edinburgh some of this was filtering through, as Angus was proving to be very useful if discreet local ear up north. Following consultation with the gang, it was decided that Ronald could play devil's advocate, by using his weekly column in a national paper Saturday supplement, to add weight to the concerns of the local people and rattle a few cages with the landed estates` fraternity. He`d built up a good following for this column; his readers seemed to warm to his people`s approach, and a nice political edge to it that he would weave in, when appropriate.

Ronald also got busy to be sure he`d meet the submission deadline for his copy. What he came up with was a comment about a fine community up north now rallying around the recent mysterious reappearance, on their former common land, of a long lost and very symbolical ancient stone. That was the gist of what he then expanded on, in a similar thought-provoking vein. On the day of publication, the local shop in Lochhead quickly ran out of copies of the newspaper, so some neighbours resorted to photocopying the article, whilst others found it online.

The estate factor groaned into his porridge.

Ronald then went off and climbed a mountain or two with his phone switched off.

Angus decided he was due himself a holiday, so flew off to Dublin to enjoy some Irish hospitality.

Lizzie and Andy were busy installing a new and much needed, computer system in their office room in their top floor flat, using the very last of the wee bit of money that he`d inherited. They didn't see the paper until much later in the day, following a call from Marissa asking if they`d seen what Ronald had written.

Far more people turned up in the village pub that evening than was normal. It was buzzing.

The following day, Sunday, the church was quieter than usual. Whilst up on the Muir many of the villagers were making the most of the especially mild autumn weather and had walked all the way to the Darach Stane, to

175

see it for themselves. It was photographed, again and again, touched almost in reverence, admired, and eagerly discussed. Many had selfies taken as they stood beside it, or even embraced it. That it had been retrieved from the bottom of the reservoir, had somehow become known, and added to the sense of amazement all around. For although the water level was still very low, the remains of the kirk and its surrounding burial ground were submerged once more. Some of the visitors to the Muir and its Stane had even brought a picnic; they sat contentedly nearby, apparently more at one with their precious landscapes than ever before.

"Is the Darach Stane casting some kind of spell over us?" A member of the eco-spiritual group asked his companions.

"It almost seems like it," came the reply. "I`ve never seen anything like it. Been up here many`s a time, but there is something special about this, and that wonderful emblem of a Stane, must be what's doing it. We need more of this, of course, life will be the richer for it, I`m certain. But let's cherish this place, Stane, Muir, and all that it brings to us from both tradition and nature herself."

"Whoever did this deserves a medal, but isn't it strange that nobody seems to know who it was? You`d think this would have got out by now, in this close community. Secrets are hard to keep. I`d like to think that they could be here right now, to share in the impromptu occasion."

In addition to the pending interdict by the estate, several other interests were acting in response.

One of the zealous church elders on the local Presbytery, who was both a keen amateur historian and a bit out of touch with contemporary thinking, felt it his duty to make sure everything was correct and as it should be. He discovered what he thought was good evidence that the old kirk, now beneath the waters of the reservoir, had never been de-consecrated.

On reporting this, however, he was tactfully advised, by the convenor, "it's a bit late now."

"Yes, but we really can't have amateur people digging around in consecrated sites. That would be most irregular, in any event."

"I don't think we can do anything; the deed has been done. From what I gather, the reservoir is rapidly filling up again, so the site of that old kirk is now well underwater. Who knows when it will appear again? And I don't want to stir anything up here, because as you surely know, Rev. Ebenezer Snoddy who apparently put the stone in the kirk, was what we would now regard as a dangerous fanatic. It would serve the church today much ill, were we to remind people in any way, of the deeds of that man."

"Hm, this is a sad compromise on all that is surely correct and proper."

The factor groaned even more, into his whisky this time, when he heard that a couple of local botanists had formally approached Nature Scotland with a request that Darach Muir and its surrounding area should be surveyed for designation as a Site of Scientific Interest. In their petition, they argued that the flora and fauna on the Muir were unusual for both its altitude and distance from the sea. In order to be sure of everything, they strongly recommended, on good authority that the site of summer sheilings should also be surveyed and protected in some way too.

At an area meeting of the Gamekeeper`s Association, a motion was passed stating, "This Branch condemns the recent activity on Darach Muir which is hurting the game thereon and potentially upsetting member`s livelihoods thereby, in breach of the access code and laws." Their chairman commented after the meeting that he felt uncomfortable with this motion, which would of course be passed on to the national council.

"It's clumsy language and an even clumsier way of doing things, but it was the will of the majority."

25.

During lunch on Sunday, Archie remarked that he was flabbergasted with the amount and diversity of reaction there had been to what had at the time seemed to be a harmless bit of nocturnal fun and otherwise perfectly legal follow-up. "Just about everyone has had to put their oar in here, some of it not very nice at all. But thankfully Ronald`s well-written column piece did, from what we hear, provide many local people with something that they have taken to very happily. There are certainly two sides to the story unfolding. I hear from my sources that the interdict submission will be heard in the Sheriff Court up there, towards the end of this week."

"How will that play out Dad?" asked Lizzie. "What's the format for such a thing?"

"Yes, will there be witnesses called?" Andy added curiously.

"It's hard to say really. But given the apparent diversity of local interests now voicing an opinion, the Sheriff may indeed have decided to hold the hearing in open court and invite representation. I`ll see what I can find out. If it is in open court, I`d quite like to be there as a somewhat anonymous member of the public, of course."

"Surely that's a long way to go for such a thing Archie dear," Marissa asked with a note of concern.

"It's kind of you to think this, but don't worry, it`ll be a nice drive, and you could come too, and visit your friends who live nearby, while I`m in court, dear."

"Yes, I suppose I could, that would be nice, I`ll get in touch with them to see if that's all right."

"We`d come too but will be up at Spurryhillock for some meetings with the planning folk," said Andy.

179

"Hey, it's all right for you lot, I`ll be at work, and I have the girls to consider," Hermione quipped. "What are your plans Malcolm, my love?"

"As you know I've just finished the elm dining furniture commission, so it needs suitable transport to deliver it. I`ll miss it because I just loved working with that wood. So, my immediate priority now is to source the oak for the doors I'm to be creating. There are a couple of specialist timber merchants I need to visit, for that."

"While we are all here folk, I just thought I`d like to tell you that I`m now expecting, I mean, Andy and I are now expecting," Lizzie blurted out excitedly. "Early days yet, but I've had a test and it's confirmed. We are so happy."

"Oh, Lizzie my dear, this is wonderful news. How are you feeling? How many weeks? Do you have a due date yet? Will you take it a bit easy on the work please?" The questions came thinks and fast from Marissa.

"Slow down Mum. All in due course I`m sure. And yes, I feel fine."

"How does fatherhood grab you, Andy?" asked Hermione, with a twinkle in her eye.

"I`m looking forward to it enormously. Lizzie and I are and will be so happy. And I`m going to be a very hands-on dad; of that, you can be sure. Though let's be patient, we have a way to go in order to get there first. Lizzie`s doing great. And I'm so proud of her."

"You can be sure that if there`s any help you want from me, then just ask. I`ll be glad to help," Marissa added.

"Does this mean we'll have a little cousin?" Monique asked excitedly. "That will be so wonderful, won't it Charlotte"

"It sure will, and I`ll help too. But not so sure about nappies, if I'm honest."

"Aw, thank you, girls. We`ll be sure to get you involved. First thing each day when you get home from school."

"But we have our homework to do then," Monique protested.

"Well babies sometimes wake early, so how are at getting up in the morning girls?"

"They are both hopeless at that," Hermione chipped in. "But you know I`ll be happy to share all of my experience in this Lizzie. And I like your hands-on approach, Andy. That's as it should be. But I know sometimes it's a bit evasive."

"You're being very quiet Dad, "Lizzie joked. "I hope you are not scared of another grandchild."

"Not a bit of it, I`m as thrilled as the rest of you, and many congratulations Lizzie dear, and Andy. Your mother will I think, confirm what's already been said though, this is the start of a journey, and we all want to see you safe all the way. So, any help that's needed, do just ask, please."

Lunch continued in a light-hearted spirit, with lots of excited chatter and laughter. "Let's go through for coffee, and you girls can, of course, leave the table and do whatever you like. You know where everything is."

The Spurryhillock Development Plan was beginning to be circulated in strategic destinations, and several meetings were set up to begin to move it forward on the initial three-month action plan. This was even more pressing because of Lizzie`s pregnancy. They headed north for a scheduled week of intensive meetings, and to set up some key partnerships.

Although it was hard work, Andy commented, "It's nice to be back here just the two of us, and the autumn colours are very special. It's sad in a way, that those who planted this place up a hundred or more years ago like a mini arboretum, never lived to see the benefit of its maturity. Though its maturity that's also part of the problem because it spills over into neglect now, which we must tackle."

"How true. I've been having a wee thought while we are here. And it's about Alex. We`ve so much to thank him for, poor man. He would have inherited this place, had he lived. Although he`s commemorated in several rolls of honour and other war memorials I'm sure, but the fact that he`s at the bottom of the Atlantic Ocean is very sad. Why don't we create something here, in his honour? Don't know what yet, or where it could be, but shall we think about it, darling?"

"Brilliant idea, I love it, Lizzie. Well done you. Yes, he was completely forgotten about for a hundred years, and but for a rather chance happening that nearly gave me a sore head, he`d have been forgotten altogether."

"Don't remind me of your close shave with that rotten roof. That nearly changed our entire future."

"Back to your idea of a memorial of some kind, can I suggest that it should be a living thing, like trees, or a garden, or pond even?"

"Yeah, that's the kind of thing I had in mind. No, you are right it must be something living,"

Lizzie picked up a copy of the Development Plan and flicked through it to get to the map of the estate. Pondering that for a minute or two, whilst Andy poured more coffee, she suddenly exclaimed, "Here`s an idea". As she put the Plan on the table for Andy to see, she pointed a moving finger at the main path that they wanted, running all the way through the estate woodland. "That path is like an artery for access to almost everything. It starts way down where we`ll have the new housing on the site of the military place. Then it winds up by the river, to the castle, stables, close to here, the pond, farm steading and right up to the top of the hill. Wow, I'm on a roll here Andy. Alex`s greatest legacy is of course the Darach Stane reinstatement, and Darach Muir, whatever becomes of that, but we don't want any plaques or cairns there because it's about nature and local people. We are incidental up there. But of course, the word Darach means oak, and the carving on the Stane is acorns, oh, and the other fragment we found, of the oak leaf. So, let's give the path here a name that relates in some way to Alex, and plant twenty-two oaks along the side or whatever number equates to his age when he died." Lizzie stopped to catch her breath.

"Wow, your creative mind is in top gear this morning, love. How about simply the Alex Way as the name for the path? Something simple like that. And being practical about it, it's not going to cost much extra, because the initial expense is in the financial plan that we have anyway. This is inspirational, Lizzie."

"Thanks. We may get a grant for the oak trees, and we could take it a wee bit further, by involving local children in planting them. A nice community link. Perhaps a small cairn and simple plaque at the pond, by way of explanation. Let's give Alex the credit he now deserves. He`s our hero."

26.

Later that day, they had a meeting with Orla the planning officer, initially down at the unsightly mess that was the old military base, and then up at the house, to discuss the overall plans over a coffee and flapjack. She was young and suitably dressed for such a site meeting.

"Ah good morning, I`m Orla Wheelwright, your planning officer for this project." She introduced herself. "Though we`ve met online already. So it's nice to meet for real, here."

Lizzie and Andy introduced themselves.

"Pleased to meet you Orla and thank you for coming out to meet us on-site. Greatly appreciated. I thought we`d start here, and then go back to the house to look at the wider plans," said Lizzie.

"Yes, that's fine. I`m conscious that a lot of the plan which we`ll discuss in more detail shortly, hinges on the use of this site."

"It does indeed," Andy replied. "As you can see the entire site is an eyesore, visible from the public road. Just a ramshackle of brick buildings and flat concrete roofs. It may have been a kind of car breakers yard at some time in its more recent past. But in our view, there`s nothing useful that could be done with what remains of the buildings. As far as we know it was constructed in about nineteen forty, so it's been part of this landscape, if I can call it that, for around eighty years. There are about two hectares in it, but that's a bit difficult to see with all that scrub over there. I did manage to battle through and find the remains of a fence around the whole site. So, as you know, the plan is to clear the entire site and use it for house building. Whether we`d be the developer, or someone else, has yet to be decided. Guess it could be individual self-build sites or something like that."

184

Orla then asked all sorts of questions, for clarification. She was non-committal to all the answers that Lizzie and Andy gave, but to their delight, she didn't give them a hard time and seemed genuinely interested in this part of the plan.

When she indicated that she was happy to conclude this part of the meeting, Andy said, "Now while we are here, can I draw your attention to those two small rough fields we can see, just a wee bit up the road? Those are one of the sites we`d like to put camping pods of some kind. We could access the power and water services that are already somewhere on this old military site and add the sewage and water treatment to the facility that would have to be created for the housing here. Since the fields are south-facing, we`d want to put in solar panels of some kind up there to provide power as well."

"Yes, thanks for showing me where those fields are. Not much use for modern agriculture. The synergy with this site makes good sense, but enough distance between, to facilitate rather different uses."

"Shall we go up to the house, now?" Asked Lizzie. "We`ll have some coffee and flapjack while we discuss the bigger picture up there. It's easy to find, up the road about half a mile, then right into the drive that's got the Spurryhillock sign."

At that, Orla stepped back a little, when suddenly, the ground seemed to give way beneath her. She sank almost up to her knees, into what seemed like an old trench covered by rotting timber, now covered in grass. She shrieked with pain or alarm; they knew not which. Both Lizzie and Andy rushed forward.

"Oh my God, are you OK Orla?" Lizzie exclaimed in a panicked tone. "Are you hurt?"

The look on Orla`s face was one of shock, indeed she`d turned ashen white with fear.

"Eh, I`m not sure. Can we get me out of this hole first?" She gasped, not sure if she`d sink further, or what might happen. Her notes clipboard had shot out of her hands and landed a couple of yards away among some brambles.

Lizzie took one elbow and Andy the other, as they steadied her, took her weight, and enabled her to take a big step out of the hole, onto what they all hoped would be terra firma. She moved slowly and very cautiously, as they eased Orla over to sit down on a convenient slab of concrete close by.

"Please sit here, catch your breath Orla," Andy said in words that he hoped would at least start to give her some reassurance. "Then let's see if you are indeed injured in any way. I`m truly sorry that you've had this accident."

Lizzie took over and kneeled beside Orla, who was clearly upset at what had happened. "Take some deep breaths first please Orla. Focus on that for a minute or two, then we`ll see the extent of your injuries."

Orla breathed deeply for a few minutes as instructed, and some colour came back into her face. She reached forward to investigate her ankles and shins first. The cords she was wearing were certainly very scuffed, but this would have given her some protection. Andy retrieved her clipboard.

"Well, I wasn't expecting that," Orla exclaimed at last. "We are trained to do a risk assessment before we enter a site, and I must have cut that corner."

"OK, but are you injured in any way?" Lizzie asked with some urgency.

 "Well, no broken bones, I`d say. Reckon my left shin has been grazed a bit, and my right ankle a bit strained. But I`m sure it could have been a whole lot worse. Perhaps I could investigate more when we get up to your house if that's OK? It's my dignity that's been the main casualty," Orla replied with a bit more confidence returning.

"Of course, you can do whatever may be necessary up at the house," Andy ventured. "Will you be OK to drive there though?"

"I think so. Could one of you come with me in my car, please? I know it's against the rules for us to take passengers in these cars, but under the circumstances, I'd value some company. It's not too far, is it?"

"I'll gladly travel with you Orla," Lizzie replied quickly.

"Here's your clipboard and the papers. I hope it's intact?" As Andy handed her what he'd rescued from the bramble patch.

"Oh, thank you. There may have been a pen, but that's unimportant."

"Do you feel ready to go?" Lizzie asked in a very caring tone.

"Yes, and I've got some water in the car, so that will perhaps refresh me. I'll not forget this place in a hurry. Oh, and I'll have to write up a wee note in what we call our Near Misses Log."

Up at the house, Lizzie took Orla into the sitting room, while Andy busied himself in the kitchen.

"Do sit here, Orla, take your time to see if there's any damage, and if need be, just gather your thoughts."

"OK, this is very kind of you Lizzie. I feel I'm somewhere between being aware of a few sore bits and feeling a bit of an eejit for not taking greater care."

"No worries, you were in shock. Let's leave the eejit bit aside and focus on the sore bits first."

That said, Orla rolled up her trouser legs, slowly and carefully, and took her shoes off. Her shins were both badly grazed, but only her left one showed any blood. "This seems to be the extent of my injuries, I`m pleased to say. Do you have any antiseptic and sticking plasters, Lizzie please?"

"Sure, give me a couple of minutes, and I`ll rustle up what you need." Lizzie left Orla as she went off to collect what was needed and came back through with a basin of warm water, cotton wool and a selection of sticking plasters. "Now, I've put a little mild disinfectant into the water here. I`ll let you tend to the damage yourself if that's OK?"

"Many thanks, yes. I`ll sort myself out."

"I`ll leave you to do that, Orla, and when you are ready to come through to the kitchen for some coffee and flapjack."

Orla was glad of the peace, as she carried out a more thorough inspection, but concluded that the only damage was what was visible. So, she cleaned it all with the cotton wool and water, dried it off, and stuck a couple of plasters on her shins, which were most necessary. Relaxing for a minute, she looked around the room and admired its homely comfort. Logs set in the hearth, ready to be lit later, she surmised. `I could cope with living here`, she thought, as she pondered the many sitting rooms, she`d visited, and this was surely the homeliest that she'd seen in a while.

She also imagined that by tomorrow her shins and lower legs would have some magnificent bruises. What would her colleagues make of that? Orla wondered.

Tearing herself away from the comfort of it, Orla made her way through to a room where she could hear voices coming from. "Thank you for taking such good care of me guys, I appreciate it. Aha, tea and flapjack, now that takes me back. This will most certainly revive me in body and spirit. Let's get back to business."

"Are you sure you feel up to it?" asked Andy, with a note of real concern.

"Yes, us Wheelwrights are made of tough stuff, though I think it's the Irish genes in me on my mother`s side, that are the toughest."

Once they were settled at the big kitchen table, and the tea had been poured, they started going over the whole of the plan, the history of the estate, concepts in the plan design, economic and public benefits, timescales, land use, and so much more. Orla seemed to take a keen interest in it, judging by both her manner and the quality of her constructive questioning. As expected, she was highly professional, in that she was still entirely non-committal.

"You know that I can't give any opinion at this stage. Your plans must go through the full planning application process. What you are proposing is significant, because it's a major change here, and involves a wide range of factors. But I`ll be your main point of contact in the Planning Department meantime, so it's my role to steer you through what may seem like a labyrinth. You`ll have seen on all the blurb about planning priorities, that positive change and development are to be encouraged wherever possible, so hopefully, you`ll find it's not a hostile environment you are in."

"Many thanks for this," Lizzie replied, we appreciate all that you are saying. "We are cautiously encouraged, wouldn't you say, Andy?"

"We are indeed. You've helped set the scene for us in a constructive manner, and we appreciate the position you must take. Be sure that we`ll be taking you up on your role, whenever appropriate. Oh, and I do hope that the image of Spurryhillock is not blighted because of your awful experience here today?"

189

"No, please don't worry about that. I have a job to do. Mind you, off the record, I`m clear about one thing folks."

What's that?" Lizzie asked somewhat nervously.

"The sooner you can get the demolition and excavation crew busy on that old military base, the better. It's almost into the realms of being a public danger."

"Be assured Orla, it's number one on the action plans lists. It's got to go." Lizzie said unhesitatingly.

"That's great, I do look forward to working with you, I do. Tell me a little more about what's behind your plan for the arterial path, I think you called it Alex`s Way. I`m intrigued."

Lizzie explained as succinctly as she could all that had led to this idea. As the planning officer avidly followed the story.

"How fascinating, and indeed how fitting to create your living memorial to Alex. You're great grand uncle if I'm correct. You are a lucky man, Andy, as I'm sure you are now aware. That roof could have killed you. Now I love connections, I've got family who live further west, and they were telling me as recently as last weekend, about what they`ve heard of the Stane and the Muir saga. They are really in the next valley, but it's all well connected, as you can imagine. Although they are rattled by the antics of the estate, they tell me they are far more interested in the positive environmental side of it, and especially the significance of the Darach Stane. So, you see, I'm quite up to date on that, and to think that the genesis of it all was when you got banged on the head, right here on Spurryhillock is amazing."

"My goodness, what a coincidence, yes, connections are fascinating indeed," Lizzie responded. "Could I ask you, however, to be very discreet about what we have just told you? For us, and I speak for the wider family

190

too, the important thing is what the local community make of it. It's all in their patch, not ours."

"Yes, of course, I`ll be discreet about this, as you ask. And I do like your approach to it. You are right. Oh, and I should add, that the full planning process usually takes at least six months, so please be prepared for that. Sometimes it depends on how many objections there are. So, it will be into next year before it could be finalised. But hey, the spring is a good time to be starting on something as big as this."

"Yeah, thanks. Now, remember, you've had a bit of a shake this morning so please just take your time travelling back to the office, or wherever you are heading Orla, "Lizzie said warmly, as they shook hands for her departure.

Planning Officer Orla`s car disappeared off down the track, while Lizzie and Andy smiled at each other and embraced.

"Job well done, I think," Andy whispered in Lizzie`s ear.

27.

Hermione crossed the lawn from her house to where Archie was sitting in the sun on the terrace in front of his own. "Oh, hello love, nice to see you, everything OK," asked Archie.

"Well, yes, but there's something I want your help with, and it's easier to talk about it with just the two of us, to start with anyway."

"Of course, dear, do go on, I hope it's not a major problem."

"It is and it isn't, but it's certainly unfinished business. As you know, I still have Jamie`s ashes, because technically at least, I was his next of kin. The undertakers were very sensitive and could see that his parents would be in no fit state to cope with anything. They were in pieces, at the crematorium. I'm glad that we decided to have no service of any kind then. But the ashes do need to be scattered somewhere, and I think down in the Borders would be best."

"Oh, this is such a difficult one for you, Hermione. But you are right, best to get it done, and involve poor David and Margaret somehow. Now that Lizzie has built a bridge there, with the girls as the focus, then yes, things can move forward a bit. What were you thinking you would want to do?"

"Don't know really, but perhaps once we`ve decided where to scatter his ashes, a simple event that both marks his life, such as it was and will enable David and Margaret to have closure when they are still able to do so. Family only probably. I`d want to discuss it with the girls, of course, he was their father, after all. Though I think in their hearts they'd rather written him off even before we left Aberlady and came here without him. This place has been a godsend, Dad. They do talk about him very occasionally, just to me I think, but Malcolm is a perfect father to them now."

"Would it be any easier for you, if you had a celebrant of some kind or even a minister to help with the event, Hermione?"

"Yes, it probably would. We are not very churchy though, are we? I think David and Margaret do have a church connection though. There`s always humanist celebrants, I`m told that they can be wonderful."

"I know of just the person for this. She`s the wife of a former client, a minister, but would do it by leaving out most of the God stuff and focusing on the positive we can find. But especially in giving David and Margaret some comfort."

"This is very thoughtful of you Dad, I know you don't need this anymore, but you are right, poor Margaret and David surely do. From what Lizzie said, their lives have shrunk so much. Mind you, she also said that the day they saw the girls was a real highlight for them. That friend of theirs, is Jean her name, she said they've never stopped talking about it?"

"Yes, that may have been a wee turning point. And the videos seem to be very well received."

"Would it be possible for you and I to meet this minister, to discuss it at least? Would that be OK, do you think, Dad?"

"Yes, of course, it would. One step at a time. I`ll see if I can invite her around here one day when the girls are at school, Malcolm will be busy, and Marissa will be at her voluntary work. Once we've had the discussion, then if it's all looking possible, we can tell the others. How could we broach the subject with David and Margaret though?"

"Lizzie will help us with that, I`m sure."

"Yes, I'm sure she`ll do that. The only thing that occurs to me now, is that this is not a good time of year for it dear. We are coming in towards the winter now. Let's suggest to Lizzie that she starts by chatting with that very kind Jean friend of theirs and see if this could be done in the spring."

"Good plan Dad. Thank you so much. This has been bugging me for a while."

"Aw Hermione dear, you should have shared it with me when it started to trouble you. But anyway, now we can hopefully move on."

Lizzie let everyone know that she`d now got in amongst the books and papers in those two crates which Malcolm had brought back from his Heriot Row excursions to the rubbish dump. "I've still a lot to go through in them, but the books, probably a couple of dozens of them, are a mixture of what we`d now call classic literature. There`s some Shakespeare of course, Scott, and a few legal-looking tomes. Then there`s a Bible, which strangely, does not have Alex`s name in it, so that set me thinking until I came to the last book I looked at, it was a personal diary handwritten by a Catriona Hyslop. And that's the name in the Bible. I`d to put it all to the side, for a week or two, as there were so many other things needing to be done.

When I came back to these two and started reading the diary, I realised to my amazement, that Catriona, had been Alex`s fiancé, before he died. So, I'm now beginning to piece together their relationship, and the many questions this poses. All very fascinating, I`m sure you'll all agree."

Andy had carefully taken the stone fragment with what appeared to be an oak leaf on it, that they found in the hole they were digging on the Muir, but now felt that they should do the right thing with it. "It is an archaeological find, after all," he said to Lizzie. "I left it with Angus, in his yard, so it's quite safe. But neither he nor I would wish to be the ones to hand it in, wherever that might be."

"Oh, I`d clean forgotten about that. I guess that Historic Scotland, or whoever put up that sign at the site, is where it should go. Could we arrange to do that anonymously? Even if that would seem to be a very strange thing to do."

"It's probably the only thing. Let's tell Angus this and see if we can come up with another nocturnal carry-on, to leave the stone at some Historic Scotland site, with a note attached to it."

28.

The drive north was uneventful for Archie and Marissa, just a long haul up the A9, with nothing to be seen but mist and rain. The mountains were there somewhere, but well hidden from sight. Archie had got word that the case would be heard in the Sheriff Court in Inverness, a bit further north than expected. But that suited Marissa, as she`d be staying with friends in Aviemore. They`d stopped for a coffee break in Pitlochry, where they found a delightful if unusual café attached to a bicycle repair and hire establishment. Both coffee and cake were excellent, they agreed.

Dropping Marissa off, with the friends, he`d said, "I`ll keep you posted, love. This case is a bit of an unknown quantity."

Staying in a comfortable hotel on the side of River Ness, Archie walked the short distance the next morning to the very new and slick-looking Sheriff Court building. The start of the case was delayed for half an hour for some unknown administrative reason, but eventually, he was allowed into the public gallery along with several other people. At one stage it looked like there wouldn't be enough seats, but finally, everyone got one and settled down. He hoped he looked suitably anonymous among this throng, in his open-necked tartan shirt, old tweed jacket with leather elbow pads, and flannels. The start of the proceedings was familiar enough to him, as the Sheriff opened this session.

Much of it, was, of course, formal courts speak, which the Clerk to the court commenced by reading out the plea from the Glenmaddy Estate, Registered Ownership in the Cayman Islands. In sonorous tones, he read that "Glenmaddy Estate pleads that there should be an interdict preventing the residents of Glenmaddy Village as defined geographically by the area of benefit of Lochhead and Glenmaddy Community Council, within the relevant Local Government Acts, and residents defined as those liable to pay Council Tax within that area, be prohibited from claiming any rights to the Darach Muir and its environs, within any long-defunct common land tradition."

There followed several hours of question and clarification, as to who would be representing what interests, and what their status as such would be, all this to set out the terms of those who would be speaking for or against the plea. The Sheriff then declared a break in the proceeding for lunch with the court re-commencing at two p.m. and the case in favour of the plea being heard first. The court rose.

By two p.m. the court was once more ready, with everyone in place, and all rose, as the Sherriff, entered, to take his place.

Archie did like how courts set out clearly, but in sometimes heavily formal ways, the seriousness of their task at hand. It was, he assumed, partly to make everyone think twice, about what they might say when asked to speak. Intimidating.

First up was Glenmaddy Estate legal representative from a heavy-duty legal firm in Edinburgh. They set out their case in quite a long-winded style, but Archie thought he noticed a very slight unease in its presentation. Were they he wondered, feeling that the case may be a weak one, and might be hard to prove? But the professionalism of the representative disguised that very well, to all but the most experienced in these matters. He was questioned thoroughly, and many points of clarification were sought, especially on the notion of common land. What was that based upon in these circumstances, and what might be the implications for the estate? Some of the answers given, which on the face of it sounded convincing, Archie could tell, lacked substance. The Sheriff gave nothing away as to what his view might be.

There followed an interrogation as to why the estate might wish to see this interdict imposed, in a grapeshot manner against everyone in the community. Was this not a bit heavy-handed, and outdated in its assumption about the place of the estate in community life? By the end of his grilling, the estate`s man looked grey and drained. He was nonetheless given one last chance to add substance to his case for the plea. He declined graciously.

The clerk of the court thanked him and said there would be one more submission, from Scottish Land and Estates, before the conclusion of business for the day.

The same process of scrutiny ensued following the presentation of its case in support of the plea. Their representation was a young woman, clearly articulate, and bristling with apparent confidence. Archie wondered to himself, which school she had attended, and which estate her family owned. She did well to start with, but when the questioning got into the area of apparent vested interests and fear of a precedent being created, she did lose her sparkle. The same procedure followed, with one last chance to reinforce her case. She too declined.

"The courts will rise and resume at 10.00 a.m. tomorrow."

Archie found a seafood restaurant overlooking the river to his liking and enjoyed a good, relaxed evening meal there. Back in his hotel room. He sent some brief updates and then sat back to reflect upon the case so far. He concluded that even at this stage it was looking a bit shaky. He also thought it was strange that some night-time goings-on by his wider family and friends should have stirred up something so big and formal. And as for Alex, he could surely never have imagined this either, but to a large extent, he had set the ball rolling. Would that war had not taken him down with his vessel all those years ago? And yes, Archie regretted not taking a bit more interest in his family history too.

With everyone in the Court and settled by 10.00, the Clerk instructed everyone to rise, which they dutifully did. The Sherriff entered, was seated, and set out his papers. The Clerk announced that the next presentations would be from the Gamekeepers Association representative. And the same process followed from the day before. Slow, meticulous, and thorough.

Strangely, Historic Scotland was next, but their case seemed to be a bit of a mix. Yes, concern for an ancient artefact and activity right beside a Scheduled site. But there also was an acknowledgement that something good had come from it.   Attempts to pin them to one side or the other were not entirely successful, despite thorough scrutiny.

The morning business concluded with, "Court will rise."

Nature Scotland led the evidence in the afternoon. Its case was that in the light of recent activity and interest in Darach Muir and the area immediately surrounding it, and on receiving a formal request from the Community Council, the process of re-survey is now underway. Even at this early stage, it was becoming evident that this site had been overlooked in the past. This matter was being put right, with a view to potential designation as a Site of Special Scientific Interest within the Nature Conservation (Scotland) Act 2004. A decision would seem likely sometime in the following year. Therefore, NatureScot advises this Court that the entire site should be protected as such, pending full designation.

In response, the Estate sought to argue during questioning that this appeared to be a knee-jerk reaction purely from local lobbying. The Sherriff, however, was having none of this and instructed the Estate to adhere to the factual evidence before the court.

The remainder of the afternoon session was devoted to a succession of what the Sherriff had deemed to be relevant local interest groups, including environmental, historical, eco-spiritual, and the Women's Institute too. Archie found all of these to be very interesting and cogent, but some of the presentations lacked polish in their delivery. The exception to this was the one that was seeking to argue the probable common land case. Archie sat up at this, as they had done their homework to build the case. He felt that they echoed briefly and succinctly the case that Alex had been working on before war called him away. He later told the gang, how heartened he was about this.

The Sherriff seemed to warm to their case judging by the constructively searching nature of his questions, and his rapid notetaking. Looking across the Court, Archie could see that the Estate representative was looking very uncomfortable. Whilst the people in the public gallery who seemed to be there to show a keen interest in the local issues seemed especially keen, judging by the level of quite an audible whispering. At one stage the Sherriff even had to bang his gavel and demand silence.

After this case, the Sherriff announced that there would be a brief resumption of the hearing at 10.00, the next morning.

"Court Rise", pronounced the Clerk.

As he was leaving, the estate representative came over and asked Archie quite pointedly, "What is your particular interest in this business?"

This rather took Archie by surprise, as he knew it was just possible that the representative knew full well who Archie was, from Edinburgh legal circles.

"Oh, I have friends in Lochhead village, and when they told me about this somewhat unusual case, my wife and I came up for a wee holiday. She`s not interested in all this legal stuff though. I`m just a fascinated bystander. Why do you ask?"

"I thought your face was a bit familiar, that's all." At this point, he walked off, clearly not a happy man.

With a little time to spare, Archie walked up the river to the Cathedral. He`d felt a sudden need to pay his respects to Alex, and somehow, this seemed like the right place to go. The warm pink stone of the building was inviting, and so he entered, leaving the noises and bustle of the city behind. In a quiet corner, he found a seat from which to reflect upon what little was known of Alex's short life and untimely death. Yes, Archie knew all too well that this was almost universally the tragedy of war deaths. The waste of a life, the pain and sorrow, and all the thoughts of what might have been too. But surprisingly, Alex had left a legacy he could never have imagined would be picked up out of almost oblivion a hundred years later, embraced so enthusiastically by his descendants and their friends, and be the cause of an action to be played out in the Sherriff Court. Archie was moved deeply by these thoughts, the poignancy of it all, and somehow the mysterious meaning of it upon him in this place. His eyes filled, as he was also transfixed by the rich mix of colours illuminating the stones of the great building, from the evening sunshine filtered warmly through the stained-glass windows.

At ten o`clock sharp, the next morning, Court was once again in session. The Clerk called the representative from the Glenmaddy Community Council, to present her evidence to the case.

"Our cause in this is quite simple really. We know that there is something almost unprecedented in an estate attempting to take out an injunction against all the local residents, it is almost unheard of. It is entirely unjustified, whatever the motive, or fear. It would seem that there is at best, a flaw in the estate`s title to and rights over the Darach Muir. They can neither prove it nor make a case that would stand further scrutiny here in this Court. We are honest people and know that equally, we cannot prove the substance of that which may be borne in tradition, legend, and local lore. But it is a foolish person who would dismiss these out of hand. To seek to saddle every local resident with an injunction which may be built on sand or prejudice is incompetent."

She sat down, visibly moved by what she had said, and that frisson was felt throughout the Court, with only a few exceptions.

"Thank you to all who have sought to present their case to this Court, and especially the Community Council, for keeping it so brief, clear, and to the point. The Court is adjourned, I will consider all that has been said, and give judgment this coming Monday at ten o`clock in the morning."

"Court rise," the Clerk announced, as the Sherriff left his dais, and disappeared through the door to his private chambers.

29.

It was unusual for Malcolm to ask Lizzie if he could pop over to see them, but of course, she happily agreed. "See you in about half an hour. Watch out for Andy, he's on his stair running for me. Though I`ll stop him as soon as he comes back and put the kettle on too."

"Ah, you are both here now, that's great," Malcolm gasped, having come up the three flights of stairs quite quickly, to prove that he could still do it, he`d said to himself.

"Come in Malcolm, let's go into the sitting room, this is a nice surprise," Lizzie said, as she ushered him through. "Coffee is ready. No flapjack this time I'm afraid, but there are a few biscuits. Do sit down and help yourself. So, what brings you over all of a sudden?"

"You`ll possibly remember I`d said a while back, that there was a chance of a cooperative to source genuine native timber?" He asked.

"Yes indeed," Andy replied, curiously. "How`s the plan progressing?"

"Quite well really, we now have eight, and that's probably going to the limit, of craftsmen like me, who are not at each other's throats competitively, as we all have our individual styles. We want to be able to go right back to the woodland, select our own trees, fell, and mill them, and then let the timber season naturally."

"My goodness, that's surely a plan with a significant timescale. From what I know, timber seasons quite slowly," Andy responded, but with a note of real interest in his voice.

"Yeah, takes a lot of forward planning. But good timber stored properly will always be an asset."

"Well, it's a wonderful plan, Malcolm. I imagine your fellow craftsmen, or craftsperson, are widely scattered throughout the country?" Lizzie enquired.

"They are but we've seen each other at various craft events. That's how it started. Oh, there`s some great timber from overseas of course, but we want a very Scottish brand if you like. And if we work together, on this, then that will make it a lot more possible. And do you know what we want to call it?"

"Eh, no," said Lizzie. "Do tell."

"Why, Darach, of course. Yes, just plain and simple Darach. And we might get you to design a logo for us Lizzie, based in some way on the Stane if you'd do that for us?"

"My God, I'd be honoured, Malcolm. Deeply honoured. What a fitting outcome from our nocturnal efforts."

"Thank you so much. And I have another request or inquiry to make of you folks."

"Do go on," Andy said with an encouraging tone.

"I've looked at your plans for Spurryhillock in detail and am so impressed. That too is a long-term project, methinks. Would it be possible at this stage to include something else in the plans?"

"Probably, as we haven't applied yet. I guess it depends on what you have in mind?" said Andy.

"We plan to go out as individuals in the cooperative, into the woods and forests and identify specific trees that we want. Then fell and extract them. We then need to take them to a yard that we`d want to establish, at low cost, of course. At the yard, each tree would need to be milled, and stacked for seasoning, all suitably labelled or tagged in some way. We`d probably go for what we might call milling days every so often, and work together on that. In essence, then, could that be included somewhere in the plan guys?"

"I suppose it depends a bit on what sort of size of a yard, as you call it, that you`d want. And how accessible?" Lizzie replied, with a mix of curiosity and excitement in her voice.

"That's hard to say at this stage, as it all needs a bit more planning, but probably about half an acre of reasonably hard standing, and accessible by truck. The actual sawmill part of it would probably not be permanent, as we`d hire in when it's needed. I suppose space for a shed or mini office would be good, too."

"Just as you were talking there," Andy quickly chipped in, "I`d a few thoughts. If we can make our plan happen, then one of the changes will be that the farm would no longer be a separate entity. We`d run the whole estate, as one. So, most of the ugly parts of the farm steading would be redundant. OK, we want to have some self-catering facilities for let there, but you can't turn a rusty corrugated iron hay barn into anything like that. And there's an old silage pit that would have to go too. It's all accessible separately from the public road, as it's always been. Oh, and I believe there's the former stackyard, but it's a bit covered in weeds and scrub now. Anyways, amongst that lot, there`s a good half-acre I`d say, probably more. Isn't it a bit out of the way though, remote?"

"Not really, for these purposes. We`d be bringing timber from all over the place, and let's just say, central belt land would be very costly, even to rent. You are just a few miles inland from the A90, which is a major arterial road, both north and south."

"The ideal will be that we continue some farming activity, within the new farming subsidy and land-use regimes. And we already have hundreds of acres of woodland that need sorting out over the next twenty or thirty years. So, the estate is a kind of mixed-use thing, in planning terms. Oh, I`m just thinking aloud here," Lizzie added. "I`m sure you'd agree Andy that we could do something here with Malcolm's request, or should I say Darach`s request? Man alive, it's great to be able to say that. It's like everything is coming together."

30.

With the usual formalities, of the start of a session in the Court, the Sherriff went straight into the matter of the bid for an interdict about Darach Muir.

"I am about to conclude this most unusual case, in which Glenmaddy Estate is seeking an Interdict against all residents of Lochhead and Glenmaddy community. My thanks to all the parties that have made submissions, and for the care and time they so clearly put into it. I will give my more detailed findings in due course, but to be clear about the outcome, I now give my judgment on the case. I find that Glenmaddy Estate has failed in its petition to this Court for an Interdict against the residents of Lochhead and Glenmaddy community as follows: seeking to prevent the residents of Lochhead and Glenmaddy community, as defined geographically by the area of benefit of Lochhead and Glenmaddy Community Council within the relevant Local Government Acts, and residents defined as those liable to pay Council Tax within that area, be prohibited from claiming any rights to the Darach Muir and its environs within any long-defunct common land tradition. I repeat, the petition has failed and that concludes the matter."

There was an immediate clamour of comments coming from the public gallery, showing lively delight with the outcome. Only the estate representative was visibly crestfallen with this pronouncement. Though he kept it to himself, however, he knew that the case would be a difficult one, but had to proceed with it, quite simply because his client instructed him to do so. He sighed, "He who pays the piper."

The Sheriff banged his gavel, "Silence, Court is adjourned for fifteen minutes."

"Court rise," the Clerk announced. And the Sheriff left into his own secret domain, backstage.

Driving back down the A9 on a much clearer day, to meet up with Marissa, Archie felt a lightness in his heart. He`d messaged the gang before he set off, so they could all share in the joy, that he had no doubt was also echoing around Glenmaddy village. He smiled as it occurred to him that social media had rather superseded the Town Crier.

Archie`s phone rang, and he rushed over to pick it up from the kitchen table.

"Hello, this is Geordie here. You`ll mind I said I`d investigate a few things for you following our earlier chat in the Club? Well, I`d noted your passing mention of the Aikenhead Papers and some reference to slavery. So, I did a brief search on that, as it rather intrigued me."

"Eh, hello, Geordie, great to hear from you. Oh, I`ll be fascinated to hear what you`ve got on that. Every family needs a dark side or has one, anyway. And slavery sure is dark."

"As soon as I started, I sensed there would be more questions than answers in this, but that was no reason to leave it aside, in fact, it fired me up."

"Do tell man, I`m all ears."

"To start with, I could see no obvious connection between Aikenhead and the Ferguson family, as Aikenhead is, or was, an estate in Perthshire. But I tracked down a digital archive catalogue reference to the Aikenhead papers in the University of Edinburgh library collections. So, I toddled along, and blagged my way in, to investigate. A box containing the papers was identified and retrieved for me. Truthfully there was not a great deal of material in it, a rather random selection of papers, that either did or did not refer to Aikenhead. At the bottom, was a tightly folded old letter. Opening it carefully, it was handwritten of course, and a bit difficult to read."

"Keep going Geordie, I feel this is leading us somewhere already."

"OK, I was able to transcribe the letter into my laptop. Photocopying it wasn't an option in the library. I`ll drop you an email with my copy of it. It's pretty much word for word. It's a letter from a Ronald Ferguson to his brother, dated 1756 and from Jamaica.

It starts, as expected, `My dearest brother Archibald`. He asks about family, and other matters back home and then goes on to talk about his own wife and children. He was obviously a slave manager of some kind, and it seems that the Fergusons were also slave owners, as there's a reference to the profits earned from this, that he has sent back to his brother. That's a summary Archie, it may not be what you wanted to receive?"

"It certainly is the start of an account of a dark era in our family history. I`ll be intrigued to receive your copy of the whole letter Geordie. The family are going to be troubled by this. I`m immediately thinking of the proceeds or compensation from the Abolition of Slavery some years later, 1837, I think. What did the family do with that, and are we still benefitting from it in some way? We may not have been perfect, but this is sombre news that you've shared, Geordie."

"Yes, I assumed that you`d not find it to be very palatable, and it certainly calls out for more investigation sometime."

"Thank you, I`m not ungrateful, just a bit shaken by it, my friend. I appreciate what you have done. And one thing is sure, we can`t hide from it. Half of Scotland has a dark shadow cast upon it, as a result of our place in the era of slavery. And beyond, indeed. Let's meet up soon to discuss it a bit more. My club be OK for that?"

"Sure thing, perhaps in a week or two. I`ll need to get my diary, so will get back in touch with you Archie."

31.

After a delicious Sunday lunch, in Hermione and Malcolm`s house, when everyone was relaxing over a convivial coffee, Lizzie introduced the subject of her research on Catriona and Alex, as far as she'd been able to put it together from the diary. "This has come as quite a bombshell folks, as we had very little information about poor Alex, and didn't even know about his fiancé at the start. In fact, I`m still left wondering if she was merely his fiancé. This degree of uncertainty may have implications that could upset several things. But after this, it may be that we need your legal expertise in particular, Dad."

"My God, what on earth have you come up with from this, Lizzie, I'm both intrigued and a bit alarmed too," Marissa chipped in, almost out of breath with it.

There were a few more murmurings in the same tone, around the room.

"Perhaps I should try and start at the beginning of what I`ve discovered from Catriona`s diary so far. It seems to cover the years 1914 – 1919, which is quite a lot for a single document. Therefore, it corresponds with the War years. It was in amongst the books and that Bible with her name on it, just inside the flyleaf. But here`s the diary," as she held up a very dog-eared volume that seemed it had suffered badly through all those years of abandonment. "Quite how it came to be amongst what I presume were otherwise Ferguson property, I can`t imagine. And it immediately begs the question as to what happened to her. Although there is much that I've been able to work out from this one-sided view of things, of the relationship, there are most surely more questions that come out of it."

"Hurry up with the story, I`m getting impatient", moaned Hermione.

"OK, I`ll give you an outline of what I`ve gathered of the bits that concern us, at this stage. It was quite hard to read in places though.

She seems to have come from somewhere in Galloway, you know, down in the southwest and was probably born in about 1895. She`d come up to Edinburgh to accompany a twin brother who was in a military administration job, perhaps in the Castle. So, in that sense, she was housekeeping for him, in a flat in Charlotte Square.

She met Alex at a ball organised by a friend of her brother`s. She was formally introduced to Alex, or in fact, it was Alexander, but seems to have felt awkward with him at first. I'm unclear why, but they did dance together. That was around Christmas 1914. The ball was in a private house somewhere, but there`s no reference to where that was. She must have made an impression upon Alex though because he contacted her himself, early in 1915. January, I think. By sending her a letter. Remember, we think he was probably working for a law firm, having graduated in about 1911. So, he may have been about four years older than Catriona. He suggested they meet in the Museum, where they were quite anonymous, and had tea and cakes together. From that meeting, she seemed to warm to him a bit, called him charming and polite, taking an interest in her.

From that first meeting, they seemed to have hit it off, as we would say. She says that she had to be a bit clever in order that they could meet without her brother`s knowledge. His name was Philip, and he seemed to be quite protective of her. Oh, and there's no indication of when, or if, she told her parents about the friendship. I have a feeling they were farmers, as she later asks about the lambing. She probably doesn't record every meeting with Alex, but by Easter of that year, that's 1915, there was a romantic touch to how she refers to him and does give a strong hint of her feelings for him.

When she hears that he is being called up later in the year, the tempo of their romance intensifies, so that by the summer, she is clear that she loves him, and hopes very much that the emotion is reciprocated. Despite this, she's circumspect in what she writes. Some of their trysts were outdoors, in the better weather.

I tried to imagine what the national mood was then because that would probably have some bearing on the urgency, they felt for each other if any. Fatalities in the War would have been mounting and be a common topic; a depressing thought for us at any rate."

"You are surely spinning this out somewhat, Lizzie?" Marissa said very impatiently.

"OK, I`ll stick to the gist of what I have to date, then. Much to Philip`s chagrin, Catriona and Alex went on holiday together in July 1915, to Oban, by train. This was a big thing for her, as she comments that she'd never been on holiday with a man before. I`m guessing that for Alex this was a first, too. I sense both great excitement, and a little bit of nervousness too in what she`s written. She makes no reference, however, to what the sleeping arrangements were. It was certainly romantic for her. She comments that he is beautiful, strong, and masculine. Also, he`s thoughtful and caring. She says she wants to please him too. We can make of that, what we will, for now, at any rate.

As the day for his departure for naval service gets closer, in the Autumn, Catriona`s mood changes and her feelings are all over the place. They do have one long weekend together in The Trossachs in October. Just a few days before he is due to leave. She tells herself before that weekend, that she is going to show her desperate love for Alex, whatever it takes. On their return, she notes that her heart, soul, and everything was for him, that weekend. And then he was gone.

There are three letters from him whilst he is away in the navy, they are tucked inside that Bible, along with a photograph of the two of them together. The letters give a brief glimpse of Alex, as he speaks to her of his endless love for her.

212

From there, we get more little snippets in Catriona`s diary. She tells us that he comes home on leave once, in mid-1916, and reading between the lines, I'd say they have a full relationship. Philip had done the honourable thing and let them have the flat in Charlotte Square together, as he`d gone back home to Galloway on holiday. One brief phrase really caught my attention in this, and that was when she says, `after the ceremony, we went out for dinner together. That's all, but my goodness, it rather looks like they got married."

Once the gasps and exclamations of amazement finally died down, and the coffee mugs replenished, Archie asked rather cautiously, "what else are we told about this new situation?"

"After the start of 1917, the entries are somewhat sparser. By April, she has certainly moved back to her parents in Galloway and talks about being unwell. News finally gets through to her, that Alex`s boat was sunk, with the loss of all hands, in February of that year. Catriona records that her whole world has fallen apart, and that mummy and daddy are still angry with her. Her baby was born in March, and she tells us it's a boy, and she has named him Alexander."

For the remainder of the War, the diary, it's deeply depressing entries about her loss of Alex and the difficulties she's having with Alexander, in a rather hostile environment. We must assume, that she and the baby remained in Galloway.

So, I don't know where we go from here folks. We may have descendant relatives that we don`t even know about, which is both gratifying, and alarming."

"Hmmm," said Archie, in his lawyer voice. "Finding the Darrach Stane was one thing, but this is potentially at any rate, an entirely different league altogether."

"Why do you say that, Dad?" asked Lizzie.

"Well just think about it. Alex as the older of two siblings would have inherited the most, had he lived. But in theory, any legitimate offspring of his, and their descendants, if there are any, could well have a claim on what my grandfather inherited. Even if they don't know it. And what's more, we need to know about what happened to Catriona`s brother Philip."

"This is serious stuff," Andy exclaimed. "All our plans for Spurryhillock could be right up in the air."

"Well, yes, but let's keep a hold of things for now. Because we don't know what happened to either Catriona or Alexander, in the first place. I`ll investigate of course and ask someone from the office to give me a hand."

"I can tell you that Alexander Peter Ferguson was born on 19th March 1917, registered in St John`s Town of Dalry, Kirkcudbrightshire, and his parents were Catriona Hyslop and the late Alexander Ferguson," Malcolm said as he read the details he had got online, on his phone.

"Now if that crate of books had never turned up folks." Archie pondered aloud.

"Oh, and there`s something else has turned up, that none of you will like. That reference to Harold Ferguson and slavery seems to be true. We were slave owners."

A silence fell over the group, as they all struggled to take this in, to weigh its significance in their hearts and minds.

32.

The otherwise quiet village of Lochhead was now a hotbed of debate as to the meaning, or indeed the opportunities which the result of the court case signalled. Just about everyone had an opinion. Those who had been done for poaching on the estate believed they saw an opportunity for a bit of revenge. Though quite what form this could take, was uncertain. The ecologists said they could see the day when Darach Muir might hold some special significance. Those in the village who held a left-of-centre political inclination sought to find a way of undoing the wrongs perpetrated upon their ancestors not long after 1715. The Women`s Institute started to plan a very special picnic on the Muir, for the following year.

Yes, Darach Muir, with its magnificent Stane, had galvanised the people of the village into a bit of a frenzy, the likes of which was quite unheard of, any time within living memory.

One lady Margaret McPherson, who just kept herself to herself most of the time, was, unbeknown to anyone else, plotting her own wee manoeuvre. Having quietly won a lot of money on the Lottery, she could both indulge herself when it suited, and distribute money to many good causes via an endowment she had placed with Foundation Scotland. She`d studied, and obtained a master's degree whilst at university, in Scottish history from the Jacobite period to the close of the 19th Century. So, she had a real conviction about the political, economic, and social injustices meted out on the native highlanders, and the consequences of it. But Margaret never chose to join any political party.

Instead, she was now in the position to hire the very best legal minds in the country, to make Glenmaddy Estate, especially its apparently anonymous owners, feel very uncomfortable. She was resolved that they would have to come out of hiding, to defend themselves. "Oh yes they would, David," she told her dog. "Darach got its Stane back, so we shall have our Muir back, my boy."

The following week, Margaret McPherson, or Maggie as she preferred to be called, entered the grand doorway of her new lawyer`s offices in one of the fine new glass-clad buildings in The Exchange area of Edinburgh, with mischief in her mind.

"Do come in, and have a seat," the lawyer welcomed her warmly. "I very much hope that you had a good journey down here yesterday?"

"Yes, I sure did, thank you. And then a very comfortable night in The Sheraton."

"I gather you have a rather strange request?"

"Yes, well strange, or not, I do have a request for your professional legal expertise. You may know of a recent case in the Sheriff Court in Inverness, in which Glenmaddy Estate sought an injunction against all the residents of the community of Lochhead and Glenmaddy. The estate failed, and the case was thrown out."

"Oh yes, we have indeed heard of this case. There`s been a lot of discussion about it."

"Good, well, as a local resident of Lochhead, as defined by the Estate, in the summary of their stated action for an injunction, I wish to act against the Estate myself. The background issue in relation to its injunction was the ancient common land called Darach Muir. Now we may not be able to prove any residual right to that common land for the people of Lochhead and Glenmaddy, but neither can the Estate prove its absolute ownership of it, or indeed disprove our claim. If you look at the detailed judgment by the Sheriff, you will see that he states, that there is insufficient evidence to prove consistent conclusive ownership of the Darach Muir, and there is, therefore, a matter of doubt as to the veracity of Glenmaddy Estate`s absolute and full title."

"Yes, I have a printout of the Sherriff`s judgment here, and can see what you are referring to, indeed, you seem to be quoting it, verbatim."

"Good, so, I want to take an action against the Estate, in which I demand that they prove I cannot exercise any of my traditional rights over the lands of Darach Muir. I`m conscious that it is a rather back-to-front action proposal, but the onus will be on the Estate to prove conclusively that I don't."

"Very good, Ms McPherson, we will act for you in this. Once we have studied the Sherriff's ruling, carried out a search, and looked for any relevant case law, which may have any bearing on it. We`ll be in touch with you, in a week or so. Safe journey home."

Archie`s Club in Abercromby Place was the chosen venue for his meeting with a former colleague. Morven who was still practising and had agreed to support him in the investigation into his family history, following the discovery that Alex had been married, and had fathered a child by his wife Catriona. Lunch was of course part of the process of the meeting, and both agreed that it was very delicious. Morven was, as Archie knew, a recovering alcoholic, and so did not drink any alcohol whatsoever. Archie fully respected this. So much to the discreet surprise of the Club staff, there was no alcohol on the table on this occasion.

With the food duly eaten and warmly expressed appreciation, they got down to business, over coffee. "In what way can I help?" Morven asked. I've already got the gist of the case, from the email, you kindly sent the other day."

"Well just to reiterate, my grandfather inherited pretty much everything, when his brother Alexander was killed in the First World War, in 1917. When I say everything, I`m referring to Spurryhillock Estate, the house I have in Edinburgh, and several investments, oh, and the sale of a house in Heriot Row. Though in reality, things were then as now, a bit run down. It's very strange, that Alex`s widow Catriona made no claim, and indeed, remained completely out of sight. We only found out about her, the marriage, and a baby quite by chance. My feeling is that given my legal background, and something as apparently innocuous as my son-in-law making an inquiry about the baby on Scotland's People or Ancestry, there is now a record of that and a link with the family. So, we can't ignore any of this."

"Thanks, yes, you are right, and in fact by involving me, and the practice, there is yet another reason for not ignoring it, Archie, whatever the outcome may be. My first course of action in this is to do a trace on Catriona, Alexander, and any descendants he may have had. I`d say I can complete this in about a week or so. Could we meet here again, here, a week from today? Sorry if I appear to be inviting you to your own Club."

"Yes, that's fine Morven, and thank you for picking this up so quickly. There`s potentially rather a lot at stake here."

After Morven had gone, Archie did have a malt or two, to while away a bit of the afternoon, he said to himself, reassuringly. It also gave him time to think about the sequence of events that had got them, and so many other people or interests, to this situation. Oh, there is still a huge amount to be done, he mused. Some of that will stretch off into the future in a way that could never have been foreseen. What had started with nothing more than the roof of an old rotten building falling in on his son in law, had now led to the discovery of an ancestor, the recovery of an ancient and symbolical stone, or Stane, stirring up an entire community, a court case, and from what he`d heard on the grapevine, another in the offing. So the list went on. Over his second malt, brought to him in such style by the waiter who knew Archie so well, he was getting into the what-ifs. Chief among them is the prospect of a living descendant from Alexander. Now whilst that troubled him a bit, the fine malt was certainly taking the edge off it. For now, at any rate.

33.

Undeterred by the potential implications of recent inconclusive discoveries, Archie and Lizzie pressed on with their plan for Spurryhillock. With a few tweaks to show a slightly more diverse use of the remains of the old farm steading, but all of it apparently relating to the estate`s woodland management, and greater clarity about camping pods, they decided to submit the outline planning application to Orla, as an act of confidence.

An architect friend of Lizzie`s drew some sketch plans for the re-use of the old castle. She even ventured some draft costs, which raised an eyebrow or two. They`d also done a fuller survey of all the estate's woodland, hedgerows, and wilder areas. Whilst they knew this wasn't conclusive, and they`d used apps on their phones for plant identification, it was Lizzie said, "a useful environmental audit, to work from." The agricultural and land use subsidy business was nothing if not confusing, "despite all the government spin on it," Andy agonised. They`d found a semi-local house builder that they felt they could probably work with, for both the new housing on the old military site and some estate building renovation. They`d even had an unannounced visit from a scrap dealer who said he could give them a good price for any old and unwanted iron. "It`ll tidy the place up for you." He`d said.

With the development plan in front of them, they tried to assess where they were on the various timelines.

"We are really stymied on any real progress until we get planning permission, and that's many months off yet," Lizzie remarked, sadly. But on the positive side, we are getting several things lined up, so that when the time comes, we can hit the ground running."

"Yes, true, but remember we need some capital from the sale of the old military place right at the start. That's for sure."

Archie and Hermione had been giving a lot of thought to the need for the event to scatter her late husband`s ashes. She knew it was long overdue but just could not bring herself to carry it out. All the old feelings of what a pillock he`d become, and the evil deeds he`d carried out, would come flooding back. And the girls, how would it affect her two lovely girls? They surely didn't deserve to have to go through all this.

One evening, Monique came into the kitchen and found her mother crying. At first, Monique was a bit taken aback because she knew her mother was made of something strong. But she quickly realised that she must act because this situation was so unusual. "What's wrong, Mummy she said," in a soft gentle voice, as she placed her hand upon her mother`s.

It's something I need to tell both Charlotte and you, and I don't know how to do it, my love. It's been troubling me for some time, but now I must break it to you both."

"That's OK Mummy, please tell me, and I`ll try to understand."

"It's about your father, darling, or more correctly, about his ashes, and something we must do with them. You know this has been unfinished business for us, and more especially for poor David and Margaret. So, the time has come, my love."

"I`ll be brave Mummy because I do love you, and I love those two-dear people, our grandparents. So please tell me what is to happen, and what can I do to help you especially?"

Hermione was once more moved by the whole experience of this. Nothing had prepared her for it, nothing could. She hated Jamie for what he had become, and what he`d done, but just knew her love for her two girls far outshone the darkest thoughts she had about Jamie. This gave her hope. "We must arrange to scatter your father`s ashes quite soon, in a very small service, which a kind lady minister will lead for us. Her name is Fiona, and I've met her. She`s the wife of one of your grampa`s former clients. Very gentle and understanding. Lizzie has been wonderful in talking with Margaret and David, and they seem to be relieved that this last thing is going to be done now."

"Oh, I am glad about this Mummy. I somehow knew that this had to be done some time, and I know you`ll feel better when it is done. Charlotte and I were talking a little bit about it not so long ago because we know that this is something that must be done when a person dies. We didn't cry when we talked about it. And it was Charlotte who said we must help you if we can, Mummy."

After another spell of uncontrollable sobbing, during which Monique held her mother tight, Hermione felt a surge of hope in her heart, because she now knew that the girls were more mature than she`d believed possible and that they were indeed ready for this step in their young lives. Dear God, young people are so resilient, she thought.

"Thank you, sweetie, for your great understanding and love. Are you ready for me to tell you what we are planning?"

"Yes, I am Mummy. Do tell me."

"In the spring, we will go down to Mellerstain, where you have been. That will be you, Charlotte, me, Lizzie and Andy, grampa, and grandma. We`ll meet Margaret and David there, as Jean has kindly said she`ll take them. And of course, Fiona the minister."

"What about Malcolm, Mummy?"

"Would you like him to be there too?"

"Yes, I think I would. He`s been so kind and lovely to us. So, he should be there."

"Thank you, darling, I`m so pleased you feel this way. Fiona will of course lead the short service, but it won't be like a church service. She has a more human plan, which is very kind of her. Do you think Charlotte and you would like to do something, like read a poem?"

"I think we probably would Mummy, can we chat about it, and see what would be best?"

"Of course, you can. You've made me feel so much better, sweetie. See, I'm not crying anymore, thank you." At which point she gave Monique a hug and a kiss. "Thank you, my sweet."

34.

On a fine midweek Autumn Day, a light breeze rustled through the dying heather, and the ever-joyous sound of a late skylark poured down upon Darach Muir. One car was parked near the start of the track, as a lone figure dressed in what looked like official issue clothing of dark blue-grey trousers, fleece, and cap, walked confidently towards the top of the small hill in the middle of the Muir. She put her backpack down against a boulder close to the Darach Stane, got out a map, studied it, and looked around slowly, taking in the location.

First, she walked slowly in a wide oval arc, about ten metres out from both the Stane and its original location, first clockwise and then anti-clockwise, stopping every so often, apparently to get a real understanding of the place, and to take a sequence of photos of everything within this arc. She took out a tablet from her pack and entered copious notes, recording what she saw, and its apparent significance. On her fleece were the words Historic Environment Scotland and a curved green and blue logo, like three stones from an arch. This was clearly an official inspection visit.

The Inspector then went over to the Darach Stane and photographed it closely from every angle, and from above. She took a small hammer from her pack, and lightly tapped the Stane, also from several different angles, noting what she took to be the integrity of the sound. After that, she ran her hand around the apparent junction where the two parts had been joined together and took more close-up photos of the joint. In one location she seemed to find something that really caught her interest, so she got a scraping tool out of her pack and loosened a very small quantity of material from the edge of the joint, letting it fall into a poly bag, which she sealed and marked for identification. The carving of the acorns on the Stane was the next focus of her attention, more photographs. Then she got a small lighting rig from her pack and placed it so that the light would cast shadows in the clump of acorns. Not content with all this, she then started taking measurements of the height and girth of the Stane, and its distance from the centre of the small hollow which may have been its original location. And finally, using a GPS, she recorded both the exact location of the Stane and its historic original position. This lady was leaving nothing to chance in her thorough survey and recording of any evidence she could find of both the Stane and any recent activity thereabouts.

Meantime, as it happened, Angus had already picked up on Andy`s request to surreptitiously donate the oak leaf stone fragment to Historic Environment Scotland, at Fortingall Church. He`d put it in a clean fertiliser bag, and placed it out of sight, at the east end of the church. Then he`d emailed a HES office, using an obscure email address that he rarely used, and notified them that a fragment of a carved stone, found on Darach Muir during the reinstatement of the Darach Stane could be found at Fortingall. They should retrieve it sooner rather than later.

This news sent a couple of HES officers scurrying halfway across Scotland to investigate. On arrival at Fortingall, they located the bag, photographed it exactly where it had been mysteriously deposited, and set off with it to the national research facility for such finds. They were thanked for their diligence and told that it would be thoroughly investigated, in due course.

The Inspectors speedy report based on her survey, and an initial examination of the oak leaf fragment prompted both an immediate conference in the Headquarters in Edinburgh, and from that a decision to move the Darach Stane to what was almost certainly its original site. All the necessary staff and equipment were mobilised for this in double-quick time. An order was also drawn up to declare a one-hectare site atop Darach Muir, as a protected Ancient Monument, thus making it an offence for anyone to go digging on it or remove anything from it.

The following week, the entire exercise swung into action. A block booking of accommodation at the Lochhead Hotel was made, for the staff. A secure portable office was located beside the end of the track, with some extra parking provided by a modest widening of the road, using hard-core. And portable track for habitat protection was rolled out over the short stretch of Muir, between the existing track and the summit. Nothing was being left to chance. A full risk assessment of every stage in the exercise had been drawn up and was understood by all.

The first task was to carry out an aerial photographic record of the entire newly protected site, by using a drone-mounted camera. This was done twice on the same day, in the early light and then the later light, in order to capture any possible shadow clues, as well as vegetation variations. The following day, a ground-penetrating radar survey was carried out using a big, red-wheeled machine with an archaeologist walking along behind it. The data collected from this was then fed into a new digital site plan and sent to an analyst in the portable site office. The photography from the previous day was added as an additional layer option to the plan. Such material as remained, from the initial survey of the small area at the summit in 1925, was provided as yet another layer choice in the high-tech picture that was being gradually assembled.

Word had of course got around the village, and from time to time, curious villagers would appear on the Muir in ones and twos, to witness the spectacle of what was happening in their backyard. All manner of speculation arose from this. One man, however, who knew rather more than anyone else, kept himself to himself but did venture out, armed with his binoculars. Angus was intrigued and gladly reported back to base in The Grange each day. Oh, would that he could somehow hack into the data being gathered in that olive-coloured site office beside the road, he sighed.

There seemed to be a slick, well-orchestrated sequence of events being played out on the Muir. The sepia-toned image of a pith-helmeted archaeologist scraping away alone, in a trench was long gone. Technology triumphed in this new scenario. It seemed they almost knew more about what may be under the ground, where, and even the material it was made of before the turf was even cut. And any subtle information gleaned from vegetation data would have started to point to dates of any possible activity too.

That evening, some of the gang assembled in Archie`s sitting room for more than just a coffee and flapjack. Ronald had joined them too, as he was just back from a journalistic foray into one of the more deprived areas of Glasgow, in order to present some constructive opinion on declining life expectancy amongst men and offer a suggestion of two as to what might be done about it. "The Scottish Government will take no comfort from what I may have to say," he commented, upon being asked what he was up to. "The whole situation is a mega tragedy, and an indictment of government policies and practice, both local and national over the last fifty years or more, but especially much more recently. Anyway, that's not what we are here for this evening I`d say."

Orla had joined in the gathering too. She`d been in touch with Lizzie, and said she was down for some professional conference, but fancied a break from that. "Could I drop in and visit you guys", she asked. "It may be a bit irregular, but hey ho, I like what you are doing."

"Of course, you can, you`ll be most welcome. And you`ll meet a few more of The Gang, as I like to call them," Lizzie replied warmly.

After the welcome and introductions, the meeting got underway.

"Who would have believed it?" Andy commented. "That roof fell in on me, and just look at what has happened, or has yet to happen, since then."

227

"Too true, and we all know what curiosity did to the cat," Lizzie snapped.

"Aye`, what started as a year to really try and get over all of the fallout from Andy`s big escapade, has taken on a life all of its own," said Archie. "And we are certainly not done with it yet."

"Where on earth is all this going to end up?" Marissa asked, in a somewhat anxious voice.

"Let's try and focus on the immediate things, for now, folks, and that's all about what's currently happening out there on the Muir. Angus`s reports have been intriguing," Hermione quickly responded. "I`m sure we`d all love to be out there, watching what's going on. Well, I would anyway. Apparently, the village is agog with it, and the hotel is doing rather well out of it too, for this time of year. Hopefully, we`ll get back there next year to see."

"There might not be much to see, though," Ronald observed. "If they are just surveying, their findings will all be in a report in archaeology speak."

"I do wonder what they are making of the Darach Stane though, cos that's what got all this going in the first place?" Malcolm pondered. "Mind you, they can`t go back to see where it came from, where we got it, because Angus tells us it's now well underwater. Don't think the hydro people would be too keen on pulling the plug on the reservoir. Can't see them putting divers down there either, can you?"

"We`ll get a report from Angus again tomorrow, I`m sure," said Archie.

And so, the conversation ranged over all the many things that had happened, in Spurryhillock, the Muir, in Court, and even down in the Borders. Such a diverse range of things made ordinary life, whatever that might be, seem mundane.

"I had a lovely chat with Monique recently, she was so kind, mature, and thoughtful, as I`d been quite upset. The business of Jamie`s ashes had been troubling me so much. Not his death at all, I`m well past that, but how the business of scattering them would affect the girls, and indeed, Margaret and David too. But it's the girls I worry about most. I`m so glad Monique and I were able to talk about it together, and I was deeply moved by how well she`s taking it. Indeed, I now know I shouldn't have got myself so upset. It's almost like I was worrying about nothing. I told her about the minister you`d found, Dad. And how the event, if I can call it that, might be organised. She seemed pleased to have been told about it in this way, said that she would certainly want to be there, and imagined that Charlotte would too. In fact, she said that she`d have a chat with Charlotte, as I must too, about them reading something, a poem perhaps. Aren`t young people amazing, they understand in a way we often don't give them credit for. They make some things easier for us, that can take us by surprise."

"This is wonderful news, darling," Marissa said warmly. "I`d wondered how you would broach this with the girls, and Monique almost seems to have beat you to it. What a wonderful child. Well, of course, she`s not a child anymore, is she?"

"Wish I`d half the courage that she seems to have, Mum. And she`s made another thing a whole lot easier too."

"What's that?" Asked Archie.

"She said, she wants Malcolm to be there. Said it, of her own accord. I was in tears once more, when she told me that, tears of joy. I`ll tell him as soon he returns from his hunt for oak for the doors, he`s about to make."

"Well, this has been a fine wee catch-up folks, thank you. Time to be calling it a day, or a night, I should say," Archie concluded. "Hope you weren`t too perplexed about the family business Orla. Lizzie will I'm sure explain later if you wish."

229

"No problem, folks, it's been a pleasure to meet you all, in your home patch. And it certainly took my mind off of the planning speak I had to endure at the conference."

35.

A bit of a bombshell communication came from Orla a few days later, in relation to the Spurryhillock plans. In it, she said that whilst much of it was progressing reasonably well, some major questions had arisen, that would need urgent attention if the full application was to be processed through to Committee. The first is related to the Castle ruins. "We need more information on plans for consolidation, security, and processing towards some form of Listed Building Consent, with a view to in principle end-use. The vehicle access arrangements at the main entrance from the public road will need to be revisited. And more information is needed regarding sewage and wastewater handling, throughout. Could you please meet with me at your earliest, to discuss these matters?"

A bombshell indeed, at this advanced stage.

Up on the Muir, the weather had turned a bit cooler, so more layers of warm clothing were donned, to try and keep out the cold breezes. The activity was now focused on two small areas, where excavations were taking place, the original site of the Stane, and its new location. From the surveys and other site investigations, a small pit was being opened at the original site. Slowly, small layers were removed, measured, recorded, and photographed. With great care. The pit was about two and a half feet square, with vertical sides. The spoil was being separated and sifted. In due course, one larger stone was appearing, so it was excavated around, with that same meticulous care. Eventually, it was time to lift it out. At which point it became clear that it had the edge of an incomplete recessed carving on one side. This was photographed and recorded, before being taken away for cataloguing in the site office.

There came a point at which the supervisor of this part of the excavation announced that it was deep enough now, as they had reached bedrock, within a rectangular hollow carved out of the rock. "This is the socket, from which the Darach Stane was removed by that Snoddy character all those years ago."

The other excavation was a trench, extending out from the back of where the Stane now stood. It received the same slow, methodical, and meticulous treatment. It was obvious where the edge of the hole dug so recently was, and the packing placed around the stone. In the area beyond that, a few small artefacts were recovered, recorded, and given the same thorough treatment for future analysis. At about a foot in depth, a rig was lowered over the Stane. It was a very robust frame, about two metre square, its weight pressing the four-pointed legs firmly into the surface vegetation. Adjustments were made by screw mechanisms, to get it level. Then four small hydraulic jacks were extended, one from each leg, and held tightly onto the Stane at a point above the acorn carving, with hard rubber pads protecting the surface of the Stane.

The excavation continued, right down to level with the base of the Stane, and then back at an angle up to surface level. Two blocks of wood were then placed in the trench, to correspond with the above and below the joint. At this point, a tracked vehicle with heavy lifting gear was drawn up alongside the Stane and trench. It had slings dangling from a hook at the end of the arm.

After due consideration and discussion, the next plan of action was implemented. Simultaneously, the jacks on the back of the Stane were eased off, and those on the front tightened. Anxiously, the Stane started to tilt back, as everyone looked on. As stones loosened from around the Stane, they were removed and set to one side. The centre of balance shifted, and the carved acorns, increasingly faced upwards, at an angle.

Midway through this part of the procedure, the webbing slings were placed around the Stane, and as it was tilted ever further back, they began to take the strain. When eventually, the jacks had done their job, the Stane rested on the wooden blocks, and the slings were adjusted to take the load evenly. The jacks were removed. With the Stane then held in the slings by the heavy lifting machine, there was a pause for further consultation amongst the archaeologists and their support team. The next plan of action was agreed upon and understood by all. Each got into his or her place.

The tracked heavy lifting machine then moved slowly towards the original site for the Stane, which now hung free, in the slings. A couple of ropes had also been put around it, one on either side, to steady it, as the vehicle moved over the uneven ground. Although the distance was not great, it took some time to travel to the newly excavated socket hole. Eventually, it was lined up. A second tracked heavy lifting machine had been manoeuvred into place, on the other side of the hole. It had a special clamp on it, to fit around the upper half of the Stane, and by careful adjustment, to take the full weight, holding the Stane in an upright position.

This too was slow, and cautiously carried out the exercise. One mistake and the Stane could fall and suffer irreparable damage. At every stage in the entire process, there had been a delegated watcher, whose role was to stand back and objectively monitor both progress and safety.

With the Stane now suspended above the socket, it was lined up for re-insertion. Lined up to undo what Rev. Ebenezer Snoddy had so crudely done, in his day. The shape of the original socket, and the shape of the very base of the Stane, combined to dictate the direction in which it would face. The gang had got it right, it transpired, it must face south.

At the signal, the Stane was slowly lowered into its socket. It was a perfect fit. Still held firmly in place by the clamp, two of the most senior of the archaeologists busied themselves with placing wedging stones in the hole around the Stane. They were of differing heights, and then smaller stones packed around them, all firmed-in, with a mash hammer. With each uneven ring of wedge stones and packing, the Stane became yet more firmly fixed in its original place.

It was reinstated exactly as its ancient creators had intended so many years ago. At a time when they knew the place of nature in their hearts, culture, and the very lives they led. A time when they felt comfortable with nature as more than just their equal, but rather, as superior. Only the absurdly literal thundering of the supposed word of God from the pulpit had confounded that balance.

The archaeologists may not have been so concerned about that truth at this time, for they had a job to do, but they knew that out of the proper completion of their task, love, and respect for the status of nature would be rekindled here.

With the final ring of stones now in place, earthed over, and some small clumps of salvaged vegetation put in place, the clamp was removed. The Darach Stane was free.

In the hotel after dinner, the HES staff toasted a job well done. All the machinery, equipment, and gear had been removed from the Muir. The air blew a blessing over the Darrach Stane and its place in man`s proper, respectful interaction with nature once more. The acorns were the symbols of that rectitude. There remained only the removal of the site office, to be done.

From the surveys of the entire area, it was clear that in order to get a fuller understanding of the place of the Darach Stane in the year-round lives of the ancients, a comprehensive excavation would be necessary, next season. For only the shadows of that living place, were evident.

Angus reported as much as he had been able to see or glean, back to the gang. From this, it was decided that a family visit to the Darach Stane must be organised.

36.

When the time came for the family pilgrimage, the car, with Lizzie, Andy, Archie, Melissa, and Malcolm in it set off north. Hermione had to stay back as the girls had several commitments to attend to. Ronald and Angus said they`d join the party, at the Stane. Orla had got wind of all this and asked if they would mind if she came along too.

"No problem," came the reply from Lizzie. "You`ll be most welcome. See you there."

To everyone's delight, they appeared to have Darach Muir to themselves. The walk across to the Stane from the road, was indeed like a pilgrimage, for this piece of ancient history that they had recovered now occupied a special place in their lives. It was Alex who had started it all off of course, but everything that he had done, could so easily have been lost forever; only some chance happenings had saved it.

At the Stane, after some friendly greetings, and with Orla being introduced to those she did not already know, the party of eight gathered around. It had been agreed, that after inspecting the Stane in its new, but original site, there should be some formality to the occasion.

Archie opened the proceedings with a tribute to Alex. "Whilst I regret that I didn't know more about Alex, within my family history, having rather sadly counted him as just one of the tragic losses in the First World War, I now have a feeling of great respect and admiration for this young man, who had found something, that for whatever reason, he knew he must investigate and record. We are all, richer for his singularity of purpose. His passion, whether borne out of some sense of historical injustice towards the local people, an interest in his own family history, or even a deeper more eco-philosophical cause, has all this time after his death, been rediscovered and reinstated. True, not everyone will know the whole story

236

about that, but for us, the important thing is that it's not all gone forever, with him, to the bottom of the Atlantic Ocean.

As the senior member of this party, the old codger, some could say, I`m just immensely proud of you, and those who helped you, with what you have done, for no other reason than you believed it the right thing to do. I thank you that you have now successfully undone the awful deeds of a misguided church, and brought this priceless symbol in stone, back to where it should be. So, thank you one and all.

Thanks to your efforts, all that this stone, this Darach Stane, represents will be discovered, visited, and probably cherished, by an unknown number of people, now, and off into the future. Reuniting a long past, with hopefully an even longer time to come. You may never have sought it, my friends, but in doing what you have done, you have made a mark in history.

As we look out together here over the Muir, see the horizons both near and far beyond, we have the captivating sounds of the skylark as our anthem, pouring its praise upon our actions and all the thoughts in our hearts, here today."

A soft silence fell upon the group, as all looked in admiration at the Darach Stane, and then to the wider landscape, in which it had a such powerful meaning for people gone before.

"Thanks for that, Dad, we really appreciate the way you've set the scene here," said Lizzie. "It's the acorns as the fruit of the oak tree, that we have in this fine, weathered carving, that moves me. They are but a stage in the cycle of life, a product of the reproduction of the tree, neither an outcome nor an end. As I look at them, in my mind's eye, I see the cold winter and the dying vegetation that they will fall into, not to die themselves, but to catch that nudge that only the winter can give, which they will need to start a new process all over again, one which transcends the centuries. Oh yes, some will have been taken as food by an animal that needs the

237

nourishment, but there is plenty to go around, in a balance of nature`s ways, that we can only wonder at.

As the days grow warmer through the turn of the season, and moisture finds its way to the acorns, there`s a stirring within which heralds new growth. Sunlight brings spring, and if the setting is right, so a little shoot breaks through the shell to send down what will become a root, and upwards toward the sky to form a leaf. And so, the genesis of a new tree begins, once more.

Then I look at the tree from which the acorn fell and see its great wide spread of branches come out from limb and trunk, all rooted so firmly in the nourishing soil. I see the leaves beginning to emerge from their buds, drawn out by sunshine and longer daylight hours. The great skeleton of the tree, which had been bare for months, takes on a green and dappled light. I see just some of what grows in and on that tree, in a rich tapestry of lichens and mosses, ferns, and all manner of small creatures that thrive on our oak. A bird flies in, and then her mate, and starts to build a nest. In no time, their wondrous cycle is being played out within the aiken amphitheatre of life. Other birds come and go, a squirrel or two, moths and butterflies, find shelter beneath the canopy. Whist somewhere down near the roots, a mouse or two, have built their nest out of last year's grasses. This oak I see, and that is represented by these precious acorns is not alone, of course. And it lives well with many other species of tree. True, the oak is king, but in nature`s ways, all the species coexist.

As the season moves into and through summer, so, modest oak flowers grow, are pollinated by the bees, and in time, new acorns form, as the fruit of the tree. The living oak has been replenished by all that lives in an around it, and with all the rich bounty of the forces of nature.

Alongside this, we stand in awe of the whole process."

Another brief silence fell upon the group, and this time they heard the soft sigh of the wind whispering through the vegetation growing around them, kissing the Stane, and moving on.

"Oh, Lizzie my love, you`ve captured so much of the essence of the oak tree and the acorns we have here, said Andy. For my part, I`m drawn to the almost mystical way in which the ancients, our wiser ancestors, knew where life dwelt in their habitat, long before the written word was shared amongst all. They created symbols carved in stone, that somehow captured the essence of that life. Here it was certainly the acorn, and possibly the oak leaf too. True, they needed the oak timber for their survival, for a shelter, or a plough to till the earth, but they respected it, they worshipped it and crowned it king amongst the trees of the forest. So, they only took what they needed, and let nature continue with the rest.

This measured wisdom was almost universal too, in every glen and coastal place, on the island and riverbank, they gave the mighty oak, which shared both male and female characteristics, real status. But evolving farming practices and wars upset that balance, so the ancient oak suffered under different regimes. The church mistakenly taught that man had dominion or superiority, so what did it matter? Now we ask, what could that god truly provide? I wonder and I doubt. Yet man chose the oak timber as the symbol of strength and endurance in building everything from a cathedral to a financial institution.

Now, the acorn has returned to its rightful place here on the Muir, and perhaps in our hearts, wherever we go. The groundswell of popular support for re-foresting and re-wilding gives the oak its true place amongst the finest native trees. As the oak returns, so does an entire ecosystem that thrives on and around it. We are giving this place back a piece of ancient wisdom, a symbol, and an icon, not for worship as Snoddy feared, but as a call to action. That call will echo across this Muir, no matter what popular changes may occur hereabouts, but also into the next glen, and the next.

We will humbly remain silent about our part in it, I hope, but the call will do fine without us because it will take on a whole new life and meaning that is drawn from deep within the best of human experience and nature, working in harmony once more."

It was Ronald who gently broke the long silence that followed all that Archie, Lizzie, and Andy had said, "There`s an ancient tradition which says that it is unwise to needlessly cut down a rowan tree. That folklore is partly rooted in the Scottish tradition that it would only bring bad luck. Well after all that you good folk have said about the oak and the acorn, perhaps we should extend the folklore belief to include the oak tree too. Here, today, you have conferred a befitting status upon it. The regeneration movement should be reinvigorated by it. And I will try to write about it in an equally moving way, but without giving the game away as to who it was that lit the spark."

37.

Andy and Lizzie both agreed that business planning was not really their forte. "I`d much rather be actually doing, than poring over a plan," Lizzie had said, as they revised yet again some of the detail in the document. Some of this was in response to questions from the Orla, and some of it was down to little, and not so little, ideas that had occurred to them along the way. But they knew that they had Spuryhillock, and they had to do something both useful and a bit profitable with it. "Quite a responsibility is this," mused Andy.

They'd been visiting it as often as possible for much of the year whilst fitting this around their respective jobs and work commitments. They were certainly enjoying it, getting to know it, and tackling a few little tasks that they could be confident would not affect the planning process. A couple more meetings with Orla seemed to be pointing toward the possibility that they were heading in the right direction. But she was giving nothing away. At least the detailed in-principle application was now in and being put through the mill, they assumed.

Although they agreed that they didn't want to have a housing development of boring look-alike buildings just down the road, they knew that the key to kicking the whole business off was the income they`d need from selling houses, one way or another. After much agonising deliberation and a couple of site meetings, they decided to increase the size of the housing area by twenty-five per cent. This would mean losing a bit of a rough field that sat alongside the old military base.

Having made approaches to several relatively local house-building companies, they settled on one that they really felt they could do business with. This company seemed to inspire confidence. Although no commitment or contract could be signed until full planning permission was obtained, they were at least happy to be in discussion with a company that they felt was on the same wavelength. Yes, money would be one thing, but so would its approach to environmental issues, and strong local roots and connections. For their part, Andy and Lizzie offered to start Alex`s Way right down in the housing. So, it would provide a nice walk all the way up through the estate to the top of the hill, for the new residents, in due course.

The builder so liked this plan, that he offered to do some of the construction and landscaping to the lower area, including a couple of footbridges across the burn. From this and other discussions locally, Andy and Lizzie felt they were gradually getting a little bit more integrated.

The pictures of other developments that the builder had done, and which he left with them, showed groups of houses each with some form of individual character. A lot of visible wood, glass, and slate. Yes, they liked the look of these houses. A nice fit for Spurryhillock.

They started looking into how they could incorporate more renewable energy into the whole development too, and how that could work out financially. Could some of it be incorporated into the housing development? Could a small solar farm be created in one of the fields now that the farm was vacant? Could there be a mini hydro in the burn? Could a wind turbine be located on the far side of the hill? And so on with the questions, all of which needed a feasibility study, costings, possible output, and much more besides. The overriding question is, could the entire estate be self-sufficient?

"Now is the time to really get to grips with this. Both because we are at the planning stages, and because we know that our future here is secure after the scare we had," Lizzie considered with some care in her voice.

"How right you are, oh learned one," Andy replied with a little touch of good humour.

That afternoon, they took a stroll down to look again at the castle ruins, as it was a bit easier to make some sense of them now that the leaves were off the trees. They walked around the ruin several times, chatting about architectural details that were still intact, pondering together the lost grandeur, the romantic image of ruins like this, and even identifying the shadow of the landscaping it had been surrounded by. It seemed that the original tower had been built on a small hill beside the burn, with the ground dropping away on three sides around it. Evidence of some subsequent landscaping around the subsequent early Victorian pile suggested a touch of grandeur. Whilst the old arched access bridge across the burn looked intact, it did appear to need something remedial.

The interior was largely unstable and dangerous, but the semi-professional report they'd had on it was not hopeless, in fact, with investment on a big scale, it offered a lot of scope.

"The more I think about this place, the more I like the castle, but the more realistic I become too, Lizzie. I don't think its restoration can form part of our development plan for the estate, however romantic a ruin it may appear to be. No, feet are firmly on the ground for this one. But, given that we are planning to reorganise so much of the estate over some period, why not take a radical look at this? We can`t very well knock it down, or just leave it be as it is, because it's a dangerous thing to have here. So here`s a thought, there`s probably some kind of informal network of people who do have money, oh, and determination, who are wanting a castle kind of building to restore and live in. In one of the more useful discussions, I did have with Jamie, he talked about this kind of thing being done on something like a ninety-nine-year lease."

"So, is that where someone negotiates a lease for a ninety-nine-year period with a landlord, does something with the ruin as part of the lease agreement, makes use of it for the duration, and then at the end of it, it reverts to the landlord?"

243

"That about sums it up, Lizzie. It could work with a single building like this, with architectural qualities on a grand scale, but not for house sites like we`ll have down the road. If we, did it, we could stipulate the use, you know, like only a private house. Or there could be exclusions too, like not a hotel. Do you think it's worth filing this away for future action, Lizzie?"

"I most certainly do, Andy. OK, there are many more immediate things on the list of priorities, but if we factor this in from the start as a possibility and organise the infrastructure accordingly when the time is right, we can give it a go."

Later, over dinner in the dining room, with the log fire burning in the hearth, Lizzie became expansive in all that she wanted to talk about. "Isn`t it amazing how much life has changed and developed this year darling?" Lizzie said with some excitement in her voice, this time. OK, we started by getting over your escapades and Jamie`s death. Then we had to get settled into our new house. You got a job you love, which is right up your street. My little business has taken off and got you running up and down the stairs so much. You nearly got yourself killed, and just look at all that has happened because of that? And all the people it now involves. Oh, I could go on and on about the changes. Then there was the miscarriage I had, and now I'm well and truly expecting again. And now we have a dilemma."

"What dilemma is that my love?"

"Where will we live and settle, of course? You've got to admit that living in a top-floor flat in Edinburgh is not going to be ideal with a baby. And babies have a habit of growing into children. You`ll be running up and down those stairs even more Andy, my boy. Are you ready for that? On the other hand, we could live here in Spurryhillock, and make this our home. But is this any better for Borthwick Junior, in terms of access to school, and being able to play with other children? I find I`m torn between these two. Our flat is close to the rest of the family, and of course, Monique and Charlotte are going to love a wee cousin around. So, what are we to do Andy Borthwick?"

"When you put it all like this, Lizzie my love, I do not know. I had given it some thought you know but got nowhere with it. It would be better to have one that really is home, rather than being kind of split between the two. Your work could I guess be anywhere but for me it's better to be in Edinburgh. Though even that`s not essential. Hmmm, we do have a dilemma all right, Lizzie dear."

"Just for your interest, I`ve been doing some arithmetic, and counting, and relating it all to my scans and dates and things, and do you know where I believe, Borthwick Junior was conceived?"

"No, I do not, but my goodness, I most certainly want to hear."

"On Darach Muir, no less."

When they returned from Spurryhillock, Malcolm indicated that he wanted to chat more about his co-op plan, so it was arranged for him to come over for dinner one evening. After all the pleasantries were done with, and an update report on the estate, he broached the subject of the Darach coop.

"I`ve been chatting with the other seven, who are keen to be part of the co-op for sourcing and processing good native timber. They are all up for it and agree that the location is grand. We are honest, in that financial considerations do come into this, so your goodwill is a valuable part of it. I did go and have a look at the area you`d talked about up at the steading, I hope that was, OK?"

"Yes, of course, absolutely fine by us," Lizzie quickly replied.

245

"That's great, I appreciate this. I measured out the area of the old rotten tin barns, and silage clamps with stackyard, and so on, and I reckon it's about an acre in total. Most of that is already some form of hard standing or foundations, though as you know there is some scrub encroachment due to sheer lack of use over the years.

One of the great things is it is all well-screened from the farmhouse, by the more substantial farm buildings, but there are no windows or doors on that side of them. Also, the access road is pretty good, with no obvious problems. We`d probably tuck the site hut or office up against the back of the farm buildings. And I see that there is both water and power on the site in one way or another. It looks good."

"That's great to hear Malcolm," said Andy. "To be on the safe side, we`d need to wait until full planning permission has been granted for things. Though I guess that the rusty old tin barn could go anytime. Cos if it's not taken down soon, the next gale might see it on its way to the neighbouring parish."

38.

Monique and Charlotte came into the sitting room, where their mother was sitting quietly relaxing, between one thing and another. It was Charlotte who spoke first, "Monique and I have been thinking about this event next year for dealing with daddy`s ashes."

"Do tell me, my loves, what have you been thinking? I hope you are not too upset?"

"Oh, not really," Monique replied. "Yes, it's so sad what happened to him, but you do know we both understood there was something wrong in his head, long before that. When we moved here Mummy, things just seemed a bit better for us. You were a lot happier Mummy, and because you were, so were we. We`ve both been doing stuff at school about mental health, so perhaps we understand it a wee bit better now. Yes, we do, don't we Charlotte?"

"I think so, Mummy. I think we know a little bit more about what can cause problems like that, and what the results of it might be. But anyway, you`ve been with us all the way Mummy, and we both love you dearly for that. Life would have probably been dark all the time for us if you`d not helped us every day. And now because you are so happy with Malcolm, and he does so much for us, it all just seems to have come right."

This all took Hermione completely by surprise, and the tears flowed freely as she held her two lovely girls closely. As her hair fell over her face, the tears clung to it and stuck to her cheeks and chin as if to add emphasis to how she felt. The warmth from these two girls after all they'd been through was almost overwhelming. "Thank you for everything you`ve said, Monique and Charlotte, my darlings. Thank you," she choked.

"We want to help you with the event Mummy, so we are writing a poem and will read it between us if that's all right?"

"Of course, it is, what a lovely idea. Is that the poem there in your hand Monique?"

"Yes, shall we read what we have written so far? We hope you`ll like it. Here goes."

"Our father`s ship has left the quayside now,

Sailing towards some distant shore.

We stand and watch, as winds fill the sails,

And wild seabirds circle her tall masts, their haunting calls echo in our hearts.

Yes, we are so sad to see him depart, but bad demons had entered his troubled mind.

Bad demons deceived him and robbed him of reality.

He took unwise decisions and paid an awful price and left some broken hearts.

So as the ship's silhouette against that bright horizon diminishes,

We know we have each other, for that is all that he has left us.

Holding hands together here, on the quay, watched over lovingly by our dear mother.

We have each other."

"What do you think? We could do more to it. Need to work out which of us will read what lines though."

"It's just perfect girls, perfect. I can`t begin to imagine how you found the talent to write something so moving. I`d say you should keep it exactly as it is because it is your beautiful special contribution to the event. Can we share it with Jean if you like, do you think? Or shall we leave it a bit longer yet?"

After a pause, Charlotte replied, "Can we leave it a little while yet, please? But we`ve also painted a little picture of a sailing ship heading towards a bright horizon. Could that go on the order of service, or whatever it's called?"

"I`m sure it could. What a wonderful idea."

39.

Margaret didn't hear much about her legal case for a while. There was of course confirmation that it was proceeding, and a few questions about some of the detail of putting the case together. She was sanguine about this. Knowing that she had the wherewithal to pay all the fees that she'd be due to pay and that she had one of the finest legal practices in the land working for her, gave her a sense of confidence. Knowing that what she was seeking in court, would be nigh on impossible for the estate to prove absolutely, she foresaw another ruling against the estate, in what might be regarded as an unsatisfactory outcome. Whether she would ever exercise any of these rights was another matter altogether. In fact, she said to herself, it doesn't really matter, regardless of how long the case may take to come to court.

She`d heard that the estate was now up for sale, so had a wry smile about that, because they could not, dare not conceal the fact that there were outstanding legal matters to be settled. Most potential buyers would run a mile at that and vanish over the horizon.

One of the things that had caused her to take the action, was not just because she could, but as a sixth or seventh-generation resident of the village, she felt bound up in its history, in the spirit of the glen, entirely at home within the landscapes. But in the culture of it, she bore a deep need for revenge. Several of her ancestors had lived relatively harmlessly on the fringes of the local economy; they`d indulged in a bit of poaching from time to time. If she were a man, she reckoned, she would probably have gone on to follow the family tradition, and proudly too.

As poachers, or takers of the bounty of the earth, as she called it, they had always had to sail close to the wind. Sometimes they failed in this unnecessary imposition and got caught. The factor and his lackeys rubbed their hands together with glee, and the local Sherriff held sway over them in court. Maggie had even heard of the odd prison sentence being dished out. That very thought filled her with rage.

So, her chance had come to have vengeance upon Glenmaddy Estate. Even if it went on well into the new year, she knew that just the sale of the property could be frustrated, despite any slick talk from their lawyers and agents.

Maggie sat back and waited for however long any of this might take.

The anxiety that now surrounded the Alex and Catriona situation had been picked up as promised, by Archie, and he`d recruited the services of a former colleague of his, who was known to be especially good at doing family traces, where there may be money, property, or some form of inheritance in dispute. He often managed to achieve a satisfactory outcome, which avoided the cost and acrimony of court proceedings. So, between the two of them, they assembled as clear and precise a picture as was possible, within a relatively short space of time, and decided to email the results to everyone who needed to know.

They reported, "that it was of course well known that Alex had died at sea in early 1917, that he had married a Catriona Hyslop in mid-1916 when he was home on leave. From this union, a baby registered as Alexander Peter Ferguson was born on 19th March 1917 in Cauldmarch Farm in the Parish of St John`s Town of Dalry, Kirkcudbrightshire. This, therefore, confirmed that she had gone back to live with her parents at some stage during the pregnancy. Alexander Peter`s parents were given as Catriona Hyslop and Alexander Ferguson (deceased).

Tragedy, it would seem, was heaped on tragedy, for from his Military record, we see that Philip Hyslop, Catriona`s twin brother, had been convicted of gross indecency in a court martial held in Edinburgh Castle

251

in early 1918. For this, he was imprisoned, as was the judgement for such an offence at the time. At the end of the War, some clemency prevailed, and he was released the following year. As far as we`ve been able to discover he died during the Spanish Flu pandemic, in a sanitorium in Kirkcudbright on the 30th of August 1920. He was buried in St John`s Town of Dalry.

From the valuation rolls and other such records, Catriona inherited the farm in about 1925 after the death of her father and she was the sole beneficiary of this. For reasons that are now long gone, she decided to set up the farm in a trust arrangement and put it on a ninety-nine-year lease to a local aristocratic family. It seems likely that they used the farmhouse for their own purposes, and Catriona and Alexander Peter lived in a cottage somewhere else on the aristocrat's landholding. She however lived off the rent received for the Cauldmarch Farm. As far as we can tell, she did have a local legal firm that set up the lease, but they may also have been acting for the aristocratic family. This we would now regard as a conflict of interest. Sure enough, the terms of the lease were not really to her advantage. So, by the time she died in 1965 at the age of seventy, she was in relative poverty, but had been tied into that lease.

Alexander Peter married Bridgid Anderson in Glasgow on 24th April 1940. It's unclear where she came from. But he was working as a groundsman in the sports field of some independent school. Why he was not called up, is not clear either. Alexander Peter and Bridgid had one child, a girl, born on 26th May 1947. Her name is Deirdre McClymont and, now lives in a council house in Glasgow. There`s no evidence of any children from her marriage to Gregor McClymont, who died in the past twenty years."

So, it's a bit sketchy, at this stage folks. There`s more we could do, and probably must do, but there are two key things for us. As things stand, unless Deirdre suddenly remarries, then Spurryhillock is safe, as there is no apparent heir to claim any part of it. It's going to take a bit of digging and delving to unravel what bits of Alex`s inheritance should in fact have gone to his widow. A greater mystery is why she never claimed any of it. We suspect that the lawyer she had who was supposedly acting in her interests, was failing to do so. There were, then as now, such things as incompetent lawyers.

The second thing will be what happens to Cauldmarch Farm when the ninety-nine-year lease expires at full term. I've asked my former colleague to handle this matter, with the lawyers who currently handle the estate down there. I would say, that if there is an asset there, as would seem likely, it should be split evenly between Hermione and Lizzie. It's probably not worth continuing the lease or renewing it. Those aristocrats by the name of Murchie-McCubbin have had more than their fair share of exploiting an asset. Yes, that is their double-barrelled name, and they live in a small castle on the estate when they are not living it up in London."

There was a lot of discussion in twos and threes, about the contents of the email which Archie and his colleague had produced. It was a mixture of great sadness, relief, some curiosity, and concern for poor Deirdre.

"I`ve written to her earlier today, in the gentlest and most thoughtful of ways, to explain what we have discovered. Some of it will of course already be known to her, and perhaps some of it will be news. My former colleague has offered to act for her should she need that support. But that offer will come directly from him to her, should she request it in due course. I would like to visit her if she wishes that too. It's worth noting, that she may already have made a will, and left the farm to the cat and dog home. That would be her prerogative, and we must not interfere."

"This is indeed a very sad account of things, Archie dear," Marissa said with a deep sigh. "Whilst we know nothing of this Deirdre`s current circumstances, by our standards, life has been rather unkind to all that part of your family, even if up until now, you knew nothing about them. If we can do anything for her, we certainly must, but we must also be careful that it doesn't seem like we are doing it just to get our hands on the farm when the time comes. Anyway, she could live for another twenty years or more. Perhaps she`s a tough old cookie. It's unknown territory we are in now."

"Yes indeed. Well, whatever happens, Alex will almost certainly be remembered in Alex`s Way that Lizzie and Andy are planning at Spurryhillock. You may remember that I told you they are planning to name a walk running right up through the estate in his honour, and planting oak trees along beside it, as a token of his work on Darach Muir, that we now know about."

"Yes, I remember that and it's a lovely plan. Perhaps a few strategically placed benches along the way would be nice too."

"A weeping willow for Philip would not go amiss, I`m thinking," ventured Hermione in sombre tone.

The family gathering dispersed in greater silence than was the norm; so many mixed feelings. For although much had been resolved, queries answered and great hope for so much in the future, the injustice meted out to poor Philip seemed intolerable to all, by today`s standards and values.

Archie had written to Deirdre. His letter was typed, as he knew his handwriting could be a bit of a scrawl. So, he printed out the copy, signed it, and sent it to her home in Glasgow. The letter was carefully worded, so as not to cause her any alarm. For although he knew her approximate age, there was no way of knowing her mental state or general welfare. Explaining a bit of the family background, what he knew of her more immediate ancestry, and the link with this to his own, he sketched out what was necessary for their relationship. Archie told Deirdre that he reckoned they were cousins by marriage, twice removed.

He then talked a little about where he and his family lived, his children and grandchildren, and what his professional job had been. "Best to leave it at that", he reckoned, so he signed off, by saying he would love to come to and visit her himself if she would be happy to meet him.

He waited for a reply; hoped for a reply.

True to his word, Ronald soon had several articles in national and local papers, and a location interview out on the Muir. The mystery of how the stone got there, was always a good opener to draw the reader in. He`d found a picture of the Rev Ebenezer Snoddy in an old book about the excesses of the reformed presbyterian church. With his black clothes, black hat, and long white beard, he looked the part. The location of the picture was in some austere church, with Snoddy apparently banging his angry, zealous fists on the pulpit. What the unfortunate congregation made of him, was just left to the imagination.

Ronald quoted, without attribution, from some of what Archie, Marissa, Lizzie, and Andy had said on the Muir because he felt that had both punch and passion to it. He knew of course that what he wrote would also help the local people to get into quite a frenzy about their Darach Muir. "And why should they not feel that?" He mused. In the greater scheme of things, "it was their common land as the first historical and identifiable source on its status attested." Ronald`s skill at writing well was clear. As he drew in his audiences, many of whom had never heard of the place before, drew them into the story, helped them to identify with it, and feel stirred by the passion he aroused. He knew which buttons to press. For sure.

From these articles and programs, the questions, and comments flooded in. Letter columns were well stirred up. The phone-in was a popular avenue for people to use to channel their responses, some of them quite heated, from the well-informed to the wildly opinionated. Ronald was

255

adept at picking out the best and most useful from this, without putting anyone down. He was clearly enjoying the whole process. This was both because he felt a strong personal and almost political interest in the topic and because he loved the Fergusons, for whom he was doing all this. They deserved the best from him, and he vowed to himself that he would deliver on that.

Social media was humming with activity and opinion too. A very varied flow, but most certainly raising awareness; and confidence within the community too.

Not everyone was entirely happy though because he did receive a few rather nasty emails, with all sorts of threats against him.

Towards the end of the year, the local jungle drums were banging loud, and the grapevine was agog with the story, that Glenmaddy Estate had been put on the market.

The Edinburgh firm of lawyers was handling the advertising and sale process.

For some, this came as no real surprise, because the place had been rife with rumours. And the Factor was nowhere to be seen. His wife and family had also disappeared off the local scene altogether. It was even rumoured that he had erred in some way and was being investigated by the professional association. Speculation everywhere.

Archie managed to dig a bit deeper in legal circles, and whilst factors like the pathetic failed court case, another one perhaps being fomented, and the sheer bad feeling locally all combined to make the situation very difficult for the estate to bear.

Someone somewhere, however, let the cat out of the bag and revealed the identity of the otherwise secretive laird. It was none other than Hamish Hammond, the local Member of the Scottish Parliament. Once this was out, the whole situation was untenable. That he`d tried to sue all the residents, his constituents, was deemed deplorable, and it now showed that his land management was at odds with even the best that his party could muster for such rural areas. The cry of hypocrite went out across the land. And the very ineffectual or out-of-touch local association, just couldn't take the bad press this generated, by the bucket load.

As each week passed and went, another nugget of scandal or political ineptitude came out, which left the whole estate situation and that of the local MSP in tatters. But the solicitors acting for the sale, just saw that as all collateral damage, because of the amount of free press that it all yielded on the pending sale. No such thing as bad news, they mused over their claret in some exclusive London Club.

In a small committee room at the rear of the village hall, an assorted group of nine local people had hurriedly convened a meeting to draft a plan. Between them, they represented many local interests, but above all, they brought their individual passions, and a commitment to work together; expeditiously.

With the advertised sale of the estate about to go live any day, they knew that they must act fast. Their goal was to do whatever needed to be done as a priority to register an interest in a community purchase of all of Darrach Muir, access to it directly from the village, and some surrounding native woodland. By chance, they appointed Angus`s cousin Molly as the chair.

"Thank you all for coming folks, and at such short notice. And thank you for having the confidence in me to be your chairperson. I hope I`ll match up with it. Can we please agree on a few things first? We need a minute taker and secretary, not least because we will quite rapidly, I hope, be communicating with some government agencies. Any takers for this essential role please?"

A young man by the name of Dave signalled his offer to do this.

"Thank you, Dave, are there any other contenders, please?"

Silence.

"OK none, Dave you are our secretary. And thank you once again. Can we now agree that we retain some confidentiality about what is happening and being discussed within this room, pro tem? Yes, it will have to be public pretty soon, but let's give ourselves the breathing space to do this properly. I've every confidence in you to formulate and drive this plan forward. There`s an absolute wealth of relevant experience and shared commitment here in this room. Are we agreed on this, folks?"

Everyone nodded their consent.

"And let's see if we can agree on a simple statement to summarise our key purpose, and delegate tasks. Let's split into two groups for this, and each does a half-hour brainstorm."

Molly was known locally as someone who got things done. So here she was in her element. And she seemed to achieve this without any acrimony or difficulty. Within the half-hour, each group had completed its interim task and reported back. Molly summarised the first group`s statement as being, "To effect a community purchase of Darach Muir, some woodland on the periphery and a route for direct pedestrian access from the village, all within the scope of the Land Reform Act of 2003."

With the other group having drafted a very similar purpose, or mission, as they called it, the allocated tasks were then dished out so that everyone in the room had an active role to play in achieving the overall purpose of the group. Lots of well-organised discussions then followed, and there was an air of determined direction to the proceedings. By the end of the meeting, Molly had set the group on a clear path, which as she put it, "would use the current regime to lay claim to that which is ours by ancient right."

A new dawn was surely going to break, over Lochhead and Glenmaddy and its traditional common land. All for a purpose that was somehow represented by that ancient Darach Stane with its acorns.

Bramble liked those daily walks and Marissa had a favourite destination on St Leonard`s Hill, with wide vistas across to all the majesty of Arthur`s Seat. How unusual, she often mused, to have a mini mountain almost in the middle of a city. No, not just any mountain, but one from her vantage point, which was like a familiar friend, girt by crags, ancient rocks, in a timeless parade.

Sitting on her usual bench, on this cold bright sunny day, she was dressed for the occasion, in a thick maroon coat. Looking down at Bramble she said, "ah, your fine black coat, will just soak up all the sunshine here, to keep you snug and warm, my friend."

Marissa`s thoughts turned first to all that had happened in the past year especially, of how chance happenings had quickly led on to so many other things, and in widely varying directions too. Yes, there had been stress and sorrow in it, but the good and happy, the optimism, far outweighed the pain. As she admired the grand vista across the valley, she felt joy and hope, in her heart. That hope was of course tinged with thoughts of unfinished business, and where that may lead. Ah, no story is ever quite ended, she pondered cautiously. The discovery of Deirdre, Jamie`s ashes, the next chapter in the Spurryhillock saga, and what of the growing realisation that the Fergusons had been slave owners? These, and other matters were all just beginning to crowd in amongst her thoughts when she sighed and drew herself up. Simply saying to Bramble, who looked up fondly at hearing Marissa`s familiar voice, "Yes Bramble, the future is another thing, another journey into the unknown, with all of the anticipations it may bring."

DID3490116

L - #0196 - 060223 - C0 - 210/148/15 - PB - DID3490116